THE EAVESDROPPERS

A NOVEL

THE
EAVESDROPPERS

ROSIE CHARD

NeWest Press

NeWest Press wishes to acknowledge that the land on which we operate is Treaty 6 territory and a traditional meeting ground and home for many Indigenous Peoples, including Cree, Saulteaux, Niisitapi (Blackfoot), Métis, and Nakota Sioux.

Library and Archives Canada Cataloguing in Publication

Chard, Rosie, 1959–, author The eavesdroppers / Rosie Chard.

Issued in print and electronic formats. ISBN 978-1-988732-44-2 (softcover).—ISBN 978-1-988732-45-9 (EPUB).— ISBN 978-1-988732-46-6 (Kindle)

I. Title.

Board Editor: Douglas Barbour
Cover and interior design: Michel Vrana
Cover images: istockphoto.com
Author photo: Nat Chard

  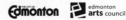

NeWest Press acknowledges the Canada Council for the Arts, the Alberta Foundation for the Arts, and the Edmonton Arts Council for support of our publishing program. We acknowledge the financial support of the Government of Canada.

NeWest Press
#201, 8540-109 Street
Edmonton, Alberta T6G 1E6
www.newestpress.com

No bison were harmed in the making of this book.

Printed and bound in Canada

1 2 3 4   20 19 18

For Nat

To those who have never visited the Whispering Gallery… it may be proper to mention… that a word or question, uttered at one end of the gallery in the gentlest of whispers, is reverberated at the other end in peals of thunder.

Thomas De Quincey,
Confessions of an English Opium-Eater, London, 1822.

CHAPTER

1

"Can you hear me? Mr. Harcourt. Can you hear me?"

I thought I was alive. My fingers were moving; my nose itched; yet I was detached from the world. Something lay on my face. A binding of sorts, it stopped me opening my eyes and seeing where I was. I felt a twinge of panic at the base of my throat.

"Everything's alright, Mr. Harcourt." A female voice beside my ear. "The surgery went well."

A voice, just a voice – sugar-coated and impatient. I couldn't judge the distance of the disembodied sound, so far away, yet I could feel breath on my cheek. I could smell coffee wafting up from a stomach. Was this person about to kiss me? I struggled to remember where I was – a faint smell of antiseptic, a rustle of rubber curtains, then yes, the details of a face poured in: tired, bloodshot eyes and eyebrows that were badly plucked. The nurse had missed a bit just above her left eye, and with sudden clarity I recalled my thoughts as the gurney had been pushed through the double doors – could a nurse with badly plucked eyebrows be trusted to hand over the correct scalpel?

"Why can't I see?" I said, trying to keep the slur from my voice.

"It's the bandage, dear." A pause. "Over your eyes."

I imagined a child in the room, so laden was her voice with condescension. I waited for the child to retort but all I heard was my own breathing and the sound of something being dragged down a nearby corridor. A bag of clean sheets perhaps? Or a bag of old bones.

"Where am I?" I said, my tongue sticking to the roof of my mouth.

"You're back in the room."

The room? I tried again to recall where I'd spent the last few hours but the only room I could remember bumped and rattled across the ground at speed. "Can I go back to sleep now?"

"Yes, you can go back to sleep. But, wait. Just a couple of questions … what year is it?"

I tried to visualise numbers. "Two thousand … two thousand and fifteen … no, eighteen."

"Correct. How old are you?"

"Thirty-four." The air held a pause. Could I be wrong?

"Also correct. Finally, where are you?"

Tight within the bandage my brain struggled to form a picture of the route to the place that now held me. Inside, yes. A hospital without doubt, but where? For how long had the siren screamed into my brain? I concentrated on my ears, my most reliable sense, so reliable they could pick up the distant throb of a black cab. "London," I said.

"Correct. You can go back to sleep now."

"Mr. Harcourt. Mr. Harcourt."

My thoughts snapped to attention. I was no longer a dullard, a woozy patient in post-op; I was sharp as a pencil. "Who's there?"

"Nurse Rigby." The sugar had melted from her throat.

"Are you the same person as before?"

I heard her chest rise and fall. "Yes, I'm the same person as before."

I tried to roll my eyes. "How long is this thing going to be on?"

"What thing?"

I couldn't halt the sarcasm. "The bandage."

"Two days."

Two days in the dark. The bandages felt tight already and, with a new twinge of panic, I tried to visualise how I'd aim straight in the bowl of the hospital toilet. "Will I be getting a dog?" I said. Faked innocence is entirely about the eyes. I realised this as I waited, trying to hear her laugh or at the very least hear a smile, but lips turning up at the corners make no noise at all.

"Is that meant to be a joke, Mr. Harcourt?"

I sighed, just like her.

Flat on my back with a bandage over my face it was impossible to be myself. That half-raised eyebrow I used so often to project sarcasm was immobilised, and it was difficult to tease someone with your nose. And it was nigh on impossible to look sheepish with a bandage over your eyes.

"I'm going to feed you now," said the nurse.

Forget pissing on the toilet seat, forget the anonymous breath on my cheek, this woman was going to feed me now. "I'm really not that hungry."

I heard the tut of her tongue. Then I heard what sounded like glue being whipped up with a spoon before the immortal words cut the air. "You need to eat to keep your strength up."

Defeat was not sweet. The five-year-old me opened his mouth and tipped back his head. Such tepid mush I never experienced from my mother, but luckily it was quickly over, my mouth wiped with a rough cloth and the rattle of bowls being put away.

Icy hands – *why always icy?* – began making the bed with me still in it. I lay stiff, mulling over the hospital protocol concerning the making of beds while still occupied. No 'do you mind if I make the bed, Mr.Harcourt?' and no, 'I'll just tuck this bit under your chin, sir,' – just strange hands glancing private parts.

"I think you're done, Mr. Harcourt," the nurse said after the sheet was tightened somewhere down by my feet, sealing me in like a piece of vacuum-packed fish. "I'll be back later to check on your temperature."

The idea of being 'done' quickly quashed all speculation on unfamiliar hands in private places, but before I could utter a comeback I heard a whoosh of hospital-starched skirts – as I imagined them – and was left alone – as assumed.

"And...." A sentence was deposited at my ear. "If you need any help, just press this."

Disturbed that the starched skirts scenario could be so wrong, I fingered a plastic object that had been placed into my hand. "Okay."

People could clearly come and go without my knowing it. I lay still for several minutes before I felt satisfied I was alone. Feeling my wrist, I found it bare. Bastards, I thought, they've nicked my watch. I gingerly tested the space beside my bed. A table was uncomfortably out of reach, but by wrenching my arm out from my sheeted bondage and stretching out I could explore its surface: a plastic cup with water inside – I surmised by sniffing it – and a card that tipped over under my touch – who'd send *me* a card? – plus my wristwatch. How cheerful it sounded pressed against my ear. But I soon grew weary of the chipper little sound and strapped it, with surprising difficulty for an activity so familiar, back onto my wrist.

For a while I lazily formed a picture in my mind of the nurse tidying her eyebrows in the Ladies loo, then I fingered the callback object, resisting the urge to press 'nurse' just for the sheer hell of it. Finally I sank back down into my pillow. It smelt funny and creaked a bit. My God, there was *nothing* to do in a hospital bed with a bandage over your eyes. Nothing to do, but lie back and listen.

"He's not going to make it."

"I know he's not."

My ears pricked up, as far as is possible for a human with a head encased. I heard a pause. Bandages on less than a day and already I knew the sound and weight of a gap in proceedings.

"How are we going to tell mum?" said a woman – young sounding.

"God knows," replied a male voice.

It was the first time I'd *heard* fingers being run through hair, but there it was, distinct as a rake through straw.

"We *have* to say something, don't we?" said the female.

"Do we?"

More raking, more silence. A knuckle cracked.

I tried to breathe quietly. It was hard to tell how much time had passed since I'd woken up the first time, but my fingers had sweat between them so I felt confident that time had moved on. I had no idea how long these people had been in the room and I felt uncomfortable that they'd entered without me knowing it. Had they befriended me in my sleep? How long *had* I been asleep? My lack of judgment was beginning to worry me.

The conversation started up again and, like a thief beneath a windowsill, I tried to angle my poor squashed ears and listen.

"We can't lie to her."

"I think we should keep it to ourselves, Jane, I really do."

Another pause, long, oh so long.

"Joe, I can hardly bear it."

"I can't bear it either, but Jane, I think we need to play for time. Let's give her a few more hours of hope, shall we?"

I could hardly bear it. I thought I heard something being rubbed, a shoulder maybe, or a knee.

"Alright."

Later – how much I'm no judge – I sensed that several people were coming into the room again in shoes with soles of varying thickness – oh, I was getting good – and muttering about the lack of chairs in this 'godforsaken place.' They took a long time to organise themselves and I lost count of the numbers. Was it three? Four? Or perhaps it was just two people who couldn't settle, the sort of people who couldn't decide where to leave their vehicle in an empty car park. Having wanted them to just sort themselves out, I was left regretful when they did just that and a horrible silence hung in the air. Were they looking in my direction? I wondered. Maybe they were reading my chart. They always did that on the telly, read the poor bastard's chart while he was asleep, then switched it with another poor bastard's – the one who was about to have a leg taken off.

"How was the bus, Mum?"

It was the same deep voice as earlier, yet different in a way I couldn't identify. I tried to think how *I'd* answer that question. I hardly used the bus if I could help it. The paired seats were never big enough for two people and there always seemed to be someone already there, oozing over the line.

"It was late. It took hours to get down the Euston Road."

Good answer.

"How are you doing, Mum?"

I heard a sniff and felt like a real shit. But in my situation I couldn't help but listen. And listening was painful. They were a family of four, it transpired, a mother, a father, two adult children who seemed to be the owners of the earlier voices, and a mute patient in a bed. I tried not to think of the mute patient in the bed and focused on the people around them. 'Joe' was clearly the one in charge. Almost every comment was followed by a, 'Don't ya reckon, Joe?' and although he sounded young he answered quickly. He was the one who had all the answers, the bloke down the pub who could sort things out.

"Is he going to get through, Joe?" asked the mother after a pause I could almost smell.

For some reason it's quite hard to hold your breath with a bandage over your eyes, but I managed it, for just long enough.

"Of course he's going to get through," said Joe.

My face reddened. I knew from the heat beneath the cloth that I was blushing like a schoolboy. Or maybe it was just my bandage, rubbing against burning ears.

"Of course he's going to get through," repeated the grown-up daughter.

I heard a slight movement, shoulders slumping perhaps.

"Thank God," said someone.

I breathed. The big sentences were over and the little ones quickly followed. Everyone was rushing out details at once, trying to get them in before another pause opened up: the terrible food, the fearsome nurses and wasn't it funny when they forgot to pay for a ticket in the car park and Dad 'made a face' at the receptionist. I tried to imagine 'Dad' making a face. Maybe he had a lopsided grin, or a ragged moustache or maybe he just had a strained look all over his face. It wasn't long before they ran dry. In my mind 'Dad' was making his 'I think we should go' face and I felt triumphant as I heard them gather themselves up and leave the room, their departure more efficient than their arrival.

That left just me. And him. Funny how they'd never mentioned his name. Was he even there? Perhaps it was all just a little play. Something to keep old Bill amused while his eyes healed up. He was certainly very still. Not even a cough. Then I began to worry. Perhaps he was dead. Maybe the morgue was full and there was nowhere to store him? I tucked my sheet tighter beneath my chin and tried to occupy myself. But there was absolutely nothing to do. Nothing to do, but lie still and listen.

MISSY'S lounge walls were thin. Voices seeped into them like vapour through cotton, but often the sounds were muffled and she liked to imagine, as she lay on the floor of her flat, the people next door sitting in armchairs, their mouths covered with a soft layer of muslin. Her ears worked best in the horizontal position. Her sense of the world worked most efficiently with her legs stretched out and her arms limp by her sides. It was the only time she could really relax. Odd, when the floorboards were so hard. The rest of the time she held her body taut. Not that she was fit; she hated exercise and a ring of surplus fat girdled her waist, but because she had to be ready for what was around the corner. She had to be ready to run. But down there on the floor she could close her eyes and slow her heart and hear what was coming through from the other side of the wall.

Mrs. O'Malley ran up the stairs at a quarter to two every day. Missy knew it was her, the step so distinctive, chipping onto the wood with the ball of her foot. Mr. O'Malley shuffled on loose-sounding slippers and occasionally the grown-up daughter visited, rushing through the tiny flat on impatient heels. Sometimes someone would slap the wall and Missy would jump and feel anxious right through the evening.

She was lying on her back, waiting for the sound of Grandma O'Malley's eight o'clock trip to the toilet, when she heard the garden gate squeak. She angled her ears towards the window. Lightweight shoes skipped up the path, one kicked a stone. Then the sound of something being forced through the letterbox. Missy sat up, counted to ten then walked downstairs into the communal hall. She picked up the newspaper lying on the doormat and carried it back upstairs into the kitchen. Beer cans littered the countertop so she sat at the small breakfast table and opened the paper at the entertainment section. Here she would find the photographs she liked best – the ones that showed people out on the town. Londoners living it up until the small hours with feathers flying and crooked ties and tiny skirts riding up and make-up, so much make-up, shiny on their cheeks. She'd linger there. Not long, but long enough to imagine a stocking clinging to her own ample thigh, and tinsel in her hair.

Next to this section she would find the job adverts, designed by clever people to make her feel guilty. She scanned the page as she did every day, hoping that this would be the day for which she had been waiting.

CHAPTER

2

Time does pass in hospitals, but I didn't know how much.
My usual methods of measurement, glancing at my watch, checking my phone, glancing over a shoulder and checking someone else's phone, were gone in a world without eyes and now I was dependent on a new set of clues. I imagined I'd be able to actually *hear* night fall but it wasn't some godly sense that took me over, it was the lack of sound that let me know the day had ended and the ward had gone to bed. The snores creeping from a distant room were a distraction, but soon I learnt to ignore them and concentrated on the sound of the routines that divided not my night, but my day. And these routines were all about pills. What sounded like a small go-kart was wheeled down the corridors at what I gauged to be three-hourly intervals and I would be held in a state of high alert as I succumbed to the ever-increasing sounds of packages being unwrapped and lids being popped. Feeding rituals also punctured my day. A friendly, 'How are we, Mr. Harcourt?' followed by the almost imperceptible sound of plastic being wiped told me food was about to be served. Eating was a whole new world of burnt tongues and spilt drinks, but the skills came. Quickly I improved my

9

accuracy and I had managed to get my entire breakfast into the hole in the middle of my face on the third morning when I was paid a visit.

"You ready?" said a female voice close to my bed.

For someone without sight this was a terrifying question. Were they going to put a spider into my hand? Throw me a cricket ball? "Ready for what?" I said.

"The great unveiling."

Oh, yes. I was more than ready for the great unveiling.

It was a strange sensation: the gentle peeling, the slow emergence of light. My whole body felt lighter as each layer of bandage was removed. I felt self-conscious too, yet at the same time curious. Would my face be gloriously restored, or would it be puckered and yellow like a wound released from beneath a damp plaster?

"Looking good, Mr. Harcourt."

"Oh ... there's two of you."

"Yes. Welcome back."

"Could you close the curtains?" I said in the direction of the speaker, who was blurred as a hurried photograph.

"They *are* closed."

I put my hand up to my eyes.

"Don't touch!" snapped the apparition. "Put these on."

I felt something placed on my face; it was intimate, a warm hand glancing my cheek, the plastic arms of glasses sliding across my ears.

"Better?"

"Much."

"Can you see me?"

I blinked. The brightness of the windows was already receding and I could just make out a tall man with a surprisingly large head. "Yes. I can see you."

"Good. Do you remember me? I'm Dr. Treadmill."

"Ah. The man with the needle and thread?"

He laughed. "Yes. That's me. Everything went well; you'll be glad to hear. It feels strange to have the bandage off, doesn't it."

"Yes. That was a long two days. Although ..." I resisted the urge to scratch my eye, "you see things differently when you can't see, don't you?"

He laughed again. "Everyone says that."

Funny how much that cut me. Bill Harcourt, never original.

The doctor sat on the chair next to the bed. Doctors never sit on the chair next to the bed. "So, Mr. Harcourt, do you have any idea what happened?"

I blinked in the direction of his face. "I was walking home from work–"

"Alone?"

"Yes, alone. And something ... some thing hit me – in the face."

The doctor glanced at the clock on the wall. "What hit you?"

"I don't know. I didn't see it coming."

"So, there was nothing left behind ... on the street?"

I shook my head. It hurt.

"Was there anyone else about?"

"No. The street was empty."

"And you definitely didn't see anything coming?"

"No, I didn't see anything coming."

He leant towards me and gazed into my eyes. "Alright, I suppose we'll have to put it down to one of life's unexplained incidents. The nurse will go over the post-op procedures. She'll be here in a minute. Then you can go home. Have you got someone picking you up?"

"No."

"Someone'll call you a taxi." He shook my hand. Or rather picked it up from my chest and held it. "See you in a month, Mr. Harcourt."

"Yes. And thanks for patching me up."

"You're welcome, and remember the golden rule. Don't touch your eyes."

"I'll remember."

Blinking fast and desperate to scratch, I watched his back as he passed through the doorway.

The room was smaller than I'd imagined and there was only one other bed, not two or three, as I'd thought. The other bed was empty. I heaved my feet onto the floor and sat up. Then I shuffled over to it – funny how you lose control over your legs after just two days in bed. At first I just stood there like an idiot. Then I gingerly sat down. I'd heard the sound of the sheets being peeled back earlier that day, had almost felt the smack of the mattress, but only then did it sink in. The silent patient had gone. I blinked. Then I lay down on the pristine sheets and gazed up at the ceiling.

"Mr. Harcourt!" A female voice hurtled from the doorway. "Get back to your own bed."

JACK was on his way home. It had been raining all day, that warm, steady spit so typical of August in London, and the inside of the Tube had the atmosphere of a neglected greenhouse: wilted raincoats, limp newspapers and commuters sapped of their last ounces of energy. The woman directly opposite him endlessly rearranged her fringe across her forehead and Jack felt disturbed by the way she was never happy with the result.

He gazed out of the window, and then, tired of the blackness of the tunnel, he glanced at the newspaper held by the man sitting next to him. It had been folded into a rectangle and the man gripped the bulging folds in a way that suggested he repeated this action every day of his life. The train's seating allowed only tabloids to be opened wide enough to be read thoroughly so owners of the increasingly rare broadsheets had to be content with a truncated story, read in snatches as the paper was folded and refolded over cramped knees or, as with standing travellers, bent into even smaller squares and held aloft like trophies. Jack was particularly keen on truncated stories. He liked it when his news was edited by a stranger. It meant he read what the stranger did not: the car theft on a skew, the upside-down bombing, the story cut in two as the owner of the paper abruptly turned the page. But that's what he was about: finding the little pieces and putting them together to make a story.

Sometimes his news would be reduced to a single line, '*Sex-change vicar in shock horror mercy dash*,' or occasionally summarised by a lone word –'*Gotcha!*' lunging across the carriage towards him. During the rush hour, when every seat was taken and readers' elbows were jammed tight against their ribs, the newspapers would disappear completely from view and all he'd get were the expressions on the readers' faces, the dart of excited eyes across the football results, or the sad mouth of someone reading of a death in a faraway place.

That day the train was sparsely peopled and he had a chance to have a long look at what his neighbour was reading. This particular traveller was a very slow reader, his finger suspended beneath the lines as if holding the words in place. Jack watched the ink-smudged digit travel across the news pages, and then feel its way through the film reviews until it reached the classified ads. Here everything changed. The paper was opened out fully – a corner cantilevered over Jack's knees – and the man pulled a pen from his pocket and settled himself back into his seat with an air of great purpose. Then the work really started. The pen bled a dot beside each job advert as it was checked off and then the man began to underline phrases as they caught his attention – *no training required, minimum wage, start immediately.*

He seemed to be at rock bottom, the man, circling the occupations of the desperate: the early school leavers, the unqualified, the ones with skills known only to themselves. Jack had been there. Even now he wasn't so far removed from the cheap orange chairs of the Job Centre that he'd forgotten what it was like to have to apply for anything and everything. He glanced at the man's shoes; they were sturdy, but of another era – nylon laces, square toes. Jack then noticed the pen circling a job in the top left corner. He couldn't see what it was, but he felt a prick of curiosity as it was heavily ringed in ink. As if suddenly exhausted the man let out a sigh, folded up the newspaper and placed it casually down on the seat opposite. Jack fretted. It seemed a long way away to stow ones' possessions, especially on the Tube where distance suggested abandonment. Jack glanced sideways at the man who had now pulled out a Tube map and was studying it, his horizontal finger holding up the whole of the Northern Line. Jack stared at the newspaper on the seat and wondered whether he could pick it up. Discarded newspapers were public property, after all. But before he could do anything the train pulled into a station and people got on, hopping inside the carriage as if scared of the doors. His view was now just waists in every direction: belted waists, bulging waists, waists of naked skin. He stood up to let a woman holding a baby take his seat and noticed the newspaper had been chucked onto the window ledge just as the train pulled into the next station. His stop, he realised, also scared of the doors. With a glance back at the square-toed man, Jack bent forward, picked up the newspaper and stepped off the train.

CHAPTER

3

I'd seen it so many times. Someone is out of the office for a few days and when they get back their desk is covered with someone else's junk. I'd done it myself. When James, the bloke who sits opposite me, went to Majorca last year all my paperwork crept sideways and by the time he came back his desk had become my overflow filing cabinet and I'd lent out his chair. *Nature abhors a vacuum* was my favourite expression in such circumstances, but it was still a shock to see the amount of rubbish that had piled up on *my* desk in just two weeks. There were at least twenty dog-eared 'circulating' envelopes awaiting a signature – nobody ever looked *inside* those things – and a small, pink envelope, no doubt a staff leaving-card filled with smiley faces and comments, *will miss you*, or *won't miss your rubbish tea*. And there were coffee rings everywhere, on everything, as if some strange, workplace creature had run amok. And there on the corner of my desk waited the pile. Jean liked to place James' pile on the right side of his computer and place my pile on the left, so it always glanced my hand as I clicked on my mouse, a tactile reminder of what I did from nine to five – reading questionnaires from the pile, researching the social issues of the day, hunting down patterns and quirks in human opinions, drawing desires on graphs that our clients would then reconfigure, swapping X axes with Ys, and massaging the data, up and down, in and out, until it resembled the truth.

"So, what have I missed?" I said, reacquainting myself with the arms of my chair.

James looked glum. He was often more of a thinker than a talker and I knew I'd have to wait for the answer. Maybe even enough time to dash up the corridor and put on the kettle.

"Wilson's got a bee in his bonnet," he said at last.

I disliked clichés, especially those involving animals, but this one conjured up such a vivid picture in my head I let it go. Tom Wilson was the company's boss, the 'head honcho,' as he liked to refer to himself in team-building sessions and occasionally mentioned in the emails sent out to all staff by his fragrant secretary Jean. He was a classic misery-guts, his social skills so minimal he was hard pressed to meet your eye if you passed him in the corridor, let alone smile. He frequently came up with barmy ideas guaranteed to lower office morale, but he was conservative when it came to accepting suggestions offered up by his workforce. He particularly enjoyed taking things apart, gadgets he found at the back of his drawer, but unfortunately could never put them together again.

"What's the bee about?" I said, signing a circulating envelope and tossing it onto James' desk.

"He wants fresh thoughts."

"So long as it's not fresh blood he's after."

James grinned then stared at my face. "How are your eyes by the way? I thought you'd be wearing dark glasses."

"I'm past that stage. They're almost back to normal. The eye is one of the quickest parts of the body to heal. Itched like hell at the beginning, though."

"Any more news on what happened?"

"No. I ... no."

"Right. So, we've got to come up with some new proposals. By Wednesday."

"About what exactly?"

"That's for you to decide."

"You mean he's letting us think?"

James' Adam's apple was suddenly prominent. "… yeah. He is … yeah."

The office hummed on. James and I were both quiet workers but our keyboards tapped pleasantly and voices drifted down the corridor in sporadic waves so we avoided the distraction of silence. I checked my long list of emails, had a bite of a sandwich from my desk drawer (someone had nicked my last bar of chocolate) and then wandered off to see what was going on by the vending machine. I was ready. Ready for condolences, ready for interest in the gory details of the last two weeks of my life.

"Got change of a quid?" It was Sammy Gringold: data analyst: big hands, face of a teddy bear.

"You what?"

"Have you got change of a quid?"

I fished some coins out of my pocket and looked at my colleague – poor Sammy, so hard at thrift. "Here you go." I said.

"Thanks." He flipped two coins into the vending machine with a practiced finger and pressed a button; something thumped down by our knees.

"So, how are you doing?" I said.

"Not bad. You?" He reached down and pulled out a *Toblerone*.

"Almost healed." I held my head at an angle, ready for inspection.

He glanced up from unpeeling the chocolate in his hand. "What do you mean?"

"My eyes. Almost healed."

He stared at my face. "I don't get it, what do you mean, 'almost healed?'"

"I had an accident."

"Did you?" He popped a piece of chocolate into his mouth. "When?"

"Three weeks ago."

He sniffed. "Didn't hear about that. Did we send you a card?"

"Yes."

"Healing up, then?"

"Yeah, healing up."

"Want a bit of chocolate?"

"No, thanks."

"That's good." He smiled with genuine happiness. "See you later."

"See you."

I watched his back as he walked down the corridor, his collapsing trouser hems dragging along the floor. Sammy wasn't high on my list of people. I had a list. Deep in my head I categorised my colleagues into those whose opinion I cared about and those whose opinion I didn't. This made life easier – it allowed reactions to be classified, smile sizes put in order, intonation graded and time spent at home nursing only the worthiest of slights.

The fortnight spent alone in my flat had seemed longer than fourteen days. I'd felt more fragile than I really was on that first day home from hospital and had let myself slip into a vapid patient condition, sipping grey soup off a tarnished spoon and getting into my pyjamas at nine thirty at night. But even then I couldn't rest, worrying that the doorbell would ring and I'd have to explain, or somehow make the case, that wearing pyjamas soothed injured eyes. I forgot that the sight of a pale person decked out in safety glasses might be more disturbing than a grown man dressed for bed before it was dark. And in this troubled state of hospital discharge I developed a skewed sense of perspective; my cooker seemed larger than I remembered and the risers on the stairs were definitely higher than before. I could see perfectly well by then but I quickly developed a peculiar sensitivity to anything that swung even briefly close to my eyes: my T-shirt pulled over my head, the greengrocer's finger as he pointed out his latest delivery of fresh tomatoes. My mother phoned daily, but, as she became increasingly distracted by noises in her house – the squeak of the window cleaner's cloth, the whistle of the kettle – her calls became less frequent until they stopped altogether. I didn't mind. And so the two weeks passed without incident but worried by thoughts of my boss's forefinger tapping impatiently on his desk I had returned to work a week earlier than my sick note specified.

I glanced at the hem of my trousers and began walking back to my office. As I turned a corner I saw Tom Wilson coming towards me. Everything as usual – jagged smile and shifty sideward glance as if we were strangers in the street, not colleagues tied together by all the stuff of mutual employment: contracts, sick leave, Christmas lunch.

"Have you been back long, William?" he said, pausing at an unnaturally long distance from which to start a conversation.

I paused too. "Clocked back in today."

"You alright?"

"Just fine."

"James told you about the 'Fresh Thoughts' initiative, did he?"

"Yes, the thoughts are fermenting as we speak."

His lips twitched. "Good. I want something that's going to shake this company up. Put it on the map. Then shake it up again."

"Right."

I watched the back of his head as he made his way down the corridor wary of the next corner. I sighed – a long, dramatic expellation of breath that emptied both my nose and lungs. I felt too tired for upheaval. Perhaps I'd suggest that we keep the status quo. That was radical. That would put the company on the map.

VIOLET was desperate for a coffee. She'd walked up the High Street too quickly and the heel of her stiletto had got stuck in a gap in the pavement, an inelegant pause in her day that left her with puddle water on her ankle and a groove in her heel that would be impossible to repair. The insides of the cafe windows were gently dripping when she arrived and she hesitated at the door, imagining the effect on her hair, on her laptop. She pushed open the heavy door and voices poured out through the gap to meet her.

"Get yerself in here, darlin'!" A woman with an apron tied too tightly round her waist pointed to a table in the corner. "Last one's over there. Better be quick."

A whiff of coffee entered her nose and that was it, Violet was inside, every bit of her ready for her morning fix. She squeezed between the tables – taking care to lift her handbag above the surrounding heads, and forcing a man to tuck in his stomach and shuffle his chair sideways – and sat down. An abandoned plate, reeking of tomato ketchup and the remnants of a fried egg, remained in front of her so she pushed it to the edge of the table, glanced at the waitress to indicate her readiness to order and then pulled out her laptop.

Violet had a high-powered job. She adored its description; the combination of power and height was just what she liked. Promotion had come fast – too fast. Her boss, if you could describe him as a boss if you were freelance, had always fancied her and that extra dab of lipstick had done the trick. She hadn't noticed the loose button on her blouse until the ink on the contract was dry but so what, she was good at her job, she deserved it. She'd always wanted to be one of those professional women who sit in cafes with their laptops, working. No cramped commute in smelly trains for her. She was one of a different breed. The new species of worker that could be trusted to plan their own day and relied upon to work efficiently in public places, immune to the distractions of the coffee-sipping public.

"Put a sock in it, Brian! He's just a bloody kid."

Violet glanced up. It would have to be a very thin waitress who could squeeze between her and the next table, and the adjacent man sat extremely close, his arms circling his plate in a gesture of grim protection. With her finger poised on the start button of her laptop – a bona fide break in proceedings – Violet summed up the scene straight away: irritable father suffering from too much quality time with his children, sullen seven-year-old, dishevelled baby. She was good at summing situations up, always had been. She should have been a lawyer.

She readied a withering smile then abandoned it as a new conversation from the table on her other side caught her attention.

"It's gonna come back and haunt you, you know."

"Rubbish, you sound like my hundred-year-old aunt."

Violet tapped her password out on her keyboard, and then stopped.

"What can I get you?"

A waitress had squeezed herself between the corner of the table and the adjacent man's elbow.

"Coffee, please. Very hot. And very black."

The waitress's pencil hovered above her pad. "What do you mean … very black?"

Violet smiled. Always the same. They called themselves baristas but they had no idea that you could never make coffee too concentrated.

"Very strong," she said. Clarification was her strong point too. She should have been a teacher. She sat back in her chair, relaxed in the knowledge that she hadn't officially 'clocked in' yet, and surveyed the room. Heads bobbed in conversation and fingers eased fragments from between gaps in teeth. Oh, how she loved it. Nothing could beat the atmosphere of the cafe: the battles for the last chair, the bread mopping up gravy, the coats slipping from the overloaded pegs. Nothing could beat the sound of strangers' voices.

"Is that the local rag you've got there?"

Violet didn't look round.

"Oh, yeah," a second voice replied. "My mum bought it. I needed something to read on the bus."

"I can't stand local news."

"Why not?"

"It's so pathetic. Who gives a damn about what the local scouts are up to?"

"Got to admit I like the obituaries."

"Weird."

"Yeah, I know. It's hilarious though, don't you think, the way everyone's so great when they die."

"What d'ya mean?"

"Have you ever read an obituary saying no one ever liked him and he was rubbish at his job?"

Two women. They sat directly behind her so Violet could not see them but it was easy to imagine: blonde with highlights, fake leather jackets, friends from way back. Violet thought of her own obituary and let her fingers tap out some words, a warm-up for her working day. *Born of Margary and John Veil, in North London on April 1ˢᵗ 1983, Violet Veil, a woman of great intelligence and beauty, will be sorely missed by her many friends . . .*

"–Hey, look at this job advertisement, what a doddle," said the first voice. "They're looking for . . . blimey . . . good listeners."

"Counts you out then."

They both laughed. A baby from somewhere across the room laughed.

"Says 'no training needed.' I might give this is a go."

"Let me see, oh, don't bother, it's some fancy research job."

"Is it? Oh, yeah."

"Might be a laugh to have a stab at it, though. What's the phone number?"

"Erm . . . two, two, three, nine, seven, one, four."

Violet's fingers tapped on her keyboard as if by themselves . . . *who always loved her, and she received many accolades during her long life . . . 020 5555 7296. . . .*

CHAPTER 4

I had the bones of it. I'd been up half the night, the latter half when the neighbour's dog had finally stopped barking and it was so quiet I could hear my heartbeat in my ears. I never worked at night normally. I needed my full seven hours, but with the big French coffee press at my elbow and Montreal jazz playing on the radio I wrote out my pitch. *Pitch.* Such a fantastic word. I couldn't wait to see Tom Wilson's face as I slugged my idea across the conference table. It was easy to mock the company, that's how James and I got through the tedium of the day, but as my idea took shape on the page I felt a touch of affection for the freshness of these thoughts. My proposal wasn't radical. It wasn't going to make the front page of *The Journal of Social Research,* but it might ruffle a few feathers round the table. It might even get me a rise. I didn't usually work this hard, but my encounter with Sammy had disturbed me. Was I so insignificant that I could be away from work for two whole weeks and people didn't notice? Even the dramatic and mysterious cause of my absence from the office had failed to penetrate the consciousness of my colleagues and I felt narked and insignificant. My idea had to be one they'd remember me by.

Everyone looked as though they'd been up late as I walked into the meeting room, a stuffy space on the second floor that was always littered with the detritus of the previous gathering. A tray in the middle of the table formed the hub: a single pot of coffee, mugs, milk in cartons, plastic stirrers in a plastic cup and sachets of saccharin, one of which had already been torn and spilt onto the tabletop. Tom Wilson, ever the blunderer, had already knocked over a chair yet he couldn't help but launch into his opening spiel while still partly beneath the table. His opening sentences, no doubt practiced aloud to Jean the afternoon before, were disturbed by the sound of chair legs scraping on the floor and notebooks being flipped open. I missed it altogether, as I was beneath the table myself, retrieving my pen, but by the time I emerged the *great hiatus*, as James and I fondly called it, was underway.

Nobody ever wanted to go first in *Wilson Inc.* or *Wink* meetings, as we named them, thinking we were funny. We felt a certain creepiness about anyone showing too much eagerness, a hangover from our school days, so we all held back while Tom Wilson scanned us eleven eminents until he caught someone's eye. Although 'going first'– in retrospect – meant your audience wasn't entirely comatose, and noting there was only one pot of coffee on the scene and not a biscuit in sight, I cleared my throat.

"William," said Wilson, fixing me in his gaze, "fire away."

I stood up and focused on Sammy. I'd been to the public speaking class in the company's *Keep the Home Fires Burning* sessions, a much-loved baby of Wilson, and now tried out my points in groups of three. "This company is very good at social research. It's very good at qualitative research. But it's not a great player in the digital age." I paused, and rearranged my body into the 'audience encapsulator' stance – point seven on the course. "We need to forget human beings altogether."

Someone sniggered.

"Aren't human beings rather our bread and butter?" said Wilson from the important end of the table.

"If I may finish." I beamed a seamless meld of humility and superiority in his direction. "What I mean is, we don't need to waste time on meeting real people, paying their expenses, heating rooms. We can do *all* our research online. It'll be *groundbreaking*."

Wilson had a misshapen smile pinned to his face.

"And, it'll be *fresh*." I glanced round the table. My eye itched; I scratched it.

EVE stepped into the launderette. Thresholds always reminded her of how tall she was, but she managed not to stoop and slipped smartly in with great accuracy and the mindset of a shorter person. A woman was reading the notice board and as Eve headed for her spot on the bench she noted the curl on the back of the reader's hair. The notice board, the place where the inexplicable met the improbable, was overloaded with tatty bits of paper, all pinned on top of one other, vying for the customers' attention. The management sometimes attempted to clear a space for important information and once had even tried to refer to the customers of the launderette as 'clients.' They had a sign printed specially to hang at the top of the board, but it had caused a mini revolution, the man with the giant jeans pronouncing 'clients go to lawyers' offices not bloody launderettes,' and the skinny woman with the improbably small bras actually ripping it off the wall and throwing it into the bin where it sank without trace beneath the mini packets of *Tide* and bobbles of grey lint. But that was a rare blip in the usually melancholic and hushed tone of the place. There was something soothing about the quietly whirring underwear and silent folding of shirts so most people did not speak, preferring to sit quietly on the bench between washes or gaze sadly out of the window like worn-out mannequins. Yet, when someone *did* speak everyone listened. They all pretended not to; they studied their newspapers, they separated black socks from white, but with all her experience, Eve knew they were all absorbing every sigh, every sucked-in syllable, every last word. And when the last word came, with the lowering of pitch and the chug of wet clothes returning to the fore, the launderette's customers would continue in their own worlds as if nothing had happened.

But Eve never continued. After every little exchange between customers, she'd think a measured thought, take a small intake of breath, do a quick assessment – sex, age, social class – then turn to her subject. 'No problem is too big' was her favourite opener. How she liked that turn of phrase. She always felt pleased with the way it suggested her competence *and* had a tinge of friendliness, yet left room for a dignified departure should a problem – one that needed solving anyway – not actually exist. And most times it didn't exist, the problem. More often as not she'd be met with a bewildered stare or a falling smile or, on bad days, told to 'mind your own bloody business, you bloody cow.' But occasionally – and this is what made it all worthwhile – her subjects would turn to her with a look of relief on their faces and she'd take them aside, usually to the nook beside the oldest washing machine that rattled like a horse trapped in a suitcase, and commence one of her little 'chats.' In less time than it takes to cupboard-dry a full load of clothes she would identify where the worry lay, outline a plan of action, and, if time and circumstance allowed, pull the appropriate leaflet from her bag and slip it into her client's hands.

Her training as a counsellor had begun at keyholes many years earlier when she had monitored the disintegration of her parents' marriage via the aperture in the lounge door. There she discovered there was no need to view the actual scene when she could glean everything by listening to the creak of her mother's handbag as she fished out yet another handkerchief and hear the top of her father's whisky bottle twist open, again and again, and again. But she was an innovative child and with a solution to her parents' woes sitting sour in her mind she had begun to write notes. Slipped anonymously into her mother's pockets, beneath her pillow, into the back of her drawers, Eve's advice marked the beginning of a vocation. She had been born to dispense it. She had dispensed it ever since.

Eve didn't actually need to come to the launderette, she owned a perfectly good washing machine at home, its detergent drawer unsoiled, its pristine drum still a spic silver, but this place was special. Here, against the gentle rhythm of rinsing knickers and shrinking sweaters, she could focus on the sporadic snatches of conversation and give people the benefit of her experience at will. Even if people didn't say much in the launderette, when they did talk it resonated; it became a little play, a clean-smelling stage with a captive audience.

That day the launderette was busy. There was only one spot left on the bench and Eve, after loading up the remaining washing machine, squeezed herself between two girls in their twenties, both with neat hair and tinkling bracelets. It seemed to make no difference that she sat between them as they talked across her, more noisily than her usual subjects. And they laughed loudly, the woman on her left actually jogging Eve's shoulder as she threw back her head at a joke that Eve didn't understand. Eve was glad they were happy, but suddenly they grew serious, their voices lowered and their smiles dropped off their faces. Eve got up to remove her washing from the washer and piled it into a free dryer. By the time she returned to the bench the gap had closed and the girls' voices had sunk to a whisper. But whispers were no problem for Eve. Doglike, she could tune into different frequencies with ease, and as she sat on the end of the bench, listening to a long story – of what she classified as woe – she felt concern bubbling up inside her.

"Might I suggest a visit to the Citizen's Advice Bureau," Eve said, as if to the air.

"Sorry?" said the closest girl.

"The Citizen's Advice Bureau, they'll be able to sort you out. I've heard of this sort of problem before. Best to let the professionals deal with it." She bent down, deftly pulled leaflet 20E out of her bag and placed it gently in the girl's hand.

"Oh … thanks."

It was as easy that. Sometimes.

Eve got up off the bench and pulled her clothes out of the dryer, folded them up and put them into her washing bag. Both girls looked up at her as she swept by so she couldn't hold back, she just couldn't resist throwing out one of her metaphors, the *coup de grâce* of an expert counsellor. "After all," she said, turning to face them, "with a mad dog in the street why go outside with bare legs?"

Without waiting for a reply she opened the door and hitched her washing bag onto her shoulder. Then she heard it. Someone had switched on the big dryer, the noisy daddy, but she still overheard a fresh remark from beside the noticeboard.

"Hey look, there's something interesting pinned up on here. A job advertisement – they're looking for listeners, would you believe. 'Good ones,' whatever they are."

Eve lowered her bag, turned and went back inside.

CHAPTER

5

So much for going first. I'd managed to relieve the itch in my eye with a wet tissue dabbed on my lid, eaten three sandwiches and wolfed down a *Kit Kat* since the office meeting ended, but none of it eased the feeling in my stomach. Tom Wilson was hopeless at socialising with his staff, but when it came to shooting down ideas he was the king. Rather than sending a ripple of interest around the table my proposal had been pitched back at me with the force of a Surrey fast bowler and I spent the rest of the session being held up as the low standard by which all others would be subsequently judged. I'd always thought of myself as a forgiving sort of bloke, but it was hard to stop the resentment simmering, especially when Sammy Gringold's lame plan for *narratology* was held up as a model of initiative. James had stood up for me of course. He'd tried his hardest to second my ideas, but Wilson was too busy complimenting the genius of his new protégé to notice.

I was back at my desk, getting ready to do some therapeutic Internet browsing when I noticed all sorts of strange tabs crowding the top of the screen. Amongst the ads for taxidermy and blogs for hot rod cars there was one that caught my attention, mainly because it sounded like something out of the 1950s. For me that was the greatest decade; I felt I should have been a teenager back then. I had narrow feet that would look particularly good in winkle-pickers and the square sort of body born to be encased in high-waisted swimming trunks. But most of all I liked the conspiracy theories of that era, the deeply unethical government manoeuvering and dodgy data in secret files. But when I opened the tab I found it was an article about something else. Something that had begun much earlier. I read.

'*Founded in 1937 by three young men, Tom Harrisson, Charles Madge, and Humphrey Jennings, Mass Observation aimed to create an 'anthropology of ourselves.'*

"Hey, James, have you been using my computer?

"No."

"Seen anyone else messing around with it?"

"No. Why?"

"There's a bit of a trail up at the top."

James frowned. "I haven't seen anyone."

"Okay."

"Sorry you got the grilling earlier," he said. "Wilson can be a bastard."

I took my eyes off the screen. "Couldn't have been worse, could it?"

His smile shorted. "Forget about it. Wilson will be throwing another sound bite at us before Sammy's had time to alphabetise his new files."

"Yeah."

I clicked on the rogue article again and re-read the title.

Mass Observation. An Anthropology of Ourselves.

STANLEY thought he should have known that something was up. Beryl's eyes were extra beady that morning. She watched him as he walked into the kitchen, chuffed as hell and cocking her head in that irritating way of hers, as if she knew something he didn't. Trouble is she often *did* know something he didn't. That's what got to him. When his bank account went into the red she whistled at the sight of the letter in his hand before he'd even got it open. And then there was the time he couldn't find his glasses anywhere because he was wearing them. Oh yes, she spotted that right away.

Anyway, *that* morning, she had attitude. She looked him straight in the eye with that know-it-all way of hers and refused to shift when he tried to open the cage door. He clacked his lips together in the way she liked, but still she wouldn't budge. "Have it your own way," he said, turning his back on her. He put the kettle on and dropped a teabag into a mug. When he looked back Beryl was watching him.

"Wishing we hadn't been so mean now, are we?" he said. Still she didn't move. Stanley wandered back over to the cage and noticed the paper at the bottom was wet. "So that's your problem, is it?"

Beryl didn't like to get her feet wet; it interfered with her concentration. Stanley clacked his lips together again but this time in a deeper, more soothing way. She loved that; she'd always get that faraway look in her eyes when he did that, but no, not today, she just stared at him, all beady and accusing.

"Alright," he said, "I suppose my tea can wait."

He crouched down to the cupboard beneath the sink and pulled out the previous day's newspaper. Then he began the sorting. Out with the *Business*, out with the *Sport*, out with the *Culture* pages. Beryl only liked real news at the bottom of her cage. Plus the *Classifieds*. Oh, and the *Lonely Hearts*. That was what made her happiest: a new cuttlefish and a fresh page of lonely hearts beneath her feet. It's what got her through her day.

He opened the paper flat on the kitchen table – Beryl couldn't abide creases – and was about to start smoothing out the page when he noticed an advertisement in the top left-hand corner. He was always on the look out for a new job, what with his current one not being up to much, but there was one word in particular that caught his eye. 'Sociological.' What could that mean? he wondered. He knew a couple of '*ogicals*' already. 'Illogical' his mother had always called him. A bit harsh he'd thought, considering he had been so good at chess as a child. And 'pathological.' His mother had called him that too, but not to his face, just when she was whispering in other people's ears.

"We'll have to look that one up, won't we?" he said.

Beryl liked words. She secretly longed to have the pages of a dictionary lining her cage. That'd be her seventh heaven. Stanley took their *Shorter Oxford* off the shelf and it didn't take long to reach 'S' but then he got distracted by 'sod' (*oblong piece or slice of earth with grass growing on it*) and then 'soddish' (*unpleasant, despicable*) but finally, after going backwards through the alphabet his gaze landed on 'sociological' (*pertaining to the study of society*).

"It pertains to the study of society," he called over to Beryl. "*We* could do that, couldn't we?"

Beryl gazed back.

CHAPTER

6

Tom Wilson always seemed oblivious to the arrival of other human beings when they were ushered into his office. Jean's announcements were crisp enough but the boss liked to keep his eyes on his computer screen for longer than was comfortable and visitors were forced to linger in that dead space between the door and the desk until he finally deigned to look up.

"I have another new idea, Tom," I said quickly, so as to circumvent any rush attempts at civility. "I think you'll find it interesting."

He waved for me to sit down. "Better than the last one I hope."

"Much better."

So I began. My warm-up was soothing: praise for Wilson's sense of judgment followed by a finely timed compliment on his new chair. Then I revealed the full thrust of it. Social research had got out of touch with its roots, I said; it needed something to bring it back into the limelight. "What we need," I said, aware of a pompous tone rising in my voice, "is an anthropology of ourselves." Against my better nature I emphasised my final two words with my index fingers hung in the air.

Wilson's voice seemed to have lost all intonation. "Mass Observation."

"You've heard of it?"

He lowered his chin and looked over his glasses. "William. British social policy in the 1940s was founded on it."

"Ah."

"But do carry on."

So I carried on, my voice getting ever more confident, outlining my strategy, breaking down the budget, all the while skipping over the grey areas, the pockets of doubt, until I reached my triumphant conclusion " I want to hire ordinary people to eavesdrop on the public, just like they did back in the day. We'd be the new *Mass Observation*. You couldn't get fresher than that."

Wilson smiled a limp rag of a smile, arched his fingers into a triangle and leant back in his chair. Time didn't stand still. It ceased to exist.

"You know what?" he said at last. "I like it. I actually like it. But what you are suggesting is somewhat illegal. Depending on your method of course."

"Don't worry," I said. "This will be very low key, I promise. Any eavesdropping will be done strictly under the radar."

In a spirit of *Ludditism* I decided to advertise in the newspaper for my team of professional eavesdroppers. A real newspaper, made of real paper. I didn't only want to attract the computer-savvy twenty-somethings who could multitask in their sleep, I wanted to reach the full demographic: the woman too skint to buy a computer, the old man who'd never heard of email. I was looking for *ordinary* people. The benchmark for 'ordinary people' was myself of course. This had seemed a reasonable level on which to base my search until James had questioned the precise meaning of the word in that pedantic way of his. The dictionary had been of little help at first, offering up an entire page of possibilities including, a person *'who has jurisdiction in ecclesiastical cases,'* and then a person '*in charge of warships laid up in a harbour.'* It was only when I came upon '*of common or everyday occurrence'* that my faith was restored in my own banal understanding of the word. Still, the range of possibilities bothered me and I spent over an hour refining the sentences of my advertisement, before returning to the wording I had started with. Was it illegal? I wondered. I knew I'd have to be careful to preserve anonymity, no names, no addresses, no descriptions that could identify places. But the potential illegality of it added to the thrill. And at that moment I was on a high, dying to get going. The blind man's team was going to listen. And even more thrilling was the question taking shape in my head. What would they hear?

MISSY spent a long time finding a telephone box. There used to be an old-fashioned red one opposite her building and she'd enjoyed watching the comings and goings around it from her window – the desperate hunt for change at three in the morning, the irritated tapping on the glass. But it had been removed six months earlier, leaving a rectangle of stained concrete behind on the verge, and now she had to walk all the way down the Holloway Road to find one. The phone book had been ripped out and the feathered spine hung down in a way that might have made her laugh. She pulled out the page of classified ads from her pocket, unfolded it, checked the number and dialled. Although only a phone call, some buried instinct made her tidy her hair, pressing the frizziest locks behind her ears and patting down the wiry ends that protruded from her parting. She didn't use her voice during the day and when the person on the end of the line asked, 'Can I help you,' she struggled to get a sound out. "I'm calling about the job," she said.

Such relief, the man on the other end of the line was a talker. All she had to do was stand there and listen while he told her about a job she might get and answered questions she hadn't asked. And while she listened she looked towards the charity shop on the other side of the road.

A mannequin looked back at her from the window. It wore an ill-fitting dress; it held a cream girdle in its stiff fingers. A pair of silver party shoes encased its feet.

"Yes," she said, realising a question had been asked. "I can come in for an interview on Friday. What time?"

There was a lot there, in that voice inside the phone. She thought the speaker wasn't used to talking to strangers, or maybe he just wasn't used to talking to women, but she heard funny little gaps between his words, longer than you'd expect, but shorter than she liked.

Her gaze wandered down the street until it settled on a man who fished money out of his pockets, rooted through his change and bought a cup of maggots from the vending machine outside the grocer's.

"Oh, yes. Looking forward to meeting you too," she said, as if reading from a script.

She put the phone down and turned towards the direction of home. She'd never been fishing, never sat in a chair by the oily canal at Camden Lock, but she suddenly wanted, no, *needed*, to have her own cup of maggots. She glanced round, crossed the road and slipped her remaining coins into the vending machine. Then, feeling a thrill inside her chest, she carefully lifted out the writhing cupful, checked the lid was properly on and slipped it into her bag.

It was almost dark by the time Missy got home and she felt tired, in need of a treat. But first she tipped the maggots into a plastic bag, squeezed out the air, tied a knot and placed them on the top shelf of the fridge, next to the three remaining rashers of bacon, dried on the rinds. Then she pulled out a stool and climbed up. She reached to the back of the kitchen cupboard, past the elderly tins of tuna, past the packet of instant gravy, until her hand came to rest on the light bulb.

Back in the living room, she removed the packaging, then placed the bulb gently on the sofa. After dragging the kitchen stool into the middle of the room, she collected the bulb, climbed up and removed the clear bulb hanging from the ceiling and replaced it with the new one. She stepped down and switched on the light. Red. Everything red.

She lay on the floor; she needed a treat. Red light made her beautiful. Red light made her sofa clean, her shoes new, the ragged nails on her fingers rounded and smooth. Yet when she held up her arms and looked at the back of her hand she saw her veins; they rippled across her skin from wrist to knuckle, knuckle to wrist. She flexed her lips, adjusted her hips on the ruddy floorboards and thought of the voice at the end of the phone. She must practice for her new job. No more random listening to conversations in bits, but professional listening where she *really* listened.

She held her breath. She waited. She tried to cock her ears, unsure of what that meant. She even squeezed her eyes shut tight, hoping that closing down one sense would sharpen another. But the air was empty of sound. The red walls were silent.

CHAPTER

7

"You are kidding, aren't you?"

I smiled. James was easy bait. Still wet behind the ears at thirty-two, he took a while to get jokes and then retold them back to the original teller with a half-remembered ending, or on bad days, spliced with a punchline from another joke. He had trouble discerning the difference between sarcasm and sincerity, which made for a confused yet pleasantly naïve life. But in spite of all this he was my mate, the bloke in the office I could go to the pub with after work and have a moan.

I sipped my beer. "I tease you not. Wilson even congratulated me on the freshness of my thoughts."

"So," James pulled his chair closer, "let me get this right. You're going to hire researchers from members of the public with no research experience–"

"They're not researchers."

"What the hell are they, then?"

"They're eavesdroppers."

"Okay, so you hire some people, Joe public and his friends–"

"And her friends."

"And *her* friends, and you get them to listen in on private conversations and … and then what?"

"They'll report back and I'll see what's out there."

"What do you mean, *out there*?"

I took another sip of beer. "Inside the chatter."

"And how are they going to record this chatter? Hidden mikes?"

"Nothing so crude. They're going to write notes in a notebook."

"Won't that be a bit obvious?"

"Not if they're good at it."

James gulped his beer – big, worried swallows that made his eyes bulge. "Am I part of this by the way?" He placed his empty glass down on the table.

"If you want to be."

He searched my face. "Bill, did you get a knock on the head too in that accident by any chance?"

I suddenly felt mischievous. "Tell you what, James, let's try it out now."

"What, eavesdrop?"

"Yes. Close your eyes for a second and listen."

"I don't want to."

"Go on. Close your eyes."

"Oh, shit. All right. But you've got to do it too."

"I will."

The pub seemed louder with my eyes shut and I immediately sensed an air of conspiracy in the room. I pictured a mouth whispering behind a hand, but when I opened one eye the room reverted to a scene of ordinary Londoners, clutching their glasses and emptying beer down their throats. James had his eyes scrunched shut like a child playing hide and seek. Feeling like a cheat, I closed my eye again and listened.

Some people are unable to speak quietly. Even in places as muted as the doctor's waiting room some people are unable to appreciate the resonance of their surroundings or adjust their vocal chords to the acoustics of a space. One such person was either at my elbow, or on the other side of the room. So many people in the pub, yet this voice lorded over them all. A man, he was telling a story – up an octave, down an octave – and it was a promising one. He'd been to Canada – a place called Winnipeg, and it was so hot he had to sleep naked. But one night an animal–

I felt a tap on my shoulder. "You awake, Bill?"

I opened my eyes to see James peering at my face as if checking for acne. "Of course."

"You looked a bit weird."

"Did I?"

"Yeah, a bit like an animal, a horse that's asleep or something."

"I was concentrating." I went to rub my eye but stopped in time. "So, what did you hear?"

"Er … just some rubbish about someone's uncle's car going in for a paint job."

"That all?"

"Yeah."

I glanced round the room. "Didn't you hear the Canadian tale of sweat on the sheets?"

He frowned, "No."

Funny that, a voice like Goliath and James didn't hear it.

"What was the story?" he said.

I suddenly didn't feel like going into detail. "Oh, something about a raccoon under a deck."

"In London?"

"No, James. In Canada."

"Hey, Bill."

"Yes?"

"Did you really get Wilson to agree to this? It's never going to work, you know. Not with amateurs."

"They managed alright during the Mass Observation."

"The mass what?"

"The Mass Observation. You must have heard of it."

"Nope."

"Well ... it was a project set up back in the 1930s by three men, Harrisson, Madge and Jennings."

James went a long time without blinking.

"They met in the newspaper."

"What do you mean, they met in the newspaper?"

I sipped my beer. "Harrison published a poem on the same day that Jennings and Madge wrote a letter and that's how they connected. On the same page."

James still didn't speak.

"Don't you see?"

"See what?"

"They were on the same page."

James searched my face as if his life depended on it.

I relaxed back in my chair. "Mass Observation was all about the man-in-the-street. The three men, Harrisson, Madge and–"

"Jennings."

"Yes, Jennings, wanted to find out ordinary people's opinions by listening in on them. In the street." James sniffed. "So, just before the Second World War people were sent out to listen in on conversations in pubs and shops and on the bus, then report back. They wanted to find out what the public really thought about the impending fighting."

James wiped condensation off the side of his beer glass with his finger. "You mean there might be a war coming?"

"James, there *always* might be a war coming. No, I want to find out what people are talking about today."

"But we have questionnaires and interviews to do that."

"But people lie in interviews."

James took a mouthful of beer, his throat comically magnified in the bottom of the glass. "How do you know?"

My left eye twitched. "I know."

James appeared to be thinking. "Hey, Bill. Are you sure it's legal? – eavesdropping."

I arranged the words in my head before I spoke. "The law is vague. But we can't help but eavesdrop. Words are out there all the time. They float in and out of our ears. They fill public space. We can't close our ears. We shouldn't close our ears. It's about survival. We've evolved to eavesdrop."

"Yeah, but that's different to making a record of what you hear. And what about the government? You know, *Nineteen Eighty-Four* – Big Brother, and all that?"

I smiled. "I'm Big Brother now. Can't you see how big and brotherly I am?"

"Seriously, Bill. Surely only certain people, you know, official organizations are allowed to listen and record?"

"Rubbish. Do you believe the government is listening to us now?"

"Maybe."

"Oh, come on. Are they really interested in listening to everyone? Recording what topping you had on your pizza last night? Noting down what you bought your grandma for Christmas."

James twisted in his seat. "Maybe the mundane hides the truth…."

I couldn't repress a slice of admiration. "I wouldn't lose sleep over it, James. Okay, I accept the government might listen in sometimes, but not to us, not to the small fry who pay their taxes and can't be bothered to go on protest marches. Government surveillance has to be focused. They'd have too much information to sort through if they worried about all of us.

"But I read an article–"

"Seriously James, there is just *too* much information out there for anyone to handle. Eavesdropping on an industrial scale just wouldn't work."

James' shoulders drooped. He liked nothing better than relaying snippets from the newspaper. I usually managed to continue writing emails as he read but occasionally I was forced to down tools and wait in suspended animation while he stumbled through a trough of journalistic analysis, sometimes mispronounced, always lacking a punchline.

"Do you believe everything you read?" I said.

"No. Do you believe everything you hear?"

A man was throwing up into a drain by the time we left the pub. James and I exchanged superior glances, and then made our way towards the Tube station. It was a damp night – the rain seemed to be everywhere, beneath my eyelashes, inside my nose, and with our collars pulled up and our necks sunk into our shoulders we walked in silence, until James spoke. "Bill?"

"Yeah."

"There was something else."

"What do you mean?"

"Back in the pub, I heard something else." He fiddled with his collar. "I heard a woman whisper something into another woman's ear. I didn't like hearing it. I felt I shouldn't be listening."

I thought of Goliath. "What did she whisper?"

He moved closer. "'I'm never going to smile again.'"

JACK sat down at his kitchen table. The chair ached out a complaint, but he liked that. He always enjoyed the sounds of the objects in his home. His cutlery drawer chattered, his blinds murmured and his copy of Hamlet whispered up to his face as he flicked through its worn pages. He made a space on the table, pushing his notebooks to one side and gathering his pencils into a pile, and then pulled the newspaper he'd picked up on the Tube out of his pocket. He opened it onto the classified ads. Two advertisements merged across a fold in the paper and for a moment he imagined life as a *sympathetic welder*. Then he spread the newspaper out fully and studied the advertisement that had been circled by the man on the train.

LISTENERS WANTED

Researchers wanted for sociological project in London.

Good rates of pay.

Flexible hours – maximum 35 per week.

All persons must be between 18-75

Ordinariness would be an asset

No experience required. Training given.

Must be good listeners.

Call 020 5555 7296 to obtain an application form

Or to arrange an interview or send your C.V. to

Bill Harcourt 29 Craven St. London.

He tried to picture the person who'd written the copy. Use of the word 'persons' suggested they were old. The absence of an email address suggested they did not know how to use a computer and were definitely old. But he liked old people. He found them easier to talk to, if he had to speak. He read the advertisement again and wondered if he had it in him. It would mean meeting new people, stranger-type people. He hadn't been to an interview since he'd got his current job and that had been a rushed affair with an interviewer who seemed more nervous than he, and the offer was probably a mistake. But he had subsequently managed to carve out a niche for himself in his current office, a private world the size of a small wardrobe. It centred on his computer screen and the few inches round it, where, in spite of the digital paintbox that could do anything with everything he still liked to lay out the tactile tools of a graphic designer at his elbow: *Rotring* pens, coloured pencils, erasers and scalpels. The small scale of his workspace allowed him to concentrate on his work without having to worry about talking to the others. He found it hard talking to the others. But he found it easy to listen. His fellow workers, the first generation of digital designers now pressing up against the ceiling of middle-age, were not so interested in the larger subjects of life, the crushing facts of global warming or the fine details of government legislation, they were interested in the mechanics of every day. Yet this was what always caught his attention. The story of the bus driver who was rude to pensioners for getting on the bus too slowly, the neighbour's problem with the dustbin lid that wouldn't stay on, and the error at the hospital when the hernia was mistaken for hip replacement because the doctor had bad writing. He liked the way each person talked, but no one really listened to what the other was saying.

Jack picked up a pair of scissors, cut out the advertisement and stuck it into his notebook with a glue stick. Then he got himself a can of orange juice out of the fridge, sat back down at the table and looked at his phone.

CHAPTER

8

James looked hung over the next morning when I arrived at the office. I knew that feeling, the fur on the tongue, the little haze round anything bright, so I turned on my heel and brewed him a strong, tar-like cup of coffee with four spoonfuls of sugar and a biscuit. I'd slipped them quietly next to his elbow, and tiptoed halfway across the room before I noticed my in tray. "Bloody hell, look at that!" Typically bare, it was almost unrecognizable as mine, so high was the tower of envelopes piled within it.

James looked up slowly from his work, as if allowing blood levels in his head to reach equilibrium. "What ...? Oh, yeah. Jean brought them in before you got here. I suspect teaming hordes of eager eavesdroppers are buried in there somewhere."

It was like Christmas. Or the St. Valentine's Day I'd imagined as a teenager. I don't know why I'd asked for handwritten applications for the jobs rather than emails. Perhaps reading about the Mass Observation project had put me back into analogue mode. Whatever the reason, it marked me as out of touch, and for a moment I regretted such a retrograde step. But then I picked up the first envelope and felt the childish thrill of receiving a real letter written on real paper. The art of fixing a stamp into the correct corner of the envelope had clearly been lost, but the handwriting was surprisingly clear – in the age of the keyboard – mostly legible and mostly straight.

I laid them all out on my desk in size order, but noting James seemed to have acquired an eyebrow that was quizzically arched, I collected them up into a rough pile and began to go through them at random. I thought of the applicants. Perhaps somewhere down there inside the envelopes would be the perfect eavesdroppers, a team of dedicated listeners who would hear what nobody else could. I'd already fashioned their characteristics in my mind: methodical, efficient, wise, but not too worldly, not too slick. I wasn't asking much, I just wanted people who could tune their ears to the right frequency and remember everything they had heard.

All the envelopes were different and it was a pleasure at first to just feel and sniff them and then grandly make use of the gold letter opener Jean had given me when she discovered she had two the same.

"Anything interesting?' asked James, through a mouthful of biscuit.

"I … don't know. It's weird, there's all sorts in here."

"You wanted 'all sorts,' didn't you?"

"Yes, but I'm not sure how I'm going to decide – hey, listen to this one: 'Crouching down beside a keyhole is my favourite position.'"

"Bloody hell!"

"I wonder if I'm going to get nothing but weirdos and stalkers?"

"Course you are."

I scanned the next letter. "James, listen to this."

"Go on."

I held up the paper, cleared my throat and read, "I've always loved to listen. Ever since the day I overheard a marriage proposal on the top of the number seven bus."

"Is that the sort of thing you're looking for?"

"Yes, I think it is – God – I don't know. What do you think?"

James had a cartoon thought, tilting his head and swivelling his eyes to the side before turning back to face me. "I think this whole thing's going to get you in trouble."

"How come?"

"Well, you're dealing with amateurs, aren't you. And it's not a proper job so there's no loyalty there. And … how do you know you can trust them?"

"Trust them with what?"

"The information."

"You mean the information they hear out on the street?"

James scratched his head.

I was beginning to see why people never showed initiative in our company. I was also starting to see why Wilson resorted to introducing banal new projects and giving them names that sounded like air fresheners. But the air round here needed some freshening. "So, I gather you're out then."

James grunted. "I'll lend an ear now and then, but I don't want to be the one transcribing details of someone's hernia into the computer. Okay?"

"Okay."

VIOLET didn't need much sleep – high-powered women generally don't. The Prime Minister got by on a couple of hours a night and Violet saw parallels with herself, with her ability during the long hours of inertia to sort the snubs, replenish the regrets and distill the stores of adrenalin, yet be alert the moment the sun broke the horizon. She could keep on running until she stopped.

It was four in the morning by the time she kicked off her slippers and lay down on her bed. Silk sheets were one of her little treats to herself, but on this night they felt uncomfortably clammy and she kicked off the duvet and spread her body out into a star shape in an effort to cool down. She went over the events of the day in her head. Like an award-winning executive she had written down the pros and cons of the listening job. Not on the computer, that was for deadbeats, but on expensive cream paper with a watermark that sang high quality when you held it up to the light. Then she had checked her bank account, rejigged her budget and applied for the job. *Professional listener* was a title that rolled elegantly off her tongue, but when precisely to make the call had been a dilemma. Eventually she had drunk a glass of iced water, loosened up her throat with some warbling exercises in the bathroom and telephoned the number in the advertisement. Obviously her manner had been impressive as the man had offered her an interview straight away. He was impressed. He was in love with her already.

She flipped the duvet back over her legs and began planning her outfit. Short skirt or long?

CHAPTER

9

I decided to walk down Whitehall at lunchtime. This part of London, with its black railings and badly parked Porsches, made me feel prickly, yet sometimes I imagined I could live in one of the massive stone buildings that lurked on the edge of the streets. But no one lived here. All embassies, churches and government ministries, it was a place to pass through, never linger too long, never imagine too much.

I glanced up at the sky as I stepped out onto the street and started along one of my well-worn paths. I crossed Northumberland Avenue, followed the swaying backsides of two police horses along New Scotland Yard before turning into one of London's most ritualistic streets. I was immediately confronted by the backside of another horse high on a plinth, its iron flank cast into a pose of strength and optimism, its gaze fixed on the Houses of Parliament which filled the distant end of the street.

I mooched along, then paused halfway up the street on a stippled square of blind persons' pavement by the pedestrian crossing and looked up at the Cenotaph, the bulky monument to war that sat stranded in the traffic. I'd seen this tomb of the *Unknown Soldier* many times on the television every Remembrance Sunday, engulfed in marching arms and marching legs, its base shored up with poppy wreaths. But now, surrounded by buses and lorries and cars, it looked incongruous, alone. I'd always assumed it was empty. 'Who *was* the unknown soldier?' I'd asked my dad as a kid. 'What did he do?' But my dad never answered me. It was as if he hadn't heard.

We'd actually attended the remembrance ceremony one year where I'd been confused by the old soldiers in black overcoats and black hats who looked too frail to carry the medals pinned to their chests let alone to haul the kit for launching rockets. And it had bothered my ten-year-old self even then. How could anyone so well known be unknown?

A glazier's van stopped in the traffic in front of the monument, but I could still see bits of it through the large sheet of glass fixed to the vehicle's side. I felt tense in the way I did these days around glass and placed my hand in front of my eyes. I dropped it back down and noticed a man pause at the monument's base beside me, one hand held on the back of his head. Thinking. Thinking about what?

I remained on my piece of blind pavement and closed my eyes. It's frightening to close your eyes when you are outside on your own. The world felt huge, yet at that moment I relished the feeling of my senses sharpening. The traffic seemed far away but also close. Something hummed. An overloaded fridge lorry maybe? Or an overloaded city? Yet between the sounds I could hear pieces of silence. I thought yet again of the soldier inside his tomb. Unknown yet *known* by everyone. The contradiction nagged me. Then I thought of the man in the hospital bed. I would never know who had slept next to me for those long nights. I wasn't sure why I cared. And finally, for reasons I understood even less, I thought of the eavesdroppers. My group of listeners would answer my questions. They would surely press their ears to the keyhole and hear things no one had heard before.

I pulled up my collar and walked to the end of Downing Street, home of our Prime Minister, prison of our leader. I slipped into the crowd gathered at the gates and admired what there was to admire: the empty street, the traffic cones, the double yellow lines kinking round a drain. Assorted tongues rippled through the crowd: French, German, Japanese and then English, clipped and recognizable.

"See the black house, yeah …?"

"Yeah, yeah, I see. Bit plain … isn't it?"

"Yeah. Got your coat? It's getting nippy."

"What's that?

"I dunno. D'ya know?"

"No. Don't know."

"That copper looks cold."

"Ha, yeah. Ha."

Three policemen stood just inside the gate, their bodies rounded by pockets bulging with notebooks and phones and unrecognizable objects. Three Mr. Plods with too much chocolate, a pistol on the thigh, machine guns held as they'd been trained to hold them, bullet-proof vests, a flash of gum between parted lips, buttons straining, too tight, everything too tight and another chew of the gum. The crowd photographed everything on their mobiles: the gum, the pistol on the thigh, the mobile phone primed to ring. Police eyes scanned the crowd, a little jump of the heels, trying to shake out the cold. We looked at them; they looked at us. I aimed my phone at my feet and switched on *record*.

EVE felt a muscle pull in her back as she reached up to the top of her wardrobe. Blankets were up there, ones that she never used, plus her old school uniform. She pulled down a shirt, the brown one for special occasions, smacked off the dust, and then eased a pleated skirt off its hanger and lay both items down on the bed. That was her. That flat person lying on the bed was her – too tired to do anything but lie down, chest deflated, hem draped over the edge.

She thought of the prospect of new job with a shiver of excitement. She had cut her hours at the Citizen's Advice Bureau to six a week.

They hadn't liked it, but the Bureau didn't pay and she needed some money. As a school administrator, she'd paid her whole life into the state pension, but when it came, the beige letter on the mat on her sixtieth birthday, she realised it was not going to be enough. Although frugality was in her blood, honed to perfection during a childhood of second-hand clothes, freezing bedrooms and plain breakfast, as the months on a pension wore on the wear and tear went unattended, and every part of her life frayed, flimsied or broke. She couldn't keep darning the holes in the toes of her tights forever.

She hovered at the end of the bed and then gently plumped her cheeks. Finally she gathered her flat self up and got dressed. She hadn't been to a job interview for thirty years. The piercing squeak of the interviewer's chair was all she remembered of the last time she'd bared her soul to a stranger. No need to bare her soul this time. They'd called for a listener. And listeners have no need to speak.

10

I hadn't done many staff interviews. James was the one who saw the bulk of our researchers; I was the one who picked the best of the crop. The whole process was a bit too much like company role-play sessions for my liking. Wilson had recently decided it would be a good idea to act out our office procedures in order to 'sharpen our corporate skills.' This meant not only instant mortification as we took turns to interview imaginary clients in the stuffy conference room at the top of the building, but it nurtured all sorts of simmering resentment among colleagues long after the sessions were complete. The only concrete result, as far as I could tell, was a spankingly written human resources manual that gilded every in tray thereafter. As I sat in the meeting room waiting for the first candidate, I realised I had never actually looked through its laminated pages so heavy with bullet points, but before I had a chance to get past the longwinded preambles someone knocked on my door.

"Your first candidate is here, Bill … I mean Mr. Harcourt."

"Send them in," I said. Pompously, I realised a second later.

"Him," corrected Jean.

I mused briefly over how *I'd* deal with *ecclesiastical cases requiring jurisdiction* when, slotting nicely into my highest age cohort, an elderly man entered the room. He seemed lost for a moment, confused by the arrangement of furniture, but then he came towards me in what could only be described as a lunge.

"Take a seat," I said, hoping to deflect him before he tripped.

"Ta." He gripped the back of the chair and pulled it close to my desk, as if about to share its surface with me, and sat down.

It was easy to identify the long-term unemployed. Apart from the jacket that didn't match the trousers – close, but not close enough – there was the inflamed piece of neck where an unfamiliar collar chafed. And there were also those forgotten corners, probably overlooked in the stress of making themselves presentable after months in loose-fitting trousers and slippers: the line of grime on the watchstrap, the sweater pills gathering at the elbow. But the long-term unemployed were the ones I admired the most, the jaded and faded ones who still had the energy to pull themselves out of the armchairs and mould their credentials to the latest set of job requirements.

He smiled blandly as I searched his face for ordinariness, and then I glanced down at the first page of the manual, but before I had a chance to find my initial question he asked, "Have you ever had a budgie?" I had. A rancid old bird with a nasty peck that terrorised my whole household up until the day it died. "His name was Trevor," I said before I could stop myself.

So my first interview began. I told him 'Trevor' stories for longer than was decent, and then he began to tell me about himself. Stanley Stipple was his name, a Londoner 'born and bred' – I'm sure I saw his chest inflate as he said it – and he'd spent his entire working life as a janitor in a school that he loved. He was heartbroken when he'd been made redundant at the age of fifty-eight. He'd been even more heartbroken when his wife Beryl died soon after. 'I miss her,' he said, in a sentence with no surface. And he missed their social

life too. He loved anything *sociological* he insisted. He had spent
the previous few years cobbling together odd jobs to augment his
pension: road sweeper, shelf stacker, shelf sweeper. I was beginning
to wonder if this man was more of a talker than a listener when he
slapped a forefinger to his lips.

"What–"

"Schhh! Please. Just a moment."

I watched in silence as he closed his eyes, crushing his eyelids
together like a constipated baby, then smiled. "There's a thrush on
the roof. It's calling for its mate."

I looked towards the window. "I can't hear it."

"That's because you haven't *learnt* to hear it. That takes time."

Then he began talking about Beryl. A couple of minutes passed
before I realised he wasn't talking about his wife any more but a
feathered version of her, a budgerigar that shared his life. This bird,
with her 'blue breast' and 'cheeky curve' to her beak, would cock
her head when Stanley spoke to her. But she never passed on secrets.
Not to *anyone*. And when Stanley had finished telling me about the
budgerigar that waited for him to come home at night he told me
about the birds in his garden. He described the whistle of the skylark,
the *kra kra* of the rook and the barely audible scratchings of the wren.
Never mind the damp in his bones from sitting too long in his hide,
he could listen to bird conversations from dawn to dusk.

I smiled to myself as I ticked a small box in the human resources
manual. My first eavesdropper had been found.

Jean betrayed anxiety in her eyes as she popped her head round
the door announcing, "a Miss Veil to see you."

There was a slight delay during which I had time to skim page
two of the manual, and then Violet Veil entered my life. A tall, rakish
woman, she sat down, swiftly plopped a large, fancy handbag on my
desk and proceeded. I don't know how she did it but before I could
utter a word she had asked me what my qualifications were. I laughed
in case it was a joke, but no, and then she launched straight into

her next question and soon I found myself nodding like an overeager schoolboy, summoning a ready smile and outlining my suitability as an employer. She seemed satisfied with my replies, nodding in a beautiful way, and even flipped open the human resources manual while I struggled with the answer to what were my 'three worst faults.' I battled to turn things round, but I was distracted by her appearance. She reminded me of a Cleopatra doll my sister had had as a child: unblemished skin, black eye-liner and bobbed black hair that I imagined would remain perfect should a crown ever be placed upon it. She wore a mannish business suit which outlined her body so rigorously I found myself wondering how she had managed to insert herself into it.

Finally, I managed to squeeze out a question of my own. "What do you currently do for a living?"

She frowned, but didn't reply.

"What's your normal job?"

Her lips seemed an odd shape. "Data entry. Freelance"

An image of Cleopatra tapping gold-leafed fingernails onto a laptop came to mind. "You mean ... ?"

"Yes, putting raw numbers into spreadsheets." She smiled. "But I can do it anywhere – in the park, in the pub, even in the cafe. That's where I do my listening. Anywhere."

"What do you hear?"

She tilted her head to one side. "Everything."

"You sound adaptable."

"I am."

"And, do you have three months to spare to work on my project?"

"Oh, yes. As I say, I am adaptable."

"Right. Well, er ... you sound quite sui–"

"I am a perfect fit." She stood up, shook my hand with silken fingers, and left the room.

I slumped back in my chair. Eavesdroppers. What sort of breed *were* they? This Violet, she'd filled the room and trodden on my toes before I had time to move my feet. I'd thought I wanted quiet people who'd blend, but maybe the bland personalities I'd envisaged didn't blend. Maybe a brash woman in a hurry was just one of life's types, the sort of person who was so loud that nobody noticed them. She had unnerved me, but she was confident. Maybe I needed some confidence in my team.

I rubbed my eye, remembered I shouldn't, even now, then rammed a square of chocolate into my mouth and chewed rapidly before the next knock on the door could come.

I decided to be a little more circumspect with my next candidate, a thready-looking woman in her sixties, wearing a brown shirt and pleated skirt rather like the outfit my mother would have worn in the 1940s, but as she settled herself down with a lot of fuss over how her pleats were arranged atop her seated legs I couldn't help but wonder what sort of pet *she* had. Not a cat for sure, no hairs impaling her jacket, yet something about her face, small black eyes, ginger hair turning grey, brought a middle-aged guinea pig to mind. I could almost see such a creature sitting on her lap, its heart racing, its distended bladder ready to give. Much to my relief the incessant fidgeting came to a halt and she looked at the wall to the left of my shoulder with a theatrical angle to her head.

"I must be frank with you," I said, forgetting the manual's insistence on *making your candidates feel at ease*, "you'll have to drop that if you want this job."

"Drop what?"

"That thing you're doing; I can tell you're listening, but pretending not to."

She laid her hands in her lap like a pair of gloves. "But you asked for a listener," she said, lifting her hands again, placing a newspaper cutting on the table and pushing it towards me. "It says, here in the advertisement."

"But you're not supposed to show you're doing it."

"Oh."

She recalibrated. I could tell by the way she rearranged her body on the chair, smoothed out another pair of pleats and looked dreamily out of the window. "Better?" she asked, without looking at me.

I smiled to myself; there was more to listening than I realised. "Much better. So…." I glanced down at her letter, "So Eve, tell me about yourself."

And she did. But she wasn't at all animated, she just kept staring out of the window as if listening to something elsewhere. Only her lips moved and she told, rather disconcertingly in the third person, the story of 'Eve.' Eve had spent forty years as a school administrator, typing out letters, filing in forms, clipping the occasional ear. Eve lived in a flat. Eve worked for the Citizen's Advice Bureau. Eve was an expert listener. Eve lived alone.

I'd always wondered about the Citizen's Advice Bureau. I could never quite believe that in a world of cynics and muggers and corrupt politicians there could be roomfuls of kind, gentle people amongst us whose sole purpose was to listen and dispense advice over lukewarm mugs of instant coffee. All for free.

"But why does she … why do *you* want this job?" I asked, seizing on a gap in her speech.

She sent out a shortfall signal, a masking gesture illustrated on page seventeen of the manual in which a smile begins then drops away, but kept her face towards the window. "I need a change."

I'm no detective but I sensed she was lying. "Okay, Eve," I said, perhaps a trifle brusquely, "I don't think I have any more questions. I'll let you know my decision in a day or so."

She turned and smiled. "Thank you. I'll be waiting."

I flicked through the manual after she had gone. Nothing in there about third person narrators. Or pleats. Just a tiresome list of misconduct issues and performance indicators, but I felt compelled to plough through a couple of pages in case it prepared me for what was coming next. I was feeling bored and exhausted by the time the penultimate candidate entered the room.

'*Missy*, not Melody,' as she insisted in her first sentence, was by far the strangest of the bunch so far. Her clothes verged on what James would have haughtily described as bohemian, a multicoloured dress, no make-up, a soily scent and grime beneath her nails. I thought I saw a petal in her hair.

Yet her handbag was spotless inside. I don't usually pay attention to the inside of women's handbags but the interior of this one was a deep, velvet red, which gaped open like a great slack mouth. As she rummaged inside for a tissue, I wondered how far my definition of ordinary was going to be stretched.

By the time she was ready I had my first question waiting. "Are you working at the moment Mel – er, Missy?"

She laughed; a spot of spit landed on my forearm. "I'm a radio analyst."

"Oh. What is that exactly?"

"Well …" she said, pausing as if she were about to translate something from another language, "they need people to give feedback on programming. Not the individual shows but the whole picture. They want to know what it's like to listen to the radio from morning till night."

"So, do you?"

"You mean listen?"

"Yes."

"I do."

"All the time?"

"When they need me, yes."

"If you don't mind me asking, Missy, how did you get a job … like that?"

She smiled. "Pure chance. I overhead two producers talking on the other side of the cafe one day – said they could do with someone who could listen to their radio station twenty-four hours a day and report on the big picture. Someone with the ears of a bat." She met my eye. "I presented myself."

"And you get paid for that?"

She flashed a wider smile. "Oh yes … but it's not enough."

"Is that why you're here?"

"Yes – no. I've always been a bit of a snoop. I like hearing about other peoples' lives."

"What about your own life?" I tried to picture her in charge of a warship.

"I don't listen in on my … friends, if that's what you mean."

"No, that's not what I mean. I mean have you …" I glanced down at the human resources manual, " … have you got any hobbies?"

"I like to barty – I mean party."

At first glance my final candidate seemed too good-looking for the job. His profile was perfectly proportioned – he tended to look to the side when he spoke – but when he turned to face me I saw his eyes were at slightly different heights and his nose was lumpy in the way that suggested time spent in a rugby scrum. Or more likely, judging by his thin frame, time spent on the receiving end of a playground bully. The potential hunk, who might have drawn unwanted attention, was actually a regular bloke when viewed full frontal. The way he moved was not so alluring either. Clearly a shy sort, he had slipped awkwardly into the room and, misjudging the height of the chair, sat down with a thump. I wondered if he would be too shy to sit by himself in a pub, but at twenty-four years old he was the only candidate to fit into the twenty to twenty-five age range.

"Got any pets?' I asked.

"None."

He had a quick smile – teeth on full display before I had even finished my sentence. And he wouldn't meet my eye, preferring to address my ear when he spoke. I could see how it might get on my nerves. I folded my arms over the manual and flashed my toothiest grin. "Got any vices?"

He showed me his profile. "I'm … writing a play."

Clearly too cocky about my powers of observation, I studied the side of his face with renewed interest; I'd labelled him a trainspotter or, at the very least, a gamer of several years standing.

"But it's not very good," he said, turning to face me.

I smiled. "So, that's why you do it, is it?"

"Do what?"

"The listening." I leant back in my chair.

"Yes."

"You're gathering information to use in your play?"

"That's right."

"How long have you been doing this, Jack?"

"Since I was a kid."

"You understand the information we gather in this project is not for use in a play."

"I understand."

"So you have a good ear?"

"Oh, yes. I hear everything – the words, the undercurrents, the things unsaid." He made eye contact for the first time. "I can hear the inside of a pause."

I felt a flash of satisfaction. "Jack."

"Yes."

"I'd like to offer you a job."

My office smelt different after they'd all gone, a mortarous mix of mothballs and nail varnish, plus something I couldn't identify. It took me a while to read all my notes as I'd got bored with writing and had tried out some half-remembered shorthand, but gradually I began to form a picture of these people who, one by one, had warmed the chair opposite me. Strange lot, I thought as I put the human resources manual back on the shelf. Strange and a bit motley. But then, strange and motley might be exactly what I needed. I wanted ordinary, but too much ordinariness might draw attention.

I looked down at the list of names. Was I going to get along with them? I wondered. I thought of how much kudos the project might bring me in the company. The corridors would be awash with people who knew who I was. And – my pen hovered above 'Eve' – I didn't have to *like* them.

STANLEY was tired by the time he reached home. He could never be bothered to hang up his coat on the hanger so he chucked it over the banister and went into the kitchen to make himself a cup of tea. Beryl seemed like an ordinary bird for a moment, one that you'd see in a tree, but then she angled an eye at him and he knew she was waiting.

"I got the job," he said quietly.

Beryl blinked.

"It's for three months and it's going to be a doddle. I even get expenses. What do you think of that?" He held his face close to the cage. "Free cups of tea, Beryl. Free."

Beryl blinked again, then cocked her head; she seemed to be listening to something in the garden.

Stanley washed his hands at the sink then went outside. His garden wasn't very big but large enough to grow a few tomatoes and build a hide. His neighbour on one side had made a fuss when it first started going up but Stanley had stood his ground and continued weaving branches through the timber frame and now it was perfect. Here he'd spend his evenings, listening to the birds as they talked to each other. They always had something to say, some long-winded report about what was going on up the street or, in moments of drama, a high-pitched command that sent every bird up into the tree tops where they'd balance on twigs and get ready to come back down. They'd been wary of the hide at first, leaving a circle round it that none dared step into, but now they all knew that the clump of dead leaves wouldn't bite and Stanley could listen without being noticed. He had brought Beryl out there to see it once, but he'd felt tears bulge up in his eyes when he saw her cage sitting on the grass. He had never done it again.

But tonight he was happy. He had a new job. And his new job involved listening to people, not to birds, who are touchy and irritable and overreact to everything, but real people, maybe even the sort of people who might be interested in an elderly man with neither money nor wife. He went inside the hide, sat on his chair and settled down to listen. The evening air was cool, the right temperature for transmitting sounds smoothly into his ears.

"Fuck you!" bellowed a male voice from the street. "I'm an arborist."

"A fucking what?" replied another.

"A fucking arborist. I cut down fucking trees."

Stanley pulled his scarf tighter round his neck, peeped through a gap in the hide and gazed up at the trees in his garden. His birds lived in trees. The canopy was their whole world. When trees were cut down, everything changed.

CHAPTER
11

It took a lot of effort to arrange the first team meeting, and I rued the day I set up a project involving so many people not born of the digital age. The group's emailing skills were idiosyncratic at best, and as a two-hour turnaround type of person I felt increasingly irritated by the white space of my inbox. Missy didn't even own a phone so I resorted to putting her invitation to our first meeting in the post, a surprisingly satisfying process of folding up a piece of paper so precisely that it fitted inside an envelope, licking the edge, (while banishing fleeting thoughts of ground-up horses' hooves) and positioning a stamp in the top right-hand corner.

Something – a desire to show my efficiency right from the start perhaps – made me line up the meeting room chairs around the table like an eighteenth-century butler, measuring the exact distance between them with the span of my hand, yet for some reason I felt worried as I waited for my new team to arrive. Would they gel instantly and be friends for life? Or would they form factions, quarrelling and backbiting and spatting over territory? And what would they think of me? I wondered. Would they see me as the morose social researcher I was or would I become their friend too?

It wasn't long before I heard the first of them coming down the corridor. Already I could identify Eve's laboured walk, not the movement of a heavy person but the weary gait of a woman who had succumbed to a life of fallen arches and feet that are trouble to lift. But it wasn't Eve who poked her head round the meeting room door, it was Violet, lips polished, eyebrows a solid brown.

"Am I early?" she said, pressing her elbows against the door frame in a semblance to a medieval yoga pose.

"No, come in. Someone's got to be first." Banal expression, I thought. Used only by people who have nothing to say.

She sat down untidily, demolishing my precious line-up, and placed a laptop on the table. She didn't speak again until she had everything booted up. "I'm ready."

"You're not planning to use that during the meeting, are you?" I said.

She looked at me as if I was three years old, but luckily any slipping into that role was halted by the sound of more footsteps massing in the corridor. The door was pushed open and four people filed in. They had the look of strangers unwittingly gathered together for a single purpose, the crowd at the scene of an accident or a group spontaneously picked to form a team at a business workshop. Laying out their personal space with great care, each sat down, pulled in their chairs and looked expectantly in my direction like a row of pale yet worldly sparrows.

I'd never done a formal pep talk before. Our researchers were normally employed singly, so I'd never had to worry about the miseries of group dynamics. How to muster enthusiasm? I glanced around to see if I could detect any signs of ordinariness breaking out round the table. I opened with a joke; it was one I'd used to reasonable effect in the pub but it went down like a lead balloon. Stanley laughed but the rest looked bewildered, or irritated, or in the case of Missy, faintly unwell.

But I ignored all this and began my spin. My tale was an intriguing one: I could see that from their eyes. They'd clearly been reared to hide their thoughts; they all fixed up their smiles and held their necks stiff, but I could see thinking was going on, just behind the expressionless foreheads. It was important to give a clear picture so I told them the instructions straight. Go out into the world with the ears of a newborn, untainted by prejudice, devoid of judgement. They had to be ordinary; they had to listen. And they had to note down the conversations they heard in a notebook with a pencil.

"Pencil!" said Violet. My eardrum quivered.

"Yes, a pencil."

I handed out a plain black notebook to each member of the group. I'd spent the previous twenty minutes sharpening the pencils and felt annoyed when Stanley broke the end off his while writing his name in the front page. "And …" the volume of my voice rose, "I want you to remember something important. Hearing is different to listening." Someone sighed. "Hearing is easy. Listening is what I'm paying you for."

The eavesdroppers closed their mouths. "And, most importantly, I don't want you to show these notes to anyone but me. Does anyone have any questions?"

"What are we looking for exactly?" asked Eve, her pencil encased in thin fingers.

"*Listening* for," corrected Violet.

I smelt perspiration in the air. "That's your job," I said. "We're trying to discover what's out there." The silence in the room made my throat seem loud when I cleared it.

Jack uttered his inaugural sentence, his voice barely audible. "You mean, you want us to feel the weave?"

I couldn't believe I'd had reservations about him. "Exactly."

"Exactly what?" said Missy, twisting a piece of wool round her finger.

I inhaled. "We're trying to get a sense of … you know, the way things are."

Missy appeared to be hugging her own waist; Stanley scratched his forehead. It made me realise the idea wasn't fully formed in my own head, let alone on my tongue.

"Do you mean you want us to listen out for something that hasn't been heard before?" said Violet.

Such clarity. "Yes!"

"But how will we recognise it?" Missy held a handkerchief to her cheek as if to dab a tear.

"He doesn't know. That's what he's paying us for," Stanley said.

I felt tearful myself. Or something was making my eyes water. But it wasn't the bewilderment seemingly felt by the eavesdroppers, maybe something else, maybe the enigma of the project. What I thought I understood, I suddenly didn't. "Look, everyone," I said, "you were chosen because you are good listeners. This is an experiment. And like any experiment we don't know what's going to happen. Just go out and listen, go out and take notes. Nothing's going to happen to you out there. It's only when you bring your notes back that we'll see if there is anything … out there."

Missy's eyes had widened, Violet's sass departed.

"There's something else I need to say." I took a breath. "You need to be … careful."

"Careful of what?" said Stanley.

"That you don't get, you know, caught."

"Is eavesdropping illegal?" Jack had become the sensible one.

"It depends on our definition," I said.

Stanley fished a small dictionary out of his pocket; a seed fell onto the table. I couldn't believe how long the silence held in the room as he thumbed his way towards the *E*'s.

"Water that drips from the eaves of a house," he announced.

"Verb, please," said Violet.

"The ground on which such water falls."

"Veeerb."

Stanley's cheeks reddened as he studied the page. "To eavesdrop. *Verb*. Listen secretly to a private conversation."

Eve spoke in a low voice. "Secretly? Mr. ... Stanley, *is* it illegal?"

Stanley seemed to have discovered the pleasurable power of a pause. We waited, oh how we waited; then we watched his thumb move imperceptibly down the page. "Formerly an indictable public offence."

"Formerly," breathed Eve.

"That means it's legal," said Stanley.

"Exactly," I said. "So long as you don't use a recording device, then it's a bit of a grey area. That's why we're using notebooks and pencils. Now ..." I glanced round the group, "I'd like to decide your locations. Any thoughts on where you'd like to station yourselves?"

"The Job Centre," said Stanley without hesitation.

"Excellent," I said. "Any other suggestions?"

"I'd like to remain in my natural habitat," said Violet.

In the hiatus that followed I sensed the others might be searching their brains as feverishly as I, but it was Stanley who ventured a conclusion first. "The shoe shop?"

Violet tutted, yet seemingly unaware of the slight proceeded to describe, in humid and loving detail, her local coffee shop, with its 'jostle and bustle and propensity for holding life in eager little clusters,' as if none of the people around the conference room table had ever heard of, let alone stepped inside, such a place. "My local cafe," she concluded. "That's where you'll find the energy of the city."

"Right," I said, depressed by the limitations of my own vocabulary. "What about you, Jack?"

"I'll be in my natural habitat, too."

A challenging little smile played on his lips but no one dared to hazard a guess, so it was left to me to ask. "And where might that be?"

"The Circle Line."

"Ah, the Circle Line," said Stanley, puffing out his chest. "Same smell and sounds since 1979, across the empty track, I half expect to see you there, or someone else from that … far distant time."

"Is that your words?" asked Eve.

"No." Stanley smiled. "It's the Underground Poem. Don't you know?"

Jack somehow caught all our attention. "I sat, a solitary man, in a crowded London shop, an open book and empty cup on the marble table-top."

"I don't think there's going to be any poetry where I'm going," Eve said.

Stanley turned towards her. "Where *are* you going?"

"The launderette."

"Oh, bravo," said Violet. "You'll hear such small talk."

I studied the side of her face for a glimmer of satisfaction, but none was there. "The launderette is a good choice. Have you been in one before, Eve?"

She flashed black eyes at me; I wondered if guinea pigs had eyebrows.

"Do I look like the sort of person who owns a washing machine?" she said.

No time to think. "No … yes … Missy, what about you? Where will you be working?"

Missy appeared to be listening to something outside the room. Her ears were larger than I remembered, wiry tufts of hair tucked behind them. "Sorry, what did you say?" she said.

"Your location? I need to know your intended whereabouts?"

She brushed a flake of dry skin off the back of her hand. "I was thinking of going to the public conveniences."

"Ah." I waited for my follow up, but nothing materialised.

"Sounds like a good idea to me," said Stanley cheerfully. "That's where people really reveal themselves."

I was impressed by his look of innocence. "You will be careful, won't you ..."

"Is taking a slash dangerous, then?" Sarcasm had replaced Stanley's cheer. It didn't suit his face.

"No, well, not usually," I said. "By the way, does everyone have a mantelpiece?"

"A *what*?" said Violet.

"It's that thing that goes over the top of your fireplace," Stanley explained. "I've got a beauty from the thirties in my house. It's–"

"I don't have a fireplace," said Violet.

"I *had* a mantelpiece," said Eve, "but a cowboy builder removed the original; it was Victorian and solid marble, but so cold to lean on. They replaced it with hideous."

'What do you mean, they replaced it with hideous?" Violet said. "That's an adjective."

"Pine," she replied, as if that was enough.

"Do you have a shelf, Violet?" I said. I hadn't anticipated this degree of detail.

"Yes, I do."

"Is that where you keep your knick-knacks?" asked Stanley.

Violet sighed.

"What I'd like you to do," I continued, "is tell me at our next meeting, just as an exercise – please indulge me – what is on your mantelpiece, or ... shelf."

I sensed movement in the room.

"You mean *everything* on it?" asked Stanley.

I laughed. "Why? Is it so full?"

He scratched his head. "It's rather ... crowded."

"With what?" asked Violet.

He smiled. "Seven decades of tat."

"Just note down the top ten," I said.

Missy seemed flustered. "The top ten?"

"Just a simple list of the top ten objects on your mantlepiece. Tat and non-tat. For the next meeting, that's all. Thank you."

Someone let out a low growl. I had no idea who it was.

MISSY liked the shipping news. On the radio so late it meant she could listen to it in bed and not feel guilty if she fell asleep before the end. Guilt was her sister. They'd been born at the same time; they slept in the same bed. Yet on this night she felt relaxed. Nothing was lovelier than the rise and fall of the broadcaster's voice, veering north, careering south, 40s, 50s, 60s, becoming cyclonic, thundery showers, poor, occasionally good. *Dogger, Cromity, Forth, Tyne, Lundy, Fastnet,* the butt of *Lewis,* veering south, rising, falling, poor, occasionally good.

Her radio listening work had dried up recently, but it was impossible not to still listen with the ears of an employee. She knew the laugh of every broadcaster, the opening notes of every show, but among the hundreds of programmes, the hours of music, her greatest love was the pips. One, two, three, four, five, six…. The hourly markers, five short, one long, had a comforting monotony, which gave her a lovely sense of calm before the turmoil of the news. *News.* She'd heard more news than anyone on earth. She didn't want to hear any more.

She'd been so tired that night she hadn't bothered to hang her dress on a hanger and it lay collapsed on the floor like a deflated lantern. A party dress, it was layered with nylon petticoats and held onto her body with thin straps that left ridges in her shoulders when she took it off.

Maybe she'd had too much to drink. It was hard to keep count, especially if the level of the glass never seemed to go down. Drinking could take its toll but burning the candle at both ends was an idea that she'd always liked. She'd tried it out once. She cut the bottom off a short white candle she'd bought in a church shop next to the cathedral and lit both ends. Just the memory of it made her smile: the two piles of wax forming on the table, the shrinking candle, the flames heating her finger on either side. She'd probably have to fine-tune her life now she was a professional eavesdropper. Mr. Harcourt might not approve of bags under her eyes or her chin resting on her hands in meetings. But come to think of it, he had bags under his eyes. And they were bloodshot. Perhaps he liked burning the candle at both ends too.

Over a late supper – a silent chew on bacon between bread – she'd pushed the memories of the first day aside, but now she allowed herself to recall the scene at her new job, the new faces, the new sets of clothes on unfamiliar bodies and the tumble of anxiety as her turn to speak had arrived. Yet it had felt good to be part of it, whatever *it* was.

Listening to the radio all day was a lonely job and the thought of hearing stories and swapping notes with others excited her. But it worried her too. Would they like her, these unknown people? Would her stories be as interesting as theirs?

She went into her sitting room and wandered over to her only shelf and observed the objects displayed on the wood. She didn't observe too long, just long enough to adjust the positions of the family living there, pull out the mother's chair a fraction, turn the father's shoulders three degrees, and push the child's tiny seat further beneath the table.

Then Missy went into the bathroom, sat on the toilet and got into her listening pose, elbows on her knees, chin resting on her palms – *The Position,* as she liked to call it. Here her bones would lock in place and her muscles hold perfect tension as seconds ran into minutes, and minutes into hours. Not many people could sit long on a toilet. The children she'd grown up with complained of aches in their backs and marks on the backs of their legs, but Missy, she'd been born in a toilet, her damp body wiped with paper from a municipal roll.

The walls of her flat were thinnest here, but the sounds of voices were often drowned out by the plumbing as the taps belched and pipes shuddered. But today there was something new in the air – a low hum, far in the distance. Or close. She listened harder; the hum carried on.

Fifteen minutes later she put on her pyjamas, got into bed, switched on the radio and lay back. She placed her hand over her stomach and closed her eyes, her head turning on the pillow, veering south, and her chest, ever so slowly, rising and falling. Life was poor, occasionally good.

CHAPTER

12

Monday was a long and frustrating day, given the onslaught of spam in my inbox and shortness of shrift handed out by the photocopier. During the dead time spent hunting down fresh supplies of toner and filling empty trays with paper I found more than a few moments to reflect on the inaugural meeting of the eavesdroppers. I'd clearly lacked the imagination to picture all five listeners within the confines of a single room when I'd interviewed them separately and was unprepared for the unfathomable frisson that had wafted between my lovingly spaced chairs. I'd envisaged a common strand, a listener's gene that had the power to govern subsequent personalities but then, as they'd gathered together for a common purpose, surprisingly different characters had emerged. Yet, the more I thought about it the more I recognised there *was* something that united them, and when I identified what it was, it concerned me. They all wanted something. Desire was an important trait for an eavesdropper I conceded, but, more than that, they all seemed to *need* something. And need, as my father liked to pronounce whenever he passed a homeless man in the street, is more dangerous than want. But the worry of the group dynamic was soon replaced by worry about the singleton, out there in the world alone, with pricked up ears and a notebook to hand. *Were* they vulnerable? Would a bolshie bore who'd had too much to drink notice the urgent scribbling and rout us? Where to put the notebook had been a crisis in itself. Under the table or on the top, disguised as a diary? Or even, as suggested by Eve, beneath a cardigan, cradled in the hand like a little hamster.

James and I discussed training at great length. Although we argued over the suitability of the word *training* when applied to show-ing someone how to sit on a chair and copy words into a book, we did agree that something had to be done before I dispatched the group to their listening posts. James preferred the word initiation but I baulked at the connotations: hot mustard, blindfolds, aprons, so we settled on *guidelining*, a word stolen from an interminable speech of Wilson's two Christmases previously, excruciating, but oh, so apt.

I decided to start with Missy. Her on-the-job guidelining was going to require the utmost delicacy so I thought of asking Jean if she'd come along with me to add a feminine perspective, but the sight of her highly-cleansed cheeks and spotless nails as I poked my head round her office door persuaded me otherwise.

I left work just before lunch, eager to feel a bit of sun on my back. There's something deeply satisfying about having an office job where you get to leave the building during working hours and continue to be paid, so I felt happy as I went outside. The great London outside, even on the most oppressive days made me feel heady, a bit shandy-drunk, and I rushed down the street feeling as if I'd kicked off my shoes in the office and left them behind forever.

Missy was late. I'd had two coffees in the forecourt cafe at Victoria Station and a pack of travel biscuits by the time she came running along from the direction of platform thirteen.

"You know, Missy, it costs thirty pence a go," I said, as she took off her scarf and draped it elaborately over the back of her chair.

"What does?"

"The Ladies loo."

She sat down. "Every time?"

"Yes. Every time." I pictured the graphics of a public toilet season ticket.

"Will the company pay?" she asked.

An image of my monthly expenses form replaced the picture of the season ticket. "Yes, but there'll be a limit." I thought of a number. "Ninety pence a day okay?"

She smiled. "That will be more than enough."

I don't know if it was her smile, or the thought of the underground toilet, or the combination of both, but I felt a shudder in my back, a creepy little finger of something. "So ... Missy ... what's your plan?"

"I thought you were here to tell me my plan?"

"Yes ... it's just a few guidelines ... basic ones."

She listened. She watched me drift further out of my depth. I had no idea what the Ladies toilet at Victoria Station looked like, let alone what its operational rules might consist of. The Men's toilet was next door, also reached through the extortionate turnstile, down the concrete steps, but there, all comparison ended. Men could not even glance into the female zone for fear of being arrested as a Peeping Tom.

"Where will you do the listening," I said at last, feeling vaguely confident I'd guided some sort of line.

"On the toilet."

Images, why so many images? "For how long?" I enquired, in the manner of a kindly cleaning superintendent.

"Most of the day. On and off."

"Won't you get ... stiff?"

"What do you mean?"

I studied the sincerity on her face. "I didn't intend this, Missy. I didn't mean you to have to do something quite so ... gruelling."

"I like it."

She did; I could see it in her face. She actually relished the idea of spending the day in a public toilet. Would I like it too? I wasn't good at empathy but I tried then, during the great impasse that had opened up over the little coffee table on the edge of Victoria Station, to visualise getting pleasure from sitting on a toilet and listening to strangers.

"Sometimes it's alright to like things," she said.

I blinked. "I know it's alright to like things but I…." I couldn't get beyond my querulousness, "I just want to make sure it's safe."

"Safe?"

"You know what I mean." Her gathering eyebrows suggested she didn't. "I'm slightly concerned … you might … you know, hear something you shouldn't."

Her eyebrows gathered more tightly. "What should I do if I hear something I 'shouldn't'?"

Bloody hell. "Just … write it down quietly."

"I'm going to write everything down quietly."

"Have you got a quiet pen?"

She seemed to be studying my eyes. Could she see scars that I couldn't?

"You gave me a pencil."

"Of course. But Missy … please don't go down there if it looks a bit dodgy."

She glanced at her watch, picked her scarf off the back of the chair, twirled it round her neck and stood up. "Mr. Harcourt. I am thirty-one-years old. I have been peeing inside the bowls of public toilets my whole life."

I watched her turn and walk back across the station forecourt. Some utterances have no reply.

I visited the other eavesdroppers one by one. My further 'rounds,' as I labelled them, turned out to be reassuring. What surprised and impressed me most was the way they had all merged so quickly into their surroundings: Violet's regal head was unrecognizable amongst the chaos of the cafe, Eve's clothes were the colour of the washing machines and Stanley looked as if he'd been unemployed for decades, standing in the

Job Centre queue with dull eyes, rounded shoulders and dry-looking hair. I thought listening without attracting attention could be difficult, but no, they all had it down perfectly. I went from location to location, having my little chats in the periphery of each, the corner of the launderette, the corner of the cafe, the intimidating corner of the Job Centre – all ripped municipal chairs and dented filing cabinets. And in each corner I had a fake run-through with each eavesdropper. We re-enacted life as a sentence was spoken, a sentence was overheard, a notebook opened with casual ease and the words noted down. But then there emerged the first difficulties. Violet couldn't spell. 'No problem' I'd said, the affable supervisor that I'd become, but Eve, she couldn't write. She could form the letters but her grasp of the pencil was loose and her speed glacial. 'Can't you write faster?' I'd said, but no, she never rushed her letters. That was her mother's most golden of rules. My own mother's most golden of rules was never rush your dinner, but try as I might I couldn't find any useful parallels and ended Eve's training with a reassurance that slow had its merits but maybe there was potential to do something with her mother's rule, not to break, but possibly bend.

Jack's guidelining was impossible. We sat elbow to elbow all the way from Bayswater to Embankment in the middle of the evening rush hour – the richest seam he insisted. Overwhelmed by the crush and the noise and the smell of clothes, I was ready to give up and suggested relocating to another place when he opened his notebook to reveal a dense page of notes, dated that day, timed over the previous hour. Again I'd underestimated him. Again, the shy one had had the most to offer.

STANLEY waited a long time to get Beryl's attention. First she had to eat some seeds from the tray, then she insisted on rubbing her beak along her cuttlefish, up and down, up and down, and finally she stared at a button on his waistcoat for a full minute before cocking her head towards him.

"Yes, it went well, Beryl. Thanks for asking. Very well." Stanley held his face up to the side of the cage. Beryl ruffled the feathers on the back of her neck, always a sign of approval.

"I heard some juicy snippets," he continued. "Oh, yes. Mr. Harcourt's going to be pleased."

Beryl stretched her wings; Stanley could see the grey underside.

"I can't tell you too much yet, though. I need to hear the full story, you know, get all the dirty little details. And actually it's supposed to be a secret. All my work is top secret now. I know how good *you* are at keeping secrets. But Beryl, my darling, we're going to have to be extra discrete. We're good at that, aren't we?"

Beryl blinked. Stanley wanted to reach out and touch the little grey eyelid.

"I could have been one of them, you know, them up at the Job Centre. I know how people look when they haven't got a job. They're tired and their clothes don't hang right. But it's good that they're tired because … can you guess … because they're too tired to notice that I'm listening to them. But not just listening, Beryl, I'm recording too. I'm so official with my new notebook and pencil. Mr. Harcourt – do you remember him? – Mr. Harcourt says we have to write in the book as if we're writing something else. What 'something else'? I asked him. Something other than what you're listening to, he said. So I've been practicing, Beryl. I've been writing something as if it's something else. I knew I'd get there in the end. It's all to do with the angle of your hand and the look on your face. Practice makes perfect. Mr. Harcourt's going to be so pleased. Even you, Beryl, are going to be extremely proud of me."

Stanley sat down at the table, sipped his tea and then looked towards the cage. "Something's bothering me though, Beryl. What if I hear something and I forget to write it down as if it's *something else*?"

CHAPTER

13

*The next day was choppy. My traditional work, analys-*ing questionnaires and looking for patterns in the results of focus groups, was woven with thoughts of the eavesdroppers. They'd be out there, all of them, somewhere. Listening. Since the project had started I was paying more attention to the air. In my little world of scraping chairs and rustling papers I'd begun to notice new sounds. Nothing of great significance at first: the sound of the blinds catching a breeze or the clunk of James dropping photographs into his online trash, but still these sounds were now actually heard, registered in my mind, as opposed to unheard and passing me by. Then there was the hum. 'Do you hear that?' I'd asked James. 'Hear what?' was his reply. 'That low hum in the background.' 'No. Never.'

He thought it would be funny to try and silence the room to see if *he* could hear the hum. But it's not so easy to silence a room. Even as we held our tongues and sat on our chairs like corporate statues, sounds kept coming in: the chug of a train in the distance, the swish of the lift door, the gentle sigh of air down our own noses. On the pretense of scientific research I'd done an informal survey of the office to see if anyone else had ever heard a humming noise in the background, but my hoped-for pie chart had remained a single colour. No one seemed to hear the nameless hum – no one but me.

Apart from unidentified sounds on the periphery, I now began a new obsession, worrying not about the overheards but about the unheards. I knew humans are good at filtering information with the eyes – we don't read every word on a page – but I didn't know if the ears also picked and chose without our ever knowing. I so hoped the eavesdroppers' sharpened ears were going to hear new sounds, but not just sounds, undercurrents, hidden pieces of information that would tell me something new. Now so reliant on a bunch of strangers' ears, I was going to look a fool if nothing original came of this. Barmy Bill I'd be christened behind the cheap doors that separated every office. Did you hear about that bloke Bill who was sacked when he got amateurs to do our jobs? Did you hear how he never got a research job again? If James, always slouching on the corner of my desk in that irksome way of his, had grilled me on the subject at that moment, I might have admitted I was nervous about what was going to happen out in the toilets, waiting rooms and launderettes of London. Eavesdropper was a polite word for snoop. Nobody likes a snoop. Yet, as a social research professional it was my job to snoop. Snoop, sift and categorise. Then extrapolate. That was the joy of my job. Finding meaning in a table of data, spotting something that no one else could see and laying it on Wilson's desk, dressed up in the delicious elegance of a graph that summed everything neatly up. But in this new plan of subterfuge and unfamiliar ears, I'd forgotten one part of the equation – people. People and their personalities. My eavesdroppers were wandering the streets in my name yet they were individuals, used to doing things their own way. The little knot of worry in my stomach began to tighten.

But my worry was misdirected that day. It was not my newly commissioned collection of ears that created cause for concern. It was something that originated further away.

I had closed down my computer for the day and was putting on my jacket when Jean rushed into the office with a letter in her hand.

"What have you got there?" I said.

"A letter for you. It came in the second post."

"I didn't know there was still such a thing as a second post."

"It depends on the time of year," she replied.

I glanced through the vertical blinds striping the window – dusk already. "Right. Thanks, Jean, I'll open it tomorrow. I've packed up for the day."

She glowed disapproval. "Aren't you going to look at it now?"

I sighed. "Okay, I suppose I could have a quick look."

The letter was in a small envelope and the address was written in a neat, italic pen. Feeling irritable and ready to dismiss such tardiness in job applicants I pulled the letter out and read.

Sea Kale Cottage
121 Battery Road
Lydd-on-Sea,
Kent
October 1ˢᵗ 2018

Dear Mr. Harcourt,

I found a copy of the London Evening Standard in my garden today, dated 3rd of September. It had been caught in the wheels of a lorry that drove past my house. I watched it fly up as the vehicle passed my open gate. Page twenty-two was open on the grass when I went outside to pick it up. There I saw your advertisement. Your advertisement worried me.

Be careful, Mr. Harcourt. Be very careful. Listening is a dangerous business.

Yours in good faith,
Raymond Watt.

"Are you alright?" said Jean.

"Huh?"

"You look pale."

Jean's perfume was right inside my nose. "Yes. I'm fine."

"Not bad news, I hope?" she said, moving closer.

The fragrance intensified. "No. Not bad. Just ..."

"Just news?"

"Yeah, just news." I placed the letter in my in tray. "I'll deal with it tomorrow."

EVE didn't go straight home after the first meeting. She felt light as she walked down the corridor, much lighter than the nine stone the scales told her. She wondered if this was what it felt like to experience an *illegal high* as they called it in the newspapers. She had never done anything illegal, not even the day she had found fifty pence rattling around the large drier and handed it over to the supervisor. And as for a high, that was something, she imagined, that came with extreme happiness. She also felt an unfamiliar throb in her chest, so unfamiliar that she hurried to the toilet on the ground floor in case she was about to be sick. But she wasn't sick. She just hummed with something unfamiliar.

The toilet seat was comfortable and she sat very still for a few minutes, listening to the sound of her own breathing and the drip, drip, drip of the cistern. She held her breath when she heard people coming into the room.

"That coffee's gone right through me. You don't mind if I go first, do you?"

"No. Go on."

A door slammed in the next cubicle, a bolt was slid.

"So ... what do you make of them?" Violet's distinctive voice was close to Eve's ear.

'Who do you mean?" Missy's voice filled the room.

"The other eavesdroppers."

"Oh. They're very—"

"Unprofessional?"

"No, they're ... nice."

"Even that old duffer, Stanley?"

"Especially him."

Violet snorted. "I suppose he might grow on you. But ..." She sniggered. "What do you think about Eve?"

CHAPTER

14

"So Bill, you've got quite the bunch working on your little experiment."

"Yeah."

"Why so gloomy?"

I met James' eye across the desk. "I got this weird letter."

James' hands hovered above his keyboard. "What sort of weird letter?"

"I'm not sure how to describe it. It was a bit threatening, and ... a bit ... weird."

He swivelled his chair to face me. "I knew it! I knew this plan was dodgy from the start. Don't tell me, one of your eavesdroppers has got themselves in trouble already."

"Actually, it's not them." I pulled the letter out of my drawer and passed it to James. "It's from some bloke down on the south coast."

James was a slow reader. He had a habit of twitching his nose while he read and I was ready to snatch the letter out of his hands by the time he laid it down on the desk and raised his eyebrows in my direction. "Lunatic," he pronounced.

"Well, yeah. I know that. But why is the lunatic writing to me?"

"He's probably a stalker. He saw the ad, thought, 'here's someone I can have a little fun with.'"

"Maybe, but I don't like that 'caught in the wheels of a lorry' bit.'"

James glanced back down at the letter. "Shit, you're right. Is it a code for something?"

I shrugged. "I don't know. Do you think I should tell Wilson?"

"God, no! He'll freak out. Just put it back in your drawer and pretend you never received it. He'll get bored when he doesn't get an answer."

"D'ya reckon?"

"Yeah, I reckon. And anyway you've got enough to deal with keeping tabs on that crazy gang of yours."

"D'ya reckon?"

"Yes Bill, I reckon."

The eavesdroppers appeared restless. They shuffled their papers; they looked in their bags; each one of them seemed to be checking their pockets for something lost. Only Jack sat still, resting his hands squarely on the table and fixing his eyes on something behind my head. The infection reached my side of the table and I found myself rummaging through the packets of saccharin beside my notebook before scanning the faces round me. Once again I was struck by how peculiar they seemed as a group. As individuals they were plain – regular citizens who might sit beside you on the bus and make no impression – but as a group they were something else: the old bird man, the queen, the frizzy-haired hippy, the pleated lady, the bloke who showed his shyness with every step.

A week had passed since I'd sent my unaccompanied brood out into the world and now they finally managed to settle themselves into the office chairs.

"Good morning, everyone."

"Morning," they chorused.

I had to smile. Already they were my children, my band of enthusiasts, willing participants in a scheme of my making. I opened my folder and spent rather too long running the side of my hand along the seam before turning to face them and beginning my speech. I felt irritated when other people in my department commenced a spiel, a corporate monologue packed with unnecessary detail and verbal logos, but I couldn't help myself and it wasn't until Violet started to examine her nails that I decided to bring up the subject of mantelpieces. "Before we start sharing our notes can you please get out your mantelpiece lists," I said. "I'd like you to read your list out loud …" I glanced round the room, "Eve."

Eve shrank visibly. "I didn't do one, sorry."

"Oh …" I cast my glance round again. No one met my eye, except Stanley, who smiled and winked.

"Shall I begin?" he said.

"Just the first chapter," said Violet, staring glumly down at her notebook.

Stanley stood up and held his book out in front of him. "One bus ticket, one set of tweezers, one unopened letter, one button, one razor blade, one piece of string, one safety pin, one washer, one photograph, one coronation mug." He sat down.

"What's a washer," said Violet.

"Oh, Vi." He looked genuinely sad. "It's the bit that goes between the bolt and the thing you are fixing it to. It stops pressure building up where it shouldn't. Washers are an essential part of life."

Violet tossed her head like an impatient horse. "*I've* never needed one."

Stanley's face oozed admiration.

I'd come to the conclusion I wasn't very skilled at being in charge of meetings, but even I could see we were going to need more focus. "Missy, can you tell me what is on your mantlepiece?"

Missy opened her notebook and read without intonation: "One table, three chairs, three plates, three sets of knives and forks, three—"

"Wait, Missy," I said. "How big is this mantlepiece?"

She glanced fleetingly in my direction. "Normal size."

"So … how big is the table?"

She lifted her hand slowly and pinched a length of air between her fingertips. "About this long."

Stanley glanced up. "Miniatures."

"What's 'miniatures'?" I said.

Violet sighed. "Miniature things … from a miniature world."

"I … see."

"Shall I continue?"

"Yes, please continue."

She pushed a wedge of hair behind her ear. " … and two cocktail umbrellas." She glanced round the table. "Full size."

"Mr. Harcourt." It was Jack speaking. I could hardly catch what he said. "Why did you ask us to do this list?"

"Bill. Please call me Bill. I thought it would be a good way of getting to know each other. I think what you have on your mantelpiece says a lot about you. And I also wanted to test your powers of observation."

A baby frown crossed Jack's forehead. He nodded.

"So, could you tell us what's on your mantelpiece, Jack?" I said, in a tone that to my ears sounded gentle.

He stopped nodding. "Nothing."

"Not even a clock?" asked Stanley.

Jack looked diagonally at us. "Not even a clock."

"May I ask what's on *your* mantelpiece?" said Stanley, turning to face me.

I felt the weight of their communal gaze. "It's being reorganised at the moment." I glanced down at my watch; I'd forgotten to put it on. "Could we move on? I'd like us to share some of what you heard over the last week."

Violet was not of the shrinking type and she stood up and began to read from her notebook in a deadpan voice. "Fourth year's all about weed. Fifth year's all about ecstasy. This year's … all about doing coke."

"Where the hell did you hear that?" I said.

Violet didn't flinch. "Some kids in the cafe."

"Sorry," I said. "Sorry, Violet. Please carry on."

"It's quite poetic, isn't it," said Stanley before Violet could open her mouth again. He'd spread his hands on the table as if to count his knuckles.

"If you call rotten noses half fallen off poetic," said Eve. She'd fished something out of her bag. I couldn't see what it was.

Stanley seemed to be straightening out the wrinkles on the back of his hand. "*Sixth year's* all about doing coke." he said, evenly. "Helps the rhythm."

"It's not a poem," said Eve. "It's a sad indictment of society today."

"Could still be a poem," murmured Jack into his notebook.

I shifted in my seat. Static seemed to be in the air but I had no idea what was causing it. "I think it would be good to get an overall feel for what you've all heard," I said, indicating for Violet to sit down. "How did you get on at the Job Centre, Stanley?"

Stanley was pretending to smoke with his pencil. "It was more crowded than I remembered, and there was a lot of talking and … it was hard to hear."

"How so?" asked Violet.

"Their sentences, they weren't proper."

"You mean not proper English?" said Eve.

'Yes." He tapped his pencil on the side of an imaginary ashtray. "Some words I didn't know … " He opened his notebook and placed his finger on a line of writing. "*Diss* was one."

"Disrespect," said Violet, her face utterly charming.

Stanley gave her a sharp look. "And … '*fam*.'"

"Family."

It was Eve who spoke. I felt something twinge in my gut.

"Maybe if we could have a little look …?" I said, stretching my hand towards his notebook.

"No!" He snatched the book out of my reach. "I'll fix it. Just give me some time to work it out."

"Okay, Stanley," I said. "Maybe we should move on. Eve?"

Eve was rummaging in her bag again. She pulled out her notebook. It was filthy and dog-eared and from my table-width glance, full. She slapped it down then dragged out a pocket dictionary, equally spent. "I'll be needing a new notebook," she said. "This one's full."

"Looks like you covered a lot of ground," I said.

"Just a normal day." She pushed the book towards me.

"Aren't you going to give your report?" I said.

She looked out of the window, locked into her listening pose. "No. You do it, please."

It was like being offered someone's diary. I flicked gingerly through the pages, every one filled with short blocks of writing drowning in childish sketches: a cleavage detached from its body, a face covered with tangled hair, a very detailed pair of underpants, its seams gone over in thicker pen.

"What is this, Eve?"

"My notes," she replied, still not meeting my eye. "Read them, please."

I speed read the first paragraph.

"What's it say?" said Stanley, craning his neck in my direction.

"It's a bit … explicit."

"We're all grown up," said Violet.

I cleared my throat. "He placed his hand between …"

Somehow, when writing my pitch, in what seemed like weeks ago, I hadn't imagined a scenario such as this. No doubt it was an innovative idea, but what had I really imagined my group might hear when I'd sat down in Wilson's office and asked for permission to proceed? I wanted insight for sure; I wanted pithy comments that summed up the zeitgeist of the day. I'd wanted to hear something that no one else did. But now

I couldn't face what they were coming back with. The prude in me exposed, I glanced at the final line and felt heat wash over my cheeks.

It was Stanley's chance to be worldly. "You're going to have to get used to this Mr. B. It's a crude and filthy world out there. When people are being themselves they revert to the language forbidden by their mothers. We're going to have to learn how to spell swear words. We're going to have to talk about things that we don't usually talk about. Except in private."

Jack levelled his eyebrows; Stanley looked appreciative; I felt idiotic. Of course he was right. It was real life that they'd be listening to. The intimacy of close friends would be laid bare; the private talk of lovers would be recorded in Eve's square handwriting, the secrets, oh God, all the confessions, that's what we would be discussing round the big table at the top of the building.

"There's going to be a *lot* of secrets," said Violet, her eyes smiling.

My mouth felt dry. "The sources of our data will remain anonymous so any secrets will remain secret." I looked at my wrist. "Missy, we're running of time. I'd like you to finish off with a quick summary of what you heard. Where did you carry out your assignment?

"I went to the public toilets in Camden High Street," she said. "The underground ones."

Oh shit. There are public toilets and there are public toilets. The ones at Victoria Station were benign and airy stopping off points for weary commuters and tourists, the ones in Camden Town were Victorian lavatories deep beneath the street, a subterranean world of drugs and propositioning, or so I imagined when my mind called for high drama. I'd never actually been to the underground toilets beneath Camden High Street. I'd never been quite desperate enough to brave the rank smell of cheap floor cleaner that wafted out of the entrance, but I knew people who had. Mates from the pub had been known to run back up the stairs, hand over mouth, before dashing across the street and begging access to the staff toilets in the Tube station. "I thought we'd settled on the loos at Victoria Station?" I said.

"Yes, but it was too noisy down there."

"Isn't that just what we need?"

"It is. I just couldn't separate the words."

"From each other?"

"From the sound of the hand driers. They were going the whole time."

"So, just paper towels down at Camden."

"Yes. Paper towels are silent."

"So, what was going on beneath Camden High Street?"

"Someone was singing."

"Down there?"

"Yes."

"What were they singing?"

"Opera."

"What, real opera, you mean?"

"Yes. *La Bohème*."

My lips felt limp. "*La Bohème*?"

"Yes. And it hurt. It echoes so much down there it hurt my ears. Then they started humming."

My lips regained their torque. "What were they humming exactly?"

"I think it was an old Led Zeppelin song."

"Who was this person?"

"I don't know. I was on the toilet."

"All the time?"

"Yes. I sat on the toilet and listened."

I looked at her notebook. There were musical notes in horizontal lines, a whole page of lines.

"Did you jot down any spoken words?"

"There weren't any spoken words. Just song lyrics."

"No spoken words?"

"None at all."

They looked expectantly at me, my eavesdroppers, waiting for a direction, a neat summing up, a lead-in to the next step. I gazed impotently round.

"I think we might have found the weave," said Jack quietly, from the end of the table, the badly lit end.

Eve turned to him, prim as a seamsmistress. "What do you mean exactly?"

"What it's all about out there." His voice dried. "Sex and drugs and rock and roll."

JACK felt a tap of tension in his chest as the tube train rumbled into the station and the doors clacked open. A compressed cross section of humankind was revealed: interlocking bodies cranked into unnatural angles, a man's head tipped right back, a child holding its mouth aloft for air, yet, he reassured himself as he eased his way through the doors, not a single person was touching another.

He drew in his limbs and inched further into the carriage, hung his weight on the metal pole and without moving his head observed his fellow travellers. A long-term student of the mechanics of personal space, he liked to watch the manoeuverings of a crowd. Outwardly it seemed brash: the defiant glare of a businessman in immaculate jacket and waistcoat, the sulky lip of a teenager who jumped into a seat the second it was vacated, yet after travelling on the Tube his whole life he could now see the subtleties of establishing territory. A single half-raised eyebrow could say, 'I know you're tired, but I'm more tired than you and I need to sit down.' And once, (he smiled at the memory), a tiny movement of a woman's thumb had cleared a double seat's worth of Hells Angels.

He hunched his shoulders and turned himself sideways to let a man squeeze past and remembered he was now at work. His ears were normally prepped for a story but Bill Harcourt wanted him to listen harder, delve deeper, find meaning in the banalities of everyday life. But the banalities *were* the stories. He'd never needed intense action. For him great drama was buried inside the small talk. But people talk less below ground than above. They constructed their own worlds inside their heads. The carriage was always noisy, always hot, and the pressure in the air that day seemed to make it noisier than usual. He'd have to lip read. But reading lips was hard. Vowels showed through with the parting and widening of lips, but the rest of the word rushed by, too fast to see. He settled on the face of a girl opposite who was speaking to a man by her side. Her head nodded emphasis, her eyebrows rose and fell and her teeth came and went. He concentrated harder, trying to match the lip shapes with words he knew, imagining the sound. Finally he wrote her words down in his notebook. As seen, as heard. *I don't love you any more.*

CHAPTER 15

I put the second letter down on my desk and observed it.
I had recognised the handwriting the moment Jean brought it into
my office, but the quiver in the font no longer charmed me and I felt
foreboding in my hands as I picked it up again, opened it and read.

Sea Kale Cottage
121 Battery Road
Lydd-on-Sea,
Kent
October 8ᵗʰ 2018.

Dear Mr. Harcourt,

The advertisement on page twenty-two of the London Evening Standard
has been moved to the table in my kitchen where I read it every single
day. And every single day I feel more worried. I repeat – be <u>very</u> careful
what you listen to. Sometimes, and I say this from experience, it is better
not to listen too hard.

But please listen to me. And please, reply to this letter.

Yours in good faith,
Raymond Watt.

I read the letter again, looking for the meaning, trawling through the words for veiled layers of threat. But was it a threat? Was it saying to *do* something or *not do* something? And who wrote so passively like that? Had the author stood back and merely observed as another moved things around him? Was Watt a gang? So polite in tone, yet it smelt off, not just of paper and ink but something musty.

I read the letter through one more time, and then slipped it into my desk drawer and went to my pin-up board to check on the eavesdroppers' whereabouts.

One idea I'd had at the end of the previous meeting was to make a sign-up sheet for the group, and as I scanned the locations I felt pleased with my forethought: October 10th: Stanley at the Job Centre, Eve at the launderette, Violet at the cafe, Jack on the Tube and Missy in the public toilets in Camden Town.

I loved Camden Town. The High Street, in spite of the recent arrival of phone shops and loan counters, still retained some dignity; the tall Victorian arcades stood aloof from their ground floors, and the above ground part of the underground toilets, built in a time of intricate ironwork and glass pavements, was still the first object to greet visitors' eyes as they were shoved through the station exit by the heaving crowds on their way to the market.

I stood at the entrance, planning my next move. Although nervous about her new choice of toilet, I rather liked the male/female conundrum that Missy's choice of listening post had presented me with. As at Victoria Station, I couldn't enter her chosen location but I could go down into its mirror image, the Men's bogs. And from there I might be able to extrapolate. Extrapolation was my forte after all. The Ladies' loos would be the same proportion as the Men's, surely? And the floor, a similar pattern. But the clientele, would there be any parallels, I wondered. I was briefly disturbed by the idea that people beneath me might be able to see up my trouser legs through the pavement glass, and I also needed to piss, so I walked down the narrow staircase to the room beneath the road.

It was another world down there. The brass handrail was sleek with the friction of decades of fingers brushing past and the black and white chequered floor looked stupidly decorative for a surface designed to be splashed with urine. But the smell of disinfectant hit my lungs before I even reached the lower level, so I held my sleeve across my mouth and made my way to the nearest cubicle and closed the door.

"That Elgin Marbles was shit," assailed my ears before I even had a chance to unzip my flies.

I stood still, my ears no longer passive containers but active receptors, straining to hear, aching to catch something. But the room remained silent. It was as if the sentence was the final one, the end of a conversation that had happened earlier. Suddenly desperate to know who had spoken, I opened the cubicle door and stepped outside.

"What do you mean, the Marbles were shit?" The words were out of my mouth before my mind had time to process the huge neck and bloodshot eyes of the man standing in front of me. He looked down at me; I looked up at him, my skin prickling with regret.

"I said they were shit, because they are shit," said the man. "Who are you, their dad?"

I laughed. Why the hell did I laugh? The sound just fell out of my mouth. "No." I laughed again. "I'm sorry, I was just shocked ... surprised to hear what you said. I love those Marbles, you see."

"*You* can love shit." He grinned. "But *I* don't want to. Don't expect me to look at those broken old bits of body."

It felt like a conversation was about to begin, a great debate on the beauty of Greek sculpture but no, the big man turned and started walking up the steps without another word. I watched his heels disappear from view, then saw the soles of his shoes above me as he crossed the glass above.

Bugger, I thought as I walked up the stairs to the street. How could I break my own cardinal rule so easily? I'd interacted with the person I was listening to. I'd been ready to dispute. It was so easy – too easy. Something else to mention to the eavesdroppers.

The top deck of the bus gave a majestic view of Trafalgar Square as I headed back to Stanley's Job Centre – the fountains, the pigeoned crowds, the bulky shadow of the National Gallery; it was hard to draw my thoughts in. But as we swung past St. Martin-in-the-Fields, the backs of my fellow passengers heads came into view and a question came into my mind. Why *do* some people hear some things and others don't?

Not one person was looking out of the window; the whole bus appeared to have thoughts elsewhere. Everyone – apart from those in social class D – was either reading, texting or scrolling. A hundred little messages thrown into the air and heard by none. I thought of the latest letter that had wended its way up from the south coast, passed from hand to hand, hand to bag, bag to letterbox. A certain Mr. Watt had taken the trouble to find a pen that worked, get hold of some paper, compose a terse note, fish an envelope out of a drawer, lick a stamp and post a letter to me. Why?

The woman on the seat in front of me – middle-aged, felt hat, *lower managerial* – reminded me of someone. It wasn't her appearance, nor her clothes, it was something else. It wasn't until the bus had passed Euston Station and I'd got off that I realised what it was. The way she sat in her seat, the shape of her neck and head, she was a dead ringer for Eve in her listening posture.

Stanley, king of the dole queue, was definitely working by the time I arrived at the Job Centre. As expected of a true eavesdropping professional, he failed to acknowledge my presence until I had sat down next to him. Even then he merely turned the page of his newspaper as a way of greeting and looked at me with empty eyes.

"Been waiting long?" I said.

"Nope."

His surliness impressed me and I would have nodded approvingly had he not abruptly moved seats in a sham progression towards the reception wicket. I lingered a couple of moments longer, basking in the subterfuge, then, with a neutral nod of the head in his direction, left the building and headed off in the direction of the bus stop.

I spent the next couple of hours finishing off my rounds. James would be sure to extract great amusement from my freshly crafted role as inspector of eavesdroppers, yet I rather liked how wise it made me feel: authentic, academic almost.

I found Violet holed up in Reynolds, the cafe on Angel St., where she seemed so absorbed in her computer (a cover she had suggested at the first meeting) that I swivelled on my heels without speaking to her – a movement honed to perfection on my great aunt's threshold many years earlier – and headed for the Tube station.

'Travelling the Tube: *Bayswater to Blackfriars*' had been Jack's note on the schedule and only then, as I approached the halfway point of my inspection, did I fully appreciate the uselessness of this snippet of information. But with fresh ears on my head, and sandwiched between two friends deep in conversation I began to enjoy the intensity of his laboratory as I journeyed underground to Eve's part of town.

I didn't frequent launderettes often. I didn't like the thought of strangers viewing my dirty clothes and there was something unsettling about the ragged ring of detergent that crusted around the jowls of the powder container that I only went there when my washing machine broke down, which was hardly ever. The place was humming with activity when I entered and I was hit fleetingly with guilt as I noticed the number of people wrestling with bedding, sheets all creased and duvet covers inexplicably stuffed with socks. Eve was reading some sort of leaflet when I arrived. She stuffed it into her bag when she saw me approaching.

"Hi, Eve, What have you got there?" I asked as I sat down beside her.

"Oh … hello,' she replied. "It's just some paperwork I had to look over."

I couldn't imagine, even for a second, what paperwork Eve might have to look over. "So, how are you," I said, all matey and chipper.

She fingered the clasp of her bag. "All right, thank you."

My inspector fantasies shattered round me as I suddenly realised something quite basic: the eavesdroppers did not want me around. They just wanted to be allowed to get on with their jobs like the professionals they were. "I was just passing and thought I'd drop by, but I see everything's fine."

"It is fine," she said, with minimal use of her lips.

"See you at the next meeting, then."

"Yes."

I peered back through the window after I'd left the premises. Eve sat on the bench, her back to me. I don't know what it was, the curve of her neck, the way her hair fell over her ears, but she reminded me of someone else.

VIOLET'S heel went down the same drain cover on her way home from the cafe, as if choreographed by God. It had been a long day, and this second encounter with the city's drainage system irritated her. She pulled off both shoes, held one in each hand and continued along the cold street barefoot. She was cautious at first, imagining unspeakably sharp things lurking in the pavement cracks, but it wasn't long before she enjoyed the feel of the stone beneath her feet and strode towards the bus stop with all the vigour of a young gazelle. She'd always looked elegant in bare feet. She should have been a yoga instructor. But yoga instructors have to bend their bodies for money. She was free of all that; she was a self-employed listener. She had two jobs now, the hallmark of the successful freelancer, and she knew there would be more. Once news of her time-management skills got out she'd be fighting off the offers of work.

She felt a few spots of rain on the top of her feet so she paused beneath a shop awning, put on her shoes and checked her hair in the window. Just a single bolt of static was enough to force a hair vertical and she built time into her day to spit and smooth and render herself symmetrical again. She rested all her weight on one leg and thought about her first day as a 'dropper of eaves.' That clever play on words had come to her during the first meeting at Wilson Inc., but she'd held it in. Who knew when a droll little quip like that would come in useful?

She was tired. Doing data entry in the cafe, although now only her 'bread and butter' job, took energy and a certain amount of concentration, but 'dropping of eaves,' now that was exhausting work. Conversations in the cafe, the fog of words that dipped in and out of her consciousness, had drifted easily round her before she'd taken on her new job, but now she was actually being paid to focus, to take note, to even, – and this was her learned interpretation of the task in hand – sort the wheat from the chaff. But there were trade-offs. Her status as a highly paid listener meant she could hover in the vicinity of attractive men without it being a sign of desperation. And there had been a particularly appealing attractive man in the cafe that day. She hadn't actually seen him of course, but she had heard him. Sitting somewhere behind her, he had ordered a latte with two shots of coffee and one sugar and hot, not lukewarm. But what really got him underlined in her notebook was his muttered comment as a woman entered the cafe and headed towards his table – 'I see a thing of beauty coming my way.'

She'd mouthed the sentence to herself, feeling so calm and content that even the sight of Bill Harcourt at the window had not dented the pleasure of her day. She'd seen him off with one of her special looks and felt confident he wouldn't be back in a hurry. Funny bloke, she'd thought. His eyes watered a lot and he said one thing when he really meant another. She'd had a boyfriend once whose eyes watered a lot and she'd spent their time together with a hanky balled in her fist, ready to dab.

Violet shifted her weight onto her left leg and studied her face in the shop window. Such authority, such confidence in the line of that jaw. She took out her mobile and checked the time. "Too early to go home," she said to her reflection.

Her voice had been with her for her whole life. Squeaky as a child, it had dropped drastically when she reached puberty and she'd spent countless sleepless nights worrying that she was turning into a man. But then it rose again and levelled out. Now it was smooth, so silky smooth. She should have been a newsreader. "Much … too … early … to … go … home," she said again. Would *he* like her voice? Would he find it a *thing of beauty*? She *was* beautiful, no doubt about that, but her voice, would he want to listen to her speak?

She opened her notebook, held the most recent page up to the light of the window display and read her final entry.

Woman in cafe: *Let's meet here again next Wednesday.*

Man in cafe: *Sounds good. I'll be here. We can talk privately.*

CHAPTER

16

I let a week pass. Violet sent me several emails a day requesting details of our next gathering, but I held off making any arrangements and only when Eve called requesting a new notebook did I book a meeting room, buy some chocolate biscuits and raid the stationary cupboard for pencils. I ordered extra coffee. There was no telling what mood the eavesdroppers would be in after a few days with their ears in the pricked-up position so at the last minute I rushed out and bought a second packet of biscuits which I piled up artfully on a plate on the table. I wasn't in the mood for the small talk that their intermittent arrival engendered so I went to the Gents and spent a long time washing my hands, fiddling with the hand drier and planning my entrance before returning to the room. Someone had closed the door when I got back, but I could hear the gentle rumble of voices within. And then – I can hardly bring myself to recall it – I moved forward and pressed my ear to the door. At first I heard nothing, but then a throat was cleared, and a nose blown twice in quick succession, which seemed to release conversation.

"He's got a bloody nerve." The pitch of Violet's voice resonated perfectly with the room.

"Who's got a bloody nerve?"

I didn't recognise the second voice and had fleeting thoughts of gatecrashers before I heard Violet's reply. "Him."

"What d'ya mean h–?"

I pushed down the handle and rushed in. They were all there, all of them. They'd already started on the coffee. Missy and Eve sat together at one end of the table like a pair of involuntary twins, both in yellow sweaters and coffee moustaches on matching lips, while Stanley, Violet and Jack, all assembled at the other end, dispatched a wave of communal guilt in my direction.

"Sorry I'm late," I said.

"S'okay," said someone there.

"How are you all?" I said breezily, taking a seat at the end of the table.

"Hungry," said Stanley, eyeing the biscuits.

"This is your reward," I said, "for the best report of the day."

Violet sighed; Missy twisted a tie-dye hanky round her forefinger.

"Seriously though," I said, realising before it was too late that my words implied I thought I'd made a joke. "How are things going?"

"Things are proceeding," said Violet.

"Yes," added Stanley. "Proceeding quite nicely."

Were they taking the piss? It was disturbing to think I didn't know. "Good," I said. Was I such a humourless git? A suit with no flare? "Before we start," I said, "I want to mention … something about your listening technique." They waited. "It's more a question than an instruction." Still they waited. "It struck me, it can be quite easy to talk to people, can't it."

"What do you mean, Mr. Harcourt?" Stanley said.

"When you're listening, it can be easy to say something … you know, to the person you're listening to. …"

"Why would we speak to them when you have employed us to listen?" said Violet.

I looked round my circle. "So, no one has ever got chatting to someone they have been eavesdropping in … on."

Indignation rippled around the table: Violet huffed, Eve allowed a cartoon tut to pop from her lips and Stanley projected his offence with tightly folded arms on heavy elbows.

I ducked – I was getting good at ducking. "I take that as a 'no' then." I turned to Jack. "So Jack, can you tell us something of what you heard in the last few days?"

Jack was a back-of-the-room sort of bloke, always the last to go. But he smiled an engaging if worried smile, opened his notebook and began. We all strained to hear.

His report was structured by the layout of the London Underground. It began at Leicester Square – I could see a tiny logo beneath his fingers – where he'd heard a detailed description of something swishing round in someone's mouth – continued several times round the Circle Line during which he'd recorded cries of communal complaint as someone insisted on bringing a ladder onto the train, before finishing with a quotation, quietly said, but word perfect. "It's like greengrocers' apostrophes … you only see them in … greengrocers."

"What's a greengrocer's apostrophe?" asked Eve.

Stanley seemed to glow. "It's when greengrocers get their grammar wrong."

Missy bit a fingernail. Her hair had been shoved behind her ears again; it made them stick out from the sides of her head. "Do you mean they get all their grammar wrong?" she said.

"No," Stanley said, "just their fruit and vegetable grammar."

Violet sighed. "It's where a simple plural is turned into a singular possessive."

"So," I said, worried that the conversation might be moving into uncharted waters, "anyone beginning to see a pattern out there, any hints of something we haven't heard about before?"

They all seemed to be thinking. I could almost hear it, the brains churning. "Anyone?"

"It's a bit soon to say." Stanley sharpened his pencil in a pedantic way; it was maddening.

'I agree," added Eve. "We are still in the initial training phase."

"You don't need any more training, Eve," I said. "This is meant to be about ordinary people listening to other ordinary people and making surreptitious notes."

"What does surreptitious mean?" asked Missy.

"Look it up," said Violet.

"But–"

"That's what needs the training," said Stanley.

"How do you mean?" I felt a prick of concern that I was about to be unveiled as incompetent, a dread that had plagued my whole life.

"Well," Stanley continued, "don't we need a bit of camouflage training and ... stuff?" He adjusted a cardboard poppy in his lapel.

"You're being ridiculous," said Violet, opening her notebook and clearing her throat in an elegant way. "Three percent of my overheard conversations were about how bad the coffee was, eighteen percent were about how *good* the coffee was, eleven percent were about the weather, twelve percent involved telling off children, and forty-seven percent were about ..." she glanced up from her notebook, "desire."

"That's not a hundred percent," said Eve.

"Desire," she repeated, closing her book and resting her hand on its cover.

We all waited for whatever was going to happen next, to happen.

Scared to ask, I asked, "Can you elaborate?"

Violet had a mole on the top of her lip. I noticed it for the first time as she looked back down at her notebook and began to read. Over the 'lovely shirt,' 'great tits' and 'cleavage going spare,' there was a discernible creaking of chairs and soft clearing of throats.

Yet unease over the revealing of sexual detail was not confined to the older members of the group and even Jack reddened during the unravelling of Violet's notebook. But she surged on relentlessly until she'd taken us inside an alarming amount of underwear and described every part of the human body in distinctly non-scientific detail.

"Was this was just one session in the cafe?" asked Eve, her cheeks flushed.

Violet took us all in with a single glance. "One session."

"You know what I think," said Missy, "it's not all about who fancies who. If you'll listen for just a minute, *I* have an idea about what they are all talking about out there."

"What are they all talking about out there, Missy," I said, expecting an almighty tangent.

"Themselves."

It's funny how the social mores of group situations don't often allow time for thinking, time to sit in silence and process something that someone has said, but at that moment there was a tacit agreement that that was what we needed. I could hear a creak in someone's chair but still no one spoke. Then mini conversations started up just with eyes, but *still* no one spoke, until Missy opened her mouth. "Did I say something wrong?"

"Not wrong, Missy,' said Stanley. "Profound."

Missy twisted her hanky even tighter around her finger. I worried the dye would stain her skin.

"Yes," I said, "you've really given us something to think about."

A chair groaned again.

I opened my notebook and went to make a note, but stopped. "How shall we categorise this observation?"

That silence again. But that silence was good. It was what I needed.

"Missy's big idea," said Stanley, helpfully.

"Noted," I said, writing fast, then adding a bracketed note. "So, Stanley, how did it go at the Job Centre?"

"Didn't go."

"You didn't go? Why not?"

Stanley hooked his forefinger into his mouth, pulled back his cheek and pointed at his exposed gums. "'entist."

"Are you saying 'dentist'?" Eve asked.

"Yes," he replied, releasing his cheek, which remained red. "The one on the Caledonian Road."

"You had a filling?" I said.

"Yes. I'm National Health so it wasn't a problem."

"What wasn't a problem?"

"Getting it done free."

I looked at his eyes, red and watery, as if he'd been rubbing shampoo out of them without success. "You mean getting the filling was just a ruse?"

His eyes lit up. "What a lovely word. What does it mean?" He moved his hand onto his dictionary, always within reach.

"Erm ... a trick or something ... a deceit."

"I suppose it was a trick of sorts," he said. "I told them I'd been in pain since Thursday and Aspirin hadn't even touched it." He looked round unrepentant. "How else was I supposed to get in there without making anyone suspicious?" He yanked back his cheek with his forefinger again and showed a triplet of tea-coloured teeth to everyone at the table. "Did a good job, didn't they."

Eve's mouth was open too; she appeared to have forgotten how to shut it.

"Isn't that immoral?" said Violet.

Stanley turned to her. "I know it's a bit dodgy, Vi, but Mr. Harcourt said we had to use guile to set up our positions." He turned to me. "Guile was the word, wasn't it?"

Guile had indeed been one of the words I'd slipped into my welcome speech. I'd imagined it would appeal to my team's sense of adventure, their undoubted love of James Bond films, but as I gazed at Stanley's raw gum I realised I had better choose my words more carefully in future. "I didn't intend that you spill blood for this job, you know."

"Or defraud the National Health Service," said Eve under her breath.

"Ah, but ... " said Stanley, wallowing in the pause he'd forced on the room, "you've heard about fillings, haven't you?"

"From what point of view?" said Violet.

"From a listening point of view. The metal can transmit radio waves." Stanley looked pleased with himself.

I felt faintly queasy. I flipped my notebook open. "Maybe in future you could let me know if you are planning to establish a new position."

Violet tittered; I didn't know why.

"What about you, Eve?" I said, turning towards her. "Did you get your notes in a way that was a little more, um ... moral?"

Red tinged her cheeks. "Moral? Mr. Harcourt. I ... I can't believe you asked me that. My morality is un ... impeachable.

I faked a smile. Jack seemed far away. "Feeling alright down the end there?"

He looked startled. "Yes, I was just thinking of ... something else."

"Everything alright?"

He smiled brightly. "Yes, sure. Everything's fine."

Looking back, this was the moment I should have taken note. Inside that airless room, accompanied by the sound of biscuits being crunched and notes being scribbled in notebooks, I should have stopped chewing so loudly on my chocolate digestive, and really listened.

EVE decided she didn't like the bench. Its edge, made rough rather than smooth with use, often snagged on her tights, and her back would ache after time spent without support down where she needed it, right behind her kidneys. Yet this was the best spot to catch what she needed to catch.

Jack's final word at the previous group meeting had caught in her mind, but she wasn't sure what he meant. First she'd thought of the weave of baskets that she'd made in craft classes at school. They invariably went wrong and she'd be left with a mess of missed stakes and reeds out of line. Her lounge carpet had a weave, but it was tight and impenetrable, surviving even her big scissors when she dropped them on it whilst trying to cut coupons out of the newspaper. She closed her eyes and fingered the weave of her sweater – she'd knitted it herself – what did it mean? What did *he* mean?

She pulled out her notebook and flicked through the pages, shivering when a breeze floated up on the turn. Every night she read and re-read the contents, correcting her spelling, sometimes rewriting whole sections on a new page. The days between the meetings had started to feel long. She liked to listen to the others' reports and she liked to lay her elbows on the table just like them, but in spite of her attempts to suppress it, her counselling antenna was always up. It took all her strength to keep her hands off the leaflets that lay quietly in the bag at her feet. The eavesdroppers were all in need of a leaflet. But so far she had managed not to let her mind identify who needed what.

The draft behind her kidneys increased so she pulled her sweater tighter round her body, got up off the bench and sat on the broken chair beside the big dryer. It was always cozy there. Even when the machine was empty there would be residual heat. She tucked her bag beneath her seat, leant her head against the warm metal and closed her eyes. Just as she started to make an inventory in her mind of the leaflets she'd gathered that morning, someone walked into the launderette. She couldn't see who it was as they were obscured by the dryer, but her hands were already in her bag, feeling the inside.

She was sharing the room with a man, a sixth sense told her that, but the sounds coming her way told her more: feet smearing the floor, a big sad sigh. This person was definitely in need of her type of ear, but then she remembered she was at work, withdrew her hand from her bag and peeped out from behind the drier.

A large man sat on the bench with his back to her – a particularly big back. He wore an old-fashioned tweed jacket, the threads a worn mesh of grey and brown, a bit like her father used to wear, but tight at the top of the arms. His hair looked greasy and a few straggly locks were tucked into his collar. She sat back, plucked a leaflet out of her bag, and listened for whatever might come into the air.

The blue washing machine abruptly stopped, the dryer by the door finished its cycle, and then Eve clearly heard the gentle tap of fingers on a mobile phone. Then *big back* spoke.

"Bobby? … yeah, it's me. Yeah, yeah, it's done. Ready to go. What do you mean you lost it? On the fucking bus? Tell me you're joking. Bobby … next time I see you … yeah … yeah … the next time I see you I'm gonna kill you."

Eve gazed down at her lap and tried not to breathe. Then, silently, she placed the leaflet, *Vintage Tailoring as Therapy,* back into her bag.

CHAPTER

17

Saturday came. This meant the noise of the city changed; weekend people walked the pavements in meandering groups, the small shops closed so tightly they looked as if they would never open again, and the sound of the street was turned down. Instead of hordes of gusting taxis seeking a rat-run, the air outside my building was disturbed only by the occasional lost driver, scanning the blocks of flats for numbers while grinding through low gears. This respite in my working life meant I could watch rubbish daytime TV and eat my supper on the sofa and be the slob that I was. My flat was my natural habitat, the place where I could whistle tunelessly any time I wanted and leave a half-eaten sandwich on the side of the bath.

I'd been one of the lucky ones. With *Breadline Britain* being shouted from the news stands and the Job Centre running out of chairs, I had managed to get a job which paid reasonably well and that I vaguely enjoyed. Social researcher was never an occupation that crossed my mind as a boy, but somehow I'd drifted into social sciences, got through university by the skin of my teeth and more by chance than burning ambition ended up in a research company that remunerated me enough to pay my rent, cook the occasional steak and down a pint or two in the pub on a Friday night. I'd even managed to beat down a mortgage-broker in a way that everyone said was impossible and bought my own ex-council flat in central London before the final wave of app developers came to roost. My place was never going to make the cover of *Ideal Home* magazine but I cleaned it up, painted it white, bought a few chairs that my mother disapproved of and got on with my life. That was until the Planning Application notice arrived. Nailed to the tree outside my building, the leaflet was written in letters too small for the average person to read and it had passed me unnoticed until my neighbour, an elderly lady who always smelt of fresh gooseberries, took hold of my elbow as I passed her on the stairs, guided me back outside and held her magnifying glass over its title. An entire section of the street opposite our flats was to be removed and replaced, in an 'aesthetically pleasing way,' by a large new government building that appeared, judging by the poster that was subsequently put up on the corner of the site, to have the urine-coloured walls of a building society headquarters from the 1970s. No more Victorian sash windows jammed open with a stick when the rope frayed, no more moss-encrusted roof tiles slipping out of place, just rows of gaunt workers in pale, over-lit rooms. I'd reconciled myself to progress, to the narrowing of my view, but I had not yet got used to the noise. Weekday mornings began at 7:00 am with a shout from the street, followed by a rumble in my floorboards as equipment was moved into position, started up and finished off with a thud. And every thud would be followed by another thud. Every tremble of my coffee mug would be followed by another tremble. And so it went, the shouting of workers, the piling, the digging, the endless filling, until I began not to notice the building going up opposite my home. Until that moment.

As I pressed my nose against the window, I noticed the builders had made a mistake.

Suppressing the urge to rub my eyes, I focused on the small corner of the building that had caught my attention. The wind had lifted the corner of the tarpaulin and it was flapping up and down like a giant petticoat, leaving the concrete exposed. But it wasn't straight like I had expected from the marketing poster. It was slightly curved.

I wiped my breath off the glass and returned to the room. I turned on the radio, sat at the kitchen table with my notebook and pencil and assumed the position of a casual scribe. A play was on air and a relaxed conversation slid out of the casing and wafted towards me. I scribbled frantically, but even with this gently paced dialogue it was hard to keep up and I felt new admiration for my team's recording skills. But harder than recording the words was maintaining a posture of innocence while recording the words. My shoulders kept tightening, my eyes insisted on turning towards the radio. Then another thought. What reason could the writing be for? What implied purpose would draw suspicion away from such a feverishly scribbling pencil? Too detailed for a shopping list, too fast for a letter.

I stopped writing and dragged the table and chair over to the other side of the room, opposite the full-length mirror. I sat down. Again I rushed to keep up with the words pouring out of the radio, which were faster now as the characters reached a climax of feverish recrimination. I listened; I scribbled; I looked in the mirror. In the rush to record the words I forgot to look innocent. I froze in mid-word and stared at myself in the mirror. There was a man writing something he shouldn't. No one would be fooled by that. Nobody likes an eavesdropper.

STANLEY was sure the dictionary was where he had left it – top shelf next to the tea caddy. He got it down and held it towards Beryl. She hadn't been interested in her cuttlefish that evening, gazing sadly out of the kitchen window while he tried to attract her attention to it, so he'd decided there was nothing like a good definition to perk her up. He sat in his chair, held the dictionary up and read aloud. "*Surreptitious* means, 'kept secret, especially because it would not be approved of.'"

Beryl blinked.

"A secret. Did you hear that Beryl? Does that mean it's wrong?"

Accompanied by a rush of creaking bones Stanley got out of his chair and put his face to the side of the cage. "Oh, Beryl. Just a word and I'd be happy. Please my darling, just one word."

Beryl preened her breast feathers. There was no sound in the kitchen, just the drone of a far-off plane high in the sky. Stanley made himself a cup of tea and buttered a slice of cold toast he'd found on the draining board. He addressed the cage from the kitchen table. "Actually, Beryl, I smelt a lady's blouse today." He sipped his tea. "Oh, yes. In the dentist's waiting room." He bit into his toast; the crunch startled Beryl. "She was a bit like you, Beryl." He laughed. "A bit on the haughty side." He glanced back at the dictionary and read the definition again, putting great stress on the first two words, "*Kept secret*, especially because it would not be approved of."

CHAPTER
18

Sea Kale Cottage
121 Battery Road
Lydd-on-Sea,
Kent
October 15th 2018

Dear Mr. Harcourt,

Your non-communication concerns me deeply. It suggests that things are worse than I thought, or that you doubt my integrity. I need to speak to you as soon as possible regarding this matter. I don't travel easily. The train from Victoria Station to Lydd goes every two hours. Let me know when you are coming.

I watch for the postman.

Yours sincerely,
Raymond Watt.

I felt a disagreeable churn in my stomach as I finished reading the latest letter. 'Your non-communication concerns me deeply,' concerned me the most deeply. His nibs didn't like to be ignored. His nibs didn't travel easily. I held my finger beneath the third line. Where the hell *was* Lydd, anyway?

I sat down at my computer and clicked on *Google* Maps. I zoomed in and moved sideways, then zoomed again, and there it was: Lydd-on-Sea, England. It *did* exist, it *was* beside the sea, but it wasn't a real town, it was what my geography teacher would have called *ribbon development*: a single row of houses squeezed between the sea and an area of dry-looking ground. Something big seemed to have gouged stripes into the earth.

I zoomed in further, the sea became shiny, the stripes evolved into lines of vegetation and the dots on the beach were suddenly full-grown bushes, clinging to what looked like shingle. As I activated *Street View* I thought I'd accidently clicked on the Nevada desert, but then I saw an English bungalow: red bricks, net curtains pulled to, in case a mermaid should see in. As I walked digitally down the coast road, I wondered if Watt lived in one of the little houses with tarmac gardens and broken concrete walls. Were those his kids' toys piled up by the front door? Was that his van being done up on the concrete? A Union Jack had been caught by the camera in mid flap and I couldn't help but wonder – was that his?

It's amazing how much ground you can cover in *Street View* and soon I was running along the Dungeness Road, past army training grounds, past the big horizon, along the empty ground, not a soul in sight, then zooming out. I was flying, faster and faster until I saw a brown Cortina pulled to the side of the road. I felt guilty as I zoomed back in again, but angelic surveillant that I was, I came down, down, down and looked inside. There was the face of a man at the window; he was looking straight at me.

Sometimes when you close your eyes a shape remains on the inside of your eyelids, a memory of the last thing you have seen. Just a moment, then the image fades and the object has truly gone. But that face inside the car, it lingered, it slipped inside my eyelids and stayed there. It faded, yes, it slowly vacated the sore, soft skin covering my eyes, but then it lingered in my brain. Wretched, accusing, staring face.

I opened my desk drawer and found a notepad in the back, ancient stationary that had not been exposed to light for decades, and then dug out a fountain pen. The pen was dry from lack of use and I had to shake and shake until the ink flowed and I could draft a response. A simple reply, no less and no more than was needed. The ink dried slowly on the paper.

Wilson Inc.
29 Craven St
London
October 17ᵗʰ 2018

Dear Raymond whoever-you-are,

I've never heard of Lydd and I've never heard of you.
Stop pestering me.
Do not write to me again.

W. Harcourt.

I licked the envelope and sealed it. My letter would be pushed through his letterbox. A rebuttal yes, yet contact would be made. Would it be moved to the kitchen table, placed next to the newspaper and scrutinised? Would I regret it?

MISSY rubbed a finger across the molar at the back of her mouth. It was warm back there, and for a second she sucked her thumb, trying to relive a time that was lost. She hadn't been to the dentist since one of the women noticed a brown tooth as she bit into an apple and her body was knuckled into the dentist's chair and she was left alone with the masked face, the pink water and the breath of the dentist inside her nose. Sometimes she thought about that day, and then her teeth would ache and her gums bleed. But you didn't need good teeth to sit in a public toilet for hours every night. You just needed to be able to settle your buttocks comfortably onto the seat, protect your back from any breezes drifting up from the floor, and breathe. Quietly. And only occasionally would the smell of the bleach and sound of fingers rattling the lock force her to remember her childhood and carry her back to the place where the toilet was the only sanctuary, to the place where she cut her teeth as an eavesdropper.

Her sitting position required no variation and it was only when she heard more than ten heels clicking on the tiles outside the door – she had learned to count feet in pairs – that she ever felt the need to open the toilet door and let someone else have their turn.

She chose her own footwear with care; whoever might be down there would see her coming before she saw them. A great believer in first impressions, she wanted whoever observed her feet descending the stairs to see the person she really was. So she wore party shoes – silver, shiny, sexy.

"Look at that bloody pouch, Ang. I've got to get some exercise."

Missy jumped as a voice erupted close by.

"Stop beating yourself up or you'll get a slap."

"Look at that bloody cellulite. I feel so ashamed."

"You can get vitamins for that."

Missy held her breath. This was her time, the brief moment that allowed her to draw a picture in her head of the owners of the voices. Muffin waists, she envisaged, rolls of neck, bags too full of stuff.

"Oh, Ang. That mirror's soul-destroying. I didn't feel fat before I came in here."

"I like that bag, where'd you get that?"

"Dunno. Just giving it an airing. God, look at that cellulite; it's all over the place. This blue druggy's light doesn't help either. I look like a bloody ghoul."

"Yeah, why do they have that?"

"Dunno, stops them finding a vein or something..."

"Ugh, put it away, will you. You're making me feel queasy."

"Thanks a bunch, Ang."

"You know I'm only joking. Let's get out of here. This light's making my head ache."

"Oh, Ang."

Perfume still hung in the air when Missy emerged from the toilet. She looked down at her wrists. Her veins, normally so big, were invisible. She pulled up her sleeve and looked at her arm. The freckles were gone, rubbed out by the blue tone of the light; she now had the smooth, perfect skin of a newborn. She looked at her other arm. Perfect too. Finally, she pulled up her shirt, stood on her toes and examined her naked belly in the mirror.

Five minutes later Missy emerged into the High Street. She paused, rummaged in her bag, pulled out her notebook and began to write under the borrowed light of the street lamp – choppy, slanting words that she hoped she would be able to make sense of later. Then she stopped and held her pen off the paper. How do you spell 'cellulite'?

"Not another one."

I looked up from my desk. I was reading the letter that had arrived that morning and my eyes took a second to focus. "Oh, hi James, I didn't hear you come in. Yeah, another letter came. It's the fourth."

"Fourth? What about the third, you never told me about that."

"Yeah, I know; I didn't want to make a big thing of it. I wrote back, but–"

"You wrote back! What did you say?"

"Told him to bugger off."

"And?"

"He sent yet another letter. It arrived this morning. I'm starting to feel a bit … bombarded."

James took off his coat, hung it on *his* peg, a place of past battles, and sat down at his desk. "Want to tell me about it?"

I looked at my colleague. Empathy wasn't always his strong point but quite suddenly he had it all: pleasant smile, bright eyes, non-judgemental bend to his neck. "I'll read it to you if you like."

His smile sagged. "Is it very long?"

"Three lines."

"Okay, let's hear it."

Reading aloud had never been my strong point but I scanned the letter again, practiced the pronunciation of *distrustful* in my head, then began: "Your refusal to listen to my pleas deeply concerns us. I know you might be dis ... distrustful of a stranger, but I also think that strangers are the people to which you like to listen." I paused to let the words sink in. "I implore you, Mr. Harcourt, please come to Lydd as soon as possible and I will tell you something important."

"Why are you reading in that funny voice?" said James.

"What funny voice?"

"That ... I don't know, that funny growl at the end of each sentence."

'I don't know. It's ... how I imagine him to sound."

"And who the hell is *us*? I thought this was just one potty bloke."

"Me too. Do you think it's a cult?"

"Nah, it's probably some seven-stone weakling with a chip on his shoulder trying to act tough."

I glanced at James' puny frame. "Yeah, you're probably right."

"You gonna write back?"

"I don't know. Do you think I should?"

James twirled his pencil between his fingers. It was annoying. "Yeah, I think you should. I'll give you a hand if you like."

"Sure."

James and I spent half an hour drafting the reply. First it was long, a full page rant complete with expletives in capitals and crowded with exclamation marks, then it was smaller, more circumspect, but still we weren't satisfied. Finally, after much milling of minds we boiled it down to one beautifully spare line:

Dear Jerk,
If you bother me one more time I shall report you to the police for stalking.
W. Harcourt.

We both tipped our chairs. My back muscles relaxed, but I noticed a fresh comment brewing on the other side of the room.

"Bill."

"Yeah?"

"You're certain, aren't you?'

"Certain about what?"

"That he's a nutter."

"Positive."

James looked shifty. "It's just that now we've got the envelope sealed and the stamp on I'm feeling a tiny bit curious about what he might have to say."

"Bloody hell, James. Now you've got *me* wondering."

James stood up and grabbed the letter off the desk. "Sod it! Let's send it. Get him off our backs once and for all."

It was just Eve and I in the pub. She had a manky little scarf round her neck and it bothered me, the way it was too short to tie in a proper knot and seemed to be attached to her shoulders by the force of static alone. I'd felt uncomfortable when she invited me to the pub after work, but her imploring eyes had forced me to accept, and now, with a pint of beer untouched on the table I felt unusually shy. "How's it going?" I said.

"Quite … well," she said, cupping her glass, but not picking it up.

"Enjoying it?"

"Enjoying what?"

I looked for clues her eyes. "The job, the highly paid snooping."

"Oh, yes. But … that's what I want to talk to you about."

"Okay."

"Yes." She tweaked her scarf; it just about clung to her neck. "I heard something the other day that I thought I should tell you about."

My flippancy was hard to shrug off, but eventually it dissolved by itself and I settled into the posture of an earnest listener. "Tell away." I felt a patronising urge to add 'my dear' on the end of my sentence, but held it back.

And tell away she did.

I'd expected a quick summary of her *overheards* – a collective noun I was under the impression I'd invented – but she pulled out her notebook and opened it onto a page marked with a yellow stickie. I tried to imagine what event could be down there on the page – a tussle over a drier maybe? a mismatched sock? – but as I looked up I saw her eyelashes were damp.

"Eve," I said, taking the book out of her hands and closing it, "just *tell* me what happened."

She drew in a breath. "Well ... I was sitting on the quiet seat yesterday and two people came in. You don't know the launderette very well but the quiet seat I like is round the corner, hidden behind the powder dispenser. It's where I have my little chats."

"What little chats?"

"The ... my ... I was sitting there on my own and two people came in and they ... they ... there was talk of waiting in the car, then what they had for lunch, then ... at the end, there was talk of 'duffing someone up.' Mr. Harcourt, what does 'duffing' mean?"

I remained eminently calm. "Oh, you know, a little fight, a bit of a scrap. Did you talk to them?"

"No."

"No little chat?"

"No."

"Did you see what they looked like?"

"Their backs, I only saw their backs."

"What sort of backs did they have?"

"I don't know ... big."

Big backs. Something caught my eye. Eve's hand was moving inside her bag.

"I heard something I shouldn't have, didn't I?" she said.

"It's not a case of shouldn't," I replied. "What's in the air is for anyone's ears."

"Is that true?"

I wasn't sure. "Yes, Missy. It is."

"Eve. I'm Eve."

"Oh, sorry. Eve. I apologise."

She gave me a long look. "What should I do?"

"Move to another launderette."

"Another launderette?"

"Yes, there are loads in your area, aren't there?"

"Yes. I'll do that. There are loads."

"Good. Any other worries?"

"No."

"Good, I'll see you at the next meeting, then."

"I'm looking forward to it. Thank you for your advice."

I nodded and smiled, the outside of my body a suit of ease.

I couldn't get home fast enough. I cursed the lateness of the Tube; I tripped on the kerb. Raymond Watt's latest letter was on the kitchen table when I got home. Where I had left it.

JACK had an open notebook at each elbow. One was closed and thick with writing, the other yawning and empty. He looked at the white space of his play. Not a play, just a few lines of a story, a half-formed arc. He sighed. He had the setting, he had the characters, but they would not speak. Why wouldn't they speak? He had given them a place in which to flex their muscles, a place to recoil; he had given them jobs, families, memories. He had even given them desires, fears, prejudices, but still they would not speak.

He got up from the table and switched on the TV. The evening news was on, piling on footage of Remembrance Sunday, the previous year. An aerial view of Whitehall, a glimpse of the Cenotaph, and finally, a shaky close-up of a cardboard poppy. Jack never bought a poppy badge in the weeks leading up to Remembrance Sunday for the same reason he never signed his organ donor card, he felt it brought him closer to death.

He sat back and watched the ranks of old soldiers as they marched across his TV screen. The November day was coming when half the country wore a cardboard flower pinned to their chests and the other half ignored it, or felt guilty, or uncomfortable, or a mixture of all three. Jack felt a loathing for war, not wanting to think about it, not wanting to be reminded that it was there, always there.

Mesmerised by the marching pensioners, he leant forward in his chair. The band played on but he fancied he could hear the groan of damaged limbs, the creak of geriatric shoes. Yet these were the brave ones. The heroes. He watched a close-up of a wrinkled hand clutching a programme and a row of medals hanging from a hollow chest, then the marching again, marching bravely up the safe street. Bravery, he thought. What *was* that? Where did that aura hanging on the shoulders of the trembling octogenarians decades after the event actually come from?

He looked down at his own skinny legs. Could they march in time? Did they have the strength to run from a bullet? But bravery, he thought again, needed an enemy in order to exist. Who was *his* enemy? Himself? Such was his hopeless body, it couldn't look people in the eye, couldn't raise its voice, couldn't interrupt even the most hesitant of conversationalists. Would he ever feel a desire to be the centre of attention? A lifelong master of social deflection, his only skills were merging into his surroundings and avoiding an insistent gaze. His only conversations were with the characters in his plays, but they wouldn't speak. Why wouldn't they speak?

He'd never had a girlfriend, but he lived in the hope that there was a woman somewhere who longed for a shy person. Yet, he felt disgusted at shyness when he saw it in others. Disgust followed by pity. Pity followed by sadness. Sad, shy them. Sad, shy him.

'Speak up,' his mother had urged him as a kid. 'Toughen up,' his father would beg.

And now they were gone he tried hard to remember their words, tried so hard not to be shy.

He'd spoken many times to his bathroom mirror; told it to 'shut the fuck up.' But swearing made him blush. Even in the privacy of his own home his cheeks grew warm and his voice lowered whenever it formed an expletive. And shouting. That was the hardest thing. Shouting strained the muscles of his throat and the voice that came out didn't sound like his.

He looked at the TV again and felt the drift of a daydream. He imagined a medal pinned to his chest. He imagined a bullet chasing him up his street. He imagined a megaphone pressed to his lips.

Jack walked slowly towards to Bayswater Tube Station. As he approached the entrance, he saw a lone woman, ginger hair cut like Eve's, with a tray slung around her neck, a money tin at her ankle and a look of expectation on her face.

"Poppy, Sir?"

"No, thanks."

Once inside the building he hesitated. Some invisible barrier held him back, just long enough for a swab of claustrophobia to wipe his face before he pulled his bag onto his shoulder and headed down the stairs. There was a queue at the turnstile, but he used the time productively, trying to memorise the words of the person talking loudly behind him. Then he attempted to read the lips of a woman who was at the top of the opposite escalator. *Get out of my face. Let us say grace.*

Someone stood too close behind him on the way down the escalators, breathing on the back of his neck, but when Jack turned round there was no one there. A train rushed into the station as he arrived at the platform and he slipped past a dithering woman in front of him to catch the last space on the train. A man watched him through a slit in the crowd.

The doors beeped, and then hissed shut. Just a moment without breath then Jack took hold of the pole, closed his eyes, and relaxed.

At first he could not separate the sounds in the carriage, but gradually, over the rumble of the wheels and whine of the engine, he heard voices, French first, then English.

"You'll have to work quick on that."

"I think it's difficult to do."

"Strike up a new relationship. Just strike it up."

The voice in the train changed, mechanical, intonation in the wrong place. *This is Embankment. Change here for …*

Jack opened his eyes. An empty seat had appeared half way down the carriage and, checking for the presence of elderly people around him, he slipped into it. From the comfort of his seat he observed his fellow travellers. It had been drizzling outside and the toes of every shoe were wet, eyelids were wet, and there was a smell of dog in the air. An unlikely couple looked comfortable opposite him, a young man with very black skin and an old man with the purple cheeks of an alcoholic. The short distance between their elbows suggested that they would speak. Jack opened his notebook onto a new page, gripped his pencil and waited. Then noted.

Old man: *Doing anything exciting today?*

Young man: *Nope.*

He waited again, but they would not speak. They just stared up at the Tube map as if they were trying to solve a mathematical equation.

He looked down at his notes then back up at the couple. Why wouldn't they say anything else? He could write the words for them, then they would speak. He looked down at his notes again. Was there something hidden in that simple exchange, something he'd missed?

"Hell down here, isn't it."

Glancing around the train, Jack could not see who had spoken. It was as if the play had finally started but the audience hadn't yet reached their seats. The woman beside him pulled out a mirror and held it up to her face; a little girl opposite looked at her. A man watched him through a slit in the crowd.

CHAPTER

20

The train from Victoria Station to Lydd left at eleven o'clock in the morning. I had just finished my coffee when it arrived at platform sixteen but couldn't find a bin anywhere, so I held the empty cup in my hand like a volunteer litter collector. The train smelt of plastic and was full of men in clothes smarter than mine and I was relieved to find a pair of empty seats so I did not have to rub elbows with fabric of a superior weave.

As the train passed out of the dry, dusty, concussed zone that is south-east London, I pulled out the latest letter, unfolded it and laid it down on the tray fixed to the back of the seat in front of me, and read. *I'm satisfied that you have come to your senses. I'll meet you at Lydd Station at 1 o'clock.* I glanced out of the window, the grass rushed by and the houses had separated from one another, no longer the tight terraces of Lewisham but the singletons of Sidcup, lonely-looking homes with overgrown shrubs in the gardens and shrivelled bedding plants drooping from hanging baskets. I pressed my cheek to the window and watched the rails as we trundled round a wide curve. What was waiting for me at the end of this track, I wondered. A prankster? A lunatic? A big, mean back?

As if under instructions from a distant controller, mobile phone conversations started up, ricocheting around the train: "Are you still on the Methodist pastoral circuit?" then, "I don't like fish paste sandwiches, I told you that."

For once I didn't feel like listening to what others were saying. I forced my attention inwards, recalling the evening in the pub with Eve in so much detail that I could almost see the condensation on the outside of my beer mug and smell the cigarettes that wafted through the door from the street. 'Duffing someone up' wasn't an expression I'd heard recently. I wasn't entirely sure what it meant, but I knew it involved physical force, a thrashing, a beating of sorts. But could it mean more? Could Eve have heard a plan for a murder?

The train rushed into a tunnel and the natural light in the carriage vanished, only to be replaced by sickly, temporary ones. That yellow light had always frightened me as a child. My poor mother: jigging me on her lap, wiping tears off my cheeks. I felt the same surge of anxiety at that moment, suppressed a cry in my throat, and then we shot out of the other end, unchanged. An hour went by as the fields grew longer and the horizon wider until the announcer suddenly called out 'Lydd-on-Sea' in a desperate voice. I looked out of the window. Flat out there, so flat; a huge tray of ground stretched towards a wall of sky and there were things scattered about: random bushes, clumps of grass that seemed to be clinging to the ground. And I saw shapes on the horizon, nautical silhouettes: lighthouses, masts, flagpoles. And dominating all the little things I could see the big thing, the massive angular bulk of the nuclear power station at Dungeness. It unnerved me, its grey hulk seeming to hold up the sky, its pall of radioactive smoke bent sideways by the wind, going somewhere else.

When I stepped off the train the station was empty yet an eerie feeling hung in the air, of someone having been there who had just gone. Was he hiding? I wondered. Had he squeezed himself behind a pillar, his shoulders pulled right in? I felt relieved – more time to rehearse.

"Mr. Harcourt?"

I turned. A man stood behind me. I'd pictured someone younger, but this person was old, so old his cheeks had a loose grid on them where wrinkles had formed in two directions, and his head looked too heavy for his neck. "Yes," I replied. "Mr. Watt?"

This was the moment to shake, but the man's hands were firmly by his sides.

"Are you ready to go?" he said.

"Go where?" I asked.

"To the pits."

"Pits?"

"Yes, pits. One mile." The thickness of his eyebrows barred any further comment.

I don't know what I'd expected from this encounter, but not this, not a hike. I glanced down at my office shoes; they looked newer than they really were. "Alright."

"I heard you coming," the man said, as we fell in step.

"Heard I *was* coming, you mean?"

"No. I heard you coming when I was sitting in the waiting room. Your left heel squeaked as you stepped onto the platform and that bag in your pocket, the one that's holding the doughnut or the sandwich you bought on the train, it rustled as you tried to find your ticket."

I glanced at his ear, expecting to see a state-of-the-art hearing aid, but all I saw were little grey tufts stuffed into a hole. "It had too much jam in it …" I said.

He didn't respond, just fished about in his pocket. He pulled a large handkerchief out of his left pocket and pushed it into the right one. "Your first letter wasn't very polite," he said, walking faster.

"Neither was yours," I replied.

"You didn't want to listen to me."

"I didn't know what I was listening *to*."

"That seems to be your problem."

The man increased his pace; I scurried in his wake.

Living a walker's life in the more elevated part of London I was used to exercising my legs, but not like this, not pushing against a wardrobe of wind. My companion walked unflinchingly; I panted behind. The edge between the road and pavement dissolved and I saw a caravan park coming into view. I'd always been a bit queasy about towns on the south coast, the accusing glare of seagulls from rooftops, the smell of chips held too long in the pan, and I was feeling increasingly apprehensive, wondering about the small garden gnome perched on the 'Welcome' doormat of a nearby house, when the old man took a sharp left through the caravan site's rickety gates.

"Is this where you live?" I asked.

He paused and turned towards me. "I thought you'd be wiser than this."

I tried not to display the sulk I fell into and decided to let my magnanimous side shine through. "I thought everyone lived in a caravan round here. Holiday town, and all that."

"This isn't a holiday town."

The man at my side increased his pace – I increased mine – and we walked between the caravans in silence. I couldn't imagine who lived inside the little tin dwellings. Miniature people with an obsession for satellite dishes, I guessed. As we reached the edge of the site and the man pressed a barbed wire fence down with his foot and gesticulated for me to step over, I began to wonder if this was nothing but a huge practical joke. Or, was he luring me to a quiet death behind the caravans? But a quick look at the tremble in his hand on the wire reassured me of my chances should a fight ensue.

Walking on shingle is hard, and I sorely missed the solid pavements of London at that moment. But my companion had no problem; he marched across the landscape like a long-legged coot, born to lifting his feet high and traversing shifting pebbles. And the crunch, it seemed to echo across the ground, stones rubbing and grinding beneath our soles. As the caravan park dropped behind us we skirted the edge of what looked like a flooded gravel pit. A place good for a murder, I thought again – a slow, horrible death.

Something huge, grey and round was on the horizon. It came slowly into view as we rounded a clump of trees.

"What's that?" I said, raising my voice above the wind.

"What's what?"

"The thing beyond those trees, that massive concrete thing."

He paused and peered into my face. I smelt the acrid aroma of a *Fisherman's Friend* on his breath. "You've never seen one before?"

One? "No. I've no idea what it is."

"I'll explain when we get there."

He set off again; I crunched behind. Had I been a naturalist I would have been distracted by the birdlife that busied itself round us, but with the gloomy back of my companion ahead of me and clouds sagging on the horizon I felt only irritation when a duck quacked, overly loudly I thought, in the murky water beside my heels. What did distract me was the object looming ever closer. As we passed through the trees and stepped onto the thing's grassy forecourt I realised it was not just a huge lump of concrete but something more elaborate.

"What *is* that?" I said, craning my neck to catch sight of the top. "That … thing?"

"Do you see the shape?" said the man.

"A sort of giant ball cut in half, isn't it?"

"And?"

"C'mon, mate. I've come all this way. Just tell me."

"And … ?"

I scanned the object towering above us. "It's tilted, it's … point-ing slightly upwards."

"Towards what?"

I followed his gaze. The clouds had now regrouped into miser-able bulks. "The sea?"

I looked at the side of his face as he continued to gaze skyward. His sideburns reminded me of an old dog I once had, all moulting and grey.

He turned towards me when I was least expecting it. "You know what these objects are doing, don't you?"

"No." I pursed my lips. "I don't."

He stretched the grid of wrinkles on his cheek. "They're listening."

I felt a chill on the back of my neck and turned up my collar. "What is it called, this … this … ?"

The man looked at me with sadness in his eyes. "*Sound mirror,*" he said.

The pairing of words puzzled me. Not only was the great beast utterly silent but the disc's spalled surface bore no resemblance to glass, and unless my skin was now pockmarked with black circles and dusted with cement the object had not the slightest ability to reflect. But mirrors he'd said, and as I turned my mind to this new possibility the old man looked beyond it to a long, curved wall about thirty metres away.

"What's that … wall?" I asked.

"Another mirror. They tried out different shapes. It was an experiment."

"They … ?"

The old man met my eyes, then he started a story. A story of war and listening for war.

"The first mirror was built in the 1920s," he began. "A time of national fear about the perils of being an island nation close to a fist-shaking neighbour. Back then," he moved his face closer to mine – more *Fisherman's*, more *Friends*, "after the Second World War finally broke out, listening was about survival. Even the smallest child could recognise the whine of the doodlebug and the growl of a Spitfire as it flew overhead." He paused to tighten his scarf around his neck. "Night was the worst time. Tension lay in every bed as the sounds of the night were analysed from all angles, then mentally ticked off as safe. But the limit of human ears can only stretch so far." He paused.

"So … ?"

"So the government built massive concrete ears at key locations on the coast."

"And ... ?"

"If you stop interrupting me, I'll tell you."

I listened. The wartime adjectives and dabs of emotion in his voice made his words hard to follow, but I was soon taken back so many decades that I could almost smell the cordite in the air and hear hands rubbing together in the cold.

"Every single night a team of shivering listeners had to operate the mirrors," he said. "Their numb backsides perched on stools, special stethoscopes in their ears, listening for what was coming. And something *was* coming. The German army was massing just across the English Channel, packing the planes with bombs, turning the planes in the direction of England."

"How do you know all this?" I said.

He looked disconcerted for the first time and stared at my face, stared but did not blink. "I was there, Mr. Harcourt. I was one of the listeners."

I struggled to hold his gaze. "Mr. Watt. Why did you bring me here?"

He blinked. "I needed to tell you what happened. I needed to warn you."

"What *did* happen?" I hardly wanted the answer.

"Let's get some shelter from this wind," he said, gesticulating for me to follow him to the leeward side of the mirror. Silence engulfed us the moment we turned the corner.

The old man took his handkerchief out of his right pocket, and then stuffed it into his left. Then he leant against the mirror. "There were five eavesdroppers on this site," he said. "I was their leader. We worked in shifts, took it in turns to listen. The lads were excited at first. More than excited, proud. We were proud to be part of something so important, something so ... ingenious. These mirrors, they were brilliant. Born of brilliant minds. Before the mirrors, before radar was invented, we were ignorant of the movements of enemy aircraft, until they were right upon us."

"I understand," I said. "But what has all this got to do with me?"

The old man wet his upper lip with his tongue; a small intake of breath dried it. "Mr. Harcourt, listening is exhausting. It's draining. Eventually it starts to do something to a person."

"What does it do?" Butterflies were opening wings inside my stomach.

"Too much listening starts to change a person."

The wings were moving. "In what way?"

"It can affect your mind … your character."

"Your character? You mean like your personality?"

"Yes. This wasn't casual eavesdropping. These men weren't sitting in cafes listening to people talk about the weather. They were listening for warplanes loaded with bombs. Can you imagine what that was like?"

"No … I can't imagine."

The wind crept round our side of the mirror and ruffled the old man's hair.

"We didn't notice anything at first," he continued. "War makes everyone a bit strange. People aren't themselves. When people live in constant fear they are often out of sorts. But straining to hear something important, hour after hour, day after day, gets to you. The other senses – sight, taste, – fade a little, but the ears, they get stronger. The ears more than hear. They actively listen – without being told to."

I heard a skylark cry out, high above us. Always heard, never seen. "Please continue," I said.

"The mirrors began to take their toll on the listeners. There was so much pressure. Pressure to hear the planes coming. Pressure to know precisely where they were."

"I don't mean to be rude, but again, what has all this got to do with me? Now."

"I'm about to tell you." His eyes were unforgiving. "Jimmy was the first to go. The youngest listener was the first to change. Jimmy started to close his eyes when he spoke to you. Closed eyes and a slight nod of his head. Said it sharpened his hearing. We didn't mind, just one of the wartime tics common in young recruits, but then he started listening to his wife. He followed her and listened, always listening, behind the door, an ear at the keyhole. Every time she answered the phone he was there, lurking in the corridor. She left him in the end. She didn't tell him to his face. She wrote him a note. He told me."

"What'd it say?" I could have bitten my tongue off.

His lips seem to have trouble shaping the words. "'I don't love you any more.'"

The breeze took up our conversation, humming across the face of the mirror. It slapped a leaf onto the base; it sighed.

"And the others?" I asked.

The man's cheek twitched. "Charlie went mad. Completely bonkers. He thought everyone was listening to *him*. He suspected his best friend. He suspected his mother. He even suspected me. Finally, they put him in a mental hospital. That was easily done in those days. Someone signs a piece of paper and you're rocking on your heels for the rest of your life."

I wanted to say something.

The man continued. "We didn't notice Malcolm at first. It was slow ... so slow, so subtle. Such a quiet, gentle lad, he wouldn't say boo to a goose. But ever so slowly, he took the listening into his other life. His private life. And he didn't just listen. He had to get involved. The listener spoke back."

My heart chugged up a gear. "What do you mean?"

"No one likes an eavesdropper."

"So you mean ...?"

"Yes. He got caught. He had to say his bit. Got into an argument, a scrap with a man with a temper and a knife. His retinas sliced clean off."

I flinched as the wind wiped my eyes. "And ...?"

"He lost his sight. Listening was all he had left."

"Is that ... everyone?"

"Almost. There was Trevor."

"What ... happened to him?"

"Prison."

"What for?"

"I can't give you the details, but all I can say is careless talk costs lives."

The phrase was vaguely familiar. "Do you mean–?"

"I can't tell you. It's classified."

'Still? It's been over ... what ... seventy years–"

"I can't tell you."

I looked at his gridded skin. His face seemed gentler than earlier. "What about you?"

"Me?"

"Yes. Did you survive the listening?"

He seemed to notice something on the wind. Then he spoke slowly. "I was their leader. I saw what was happening, but I left it too late, Mr. Harcourt. You are the leader now. *You* can stop this project. I know it's not about war, but all eavesdropping is potentially dangerous. You can stop the project, before it's too late. It's all up to you."

The train back to London was empty. I was glad. Not only did I get a window seat and a table to myself, but I also had a chance to sift through the events of the last couple of hours inside a peaceful head. Mr. Watt had said a lot, His story was sad. I wasn't such a heartless bastard that I hadn't been moved by it, but it was history. London had reached the twenty-first century. Ears were different back then.

I hadn't felt the need to mention *my* eavesdroppers to the old man. I didn't feel like another lecture. But back in the train I began to wonder. Wonder and doubt.

As the train crawled into the shadows of Clapham Junction I went through each listener in my head: Violet fine, Stanley, too many fillings but fine, Missy fine, Jack fine. Only Eve had brushed up against any real problem and that had been sorted out. A change of launderette, a change of scene, all it needed.

I looked out of the window. I tried to count the trees rushing by 1, 2, 3, 4 … 1, 2, 3, 4 …

I thought of the wartime eavesdroppers – 1, 2, 3, 4 …

VIOLET didn't like the notebook Bill Harcourt had given her. The beige cover, rather than allowing her to merge into the background, made her stick out in a crowd. What woman of her status, and more importantly style, would be seen dead with such an inelegant piece of stationary? Women of her calibre should be resting their delicate wrists on pink notebooks with gold-edged pages with silky ribbon bookmarks. And such a specimen now rested on the table in front of her. But even this new addition to her eavesdropping arsenal, bought in a velvet-smelling stationers' on Charing Cross Road, was hidden by her laptop, the proper tool of professional researchers, and any writing with a pencil had to be done awkwardly, quickly and with the minimum of fuss. But in a spirit of fastidiousness she noted down every single thing she heard and the book was now half full.

It had been a slow morning. There weren't that many people in the cafe and she had to move table twice in order to be in earshot of anything that was coming out of people's mouths. The first couple she listened to appeared to have run out of things to say to each other, their half hour in the cafe marked by nothing more than a cursory, 'D'ya want a bun with your tea?' followed by an even glummer, 'Nah.' The second table provided even less ear fodder as all three occupants sent text messages to friends elsewhere and Violet was so engrossed in re-reading her notes from the previous day that she didn't notice the table behind her had become occupied, until someone spoke.

"You won't want to make that client list. It's tedious work," said a man.

A man. Not *any* man, but the man she'd heard the previous day. The one with the delicious voice.

"But I like tedious work," the woman replied. "Interesting work is overrated."

"Don't be silly, you need to go for something more gutsy."

Violet heard air blown down a nose.

"What do you want?" said the woman.

"A coffee, but we need to hurry. I don't have much time."

"*I'll* fetch it, that waitress is texting."

"Okay."

Violet watched the woman's back as she walked across the room: pink sweater, black skirt, flabby bottom. Fear of being caught staring forced Violet's gaze back to her notebook and she thought of the clothes on her own back. Her ensemble had been carefully chosen early that morning; soft grey trousers, mustard sweater and a necklace made of big black beads, which matched her earrings – little jades that caught the light if she turned her head. But gutsy? Did anything she was wearing show her strong side? Did any of her clothes say – no, shout – 'I don't give a damn?'

She was alone with *him*, in their own private space, yet still she didn't look. She wanted to look; she didn't want to look. She closed her eyes and tried to filter his breathing from the other sounds in the room. But her concentration was broken as the woman returned; chair legs scraped the floor; a backside slapped onto a seat.

"This coffee's lukewarm," said the woman.

"Send it back."

"I don't like to."

Violet would have sent it back. Oh, yes. She would have had that little waitress running to their table before she'd had a chance to settle back down behind the cappuccino machine.

"Anyway ..."

Violet held her breath; *he* was speaking. His voice was beautiful – so smooth and beautiful. He must be an actor. She turned her face to the wall, closed her eyes and listened. Plunged behind the black of her eyelids, a sensuous pleasure enveloped her. The words became sounds stripped of meaning, just vibrations and air and a hidden rhythm going up and down, up and down, up and finally down. But would she look? No, she wouldn't. She wanted only his sound. She squeezed her eyes shut and waited.

"You could come to my house tomorrow and we could go over the list."

"Won't your wife be there?"

"No, she'll be out. Number twenty-seven. Suit you?"

"Okay. Lexington St., right?"

"Yes, it's the house on the corner, the one with the big tree outside which looks like it's about to fall over."

"I'll be there."

Behind a cupped hand, Violet wrote fast.

Woman: Won't your wife be there?

Man: No, she'll be out. Number twenty-seven. Suit you?

Woman: Okay. Lexington St., right?

Man: Yes, it's the house on the corner, the one with the big tree outside that looks like it's about to fall over.

Woman: I'll be there.

Violet laid her pencil on the table beside her saucer. Violet thought of the voice. Violet forgot to breathe.

CHAPTER
21

"You alright, Bill?"

"Mmm?"

"Are your eyes troubling you? They look a bit red."

"No, everything's okay. I've probably been surfing the web too long."

James looked unconvinced. "How'd it go yesterday? – out in the wilds of London."

"You're not going to believe this, but I met that bloke, that stalker bloke."

"What! You mean you went all the way down to the coast?"

"Yeah. I met him."

James straightened his back. "Why?"

"I ... curiosity. Like you said, what we don't find out, we'll never know."

"*I* said that?"

"Something along those lines."

He straightened his back further. "So, what's he like? The bloke."

"He's an old soldier – you know, the serious type you can't tease."

"Shit."

"Yeah."

"How did you get in touch with him?"

"I wrote him a letter, sent it express delivery."

"So … what did he want?"

"He told me a story."

"Didn't think you liked stories."

"I don't normally, but this one was … kind of interesting."

"What'd he say?"

I stood up, crossed the room and closed the door.

"Ooh, secret is it?"

I dispatched a withering look across our airspace. "Just don't want anyone listening in."

"Walls have ears, you know." James grew a little.

"Shut up, James. Don't you *want* to hear this?"

"Go on," he said.

I sat back down at my desk; a folder marked *Eavesdroppers* waited beneath my hand. I began to speak.

Away from the eerie coastal light and squawk of birds rummaging in the gravel pit, the story seemed plain. I tried to give my tale a bit of build up, describing the old man's black trench coat, his army surplus shoes and grey scarf in loving detail, but James grew impatient, tapping his pen on the desk, so I hurried through the caravan site, rushed across the shingle and only stopped when I reached the sound mirrors.

"Sound what?"

"Sound mirrors."

"What the hell are they?"

"Early warning system," I said expertly, "they used them to listen for approaching aircraft before radar was invented."

"When *was* radar invented?"

"1937. There are lots of sound mirrors along the south coast. Bloody great concrete things. They're crumbling a bit, and some are falling into the gravel pits around them, but there are still a few around. They don't use them any more, so they're getting derelict. Anyway, the old bloke showed me two of them. A round one and a long curved one."

I waited for James to take everything in. He had a way of folding his arms when he was thinking and I watched it now, his hands forced into his armpits like a sailor's knot, ineptly tied.

"Who are *they*?" he said at last.

"The military of course," I replied. "He was in the army. He used to man the listening post, the mirror, during the Second World War."

"Blimey, he must be really, really old."

"Over ninety, I'd guess."

"So, what did he hear?" James moved his whole body closer.

"He heard the enemy aircraft coming long before it reached the coast."

"Is that all?"

Now it was my turn to lean forward. "Don't you see? He heard something coming before it got there."

James frowned. "And that means … ?"

Our next gathering was hard to assemble. Tom Wilson had block-booked the meeting room for three mornings in a row for a re-enactment of the company core values. This was followed by a round-table analysis of the new mission statement, as revealed by the roughly penned note stuck to the door. Then Jean held an administrative jamboree in there, which involved spreading a terrifying amount of paper out on the big table and littering the floor with paper clips, broken file dividers and string tags. Such was my condescension concerning the whole affair, which I failed to suppress, I was omitted from the cakes that formed the finale and left to eat cheese crackers alone in my office. But finally, I managed to force our usual Friday booking into Jean's bulging diary (her status as a digital refusnik was legendary) and contacted the eavesdroppers.

I waited by myself in the meeting room, but this time I was accompanied by memories of sounds: the crunch of shingle beneath my feet, the slap of feathered duck breasts on water. And even after the eavesdroppers had arrived and sat down I was stuck in a solitary moment, not even disturbed by the demands of civility. I looked at each face in turn, unsure if they could read my thoughts, worried they'd noticed salt water stains on the rim of my shoes.

Stanley stirred sugar into his coffee. "You alright, Mr. B?"

"Yes, thanks." The sound of pages being turned filled the room. "Before we start our reports everyone, there's something I'd like to mention."

The pages stilled; all ears tuned to me.

"I know we've talked of this before, but I just wanted to reiterate that it is important people don't know you are listening to them."

Stanley smiled gracefully. "I think we all know that."

"I know you do. Just be careful. Please."

I watched them all as their glances fell downwards and they studied their notebooks. Most cheeks were ruddy, but one pair was pale. "You alright, Jack?" I asked.

I expected a quick response from the eavesdropper on the other side of the room, a short cluster of words tripping through his lips, but no, Jack opened his mouth, then paused and held his breath. I held my breath too. The entire table held its breath.

"I'm okay. Why do you ask?"

"You look a little … pale."

"You *do*," said Eve, fluffing herself up into a ball of concern.

"I'm fine," he said.

But he wasn't. Now that he had our communal attention I could see he was holding the weight of something.

"Your eyes are bloodshot," Eve said.

"I'm alright. I just …"

"Just what?" urged Violet.

Poor squirming lad, I felt shitty for asking, "Yes, just wh–"

"I think I'm being followed." He stared down at the surface of the table. Then he picked up a sachet of saccharin and squeezed it between his fingers. I could hear the paper crackle.

"What exactly do you mean by *being followed*?" It was Stanley who spoke. He'd been on the periphery up until then, distracted by the ribbon in his notebook that refused to lie flat, but now he was interested, the amateur sleuth with a mouthful of fresh fillings.

Jack dropped the sachet onto the table. "There's this bloke on the Tube … he's always there … when I'm there."

"Perhaps he's going the same way as you," said Stanley, his hands propped on the table in a triangle of wisdom.

"No. He's not."

I'd never heard Jack speak with such certainty.

"He's *always* there," he insisted. "I don't always go the same way. I change my route and yet, he's always there."

"Are you sure he's always the same man?" said Missy obliquely.

Jack picked up another sachet and tore the end off. "I'm sure."

Violet sighed. "Are you certain it's not just an odd coincidence?"

"He was at Oxford Circus at Tuesday lunchtime, then the Angel on Thursday evening and even today, when I took a different line to come here, he was there."

"What does he look like?" I said, wondering if Jack had always had such short nails.

"He wears a big coat and … a hat."

"That narrows it down," said Violet.

Jack looked smaller than before.

"It doesn't matter what he's wearing." He took a deep breath; it tightened his shirt over his chest. "What matters is that he is always there and he's always watching, and he's always listening."

Jack's words equalled us all out. We were no longer a boss and employees, we were a bunch of people worrying about a fellow listener. I longed to find a helpful reply but only platitudes came into my head.

It was Eve who spoke. "Why don't you give the Tube a miss for a few days."

"I don't want to," said Jack. "That's my place."

Stanley seemed to have had an inspiration. "But then you'll be able to shake him off."

"If there is a 'he,'" said Violet.

"Yes!" I'd found my tongue. "You don't know for sure that there is a *he*." The remark sounded less intelligent out than in.

"Shall I come with you next time?" said Stanley. "See what I can see?"

Thank God. "That's a great idea, Stanley. You happy with that, Jack?"

Jack nodded, miserable as sin.

"Okay. Let's move on."

It was hard to move on. Meetings are like stories. There's a beginning, a middle and an end. And sometimes the end seems to come before the middle. But there's also a tone. I realised this as I surveyed the eavesdroppers' sagging shoulders, and when the tone changes it's hard to change it back again. And when you are the one who is in charge this sapped energy is daunting. It was Violet who rescued us. She opened her notebook, passed a smile round the circle and read us tales from the cafe as if we were children. Not her own children, but rather children she had borrowed for the day. I felt I was there, smelling the coffee, tasting the egg yolk exploding beneath the teeth of the fork, and for a moment I forgot I was supposed to be analysing the eavesdroppers reports; I forgot I should be worrying about Jack.

EVE had an ache in her stomach. She rubbed it in a circle, like her mother had told her to do as a child, but it still hurt. She wished she had a mother still. People would probably scoff at that. People might laugh to hear that a person of sixty-three wanted its mother. But as well as a mother she wanted an *Eve*. She wanted someone to come to *her* rescue. But what would they be rescuing her from, people might reasonably ask. 'Life' would bore them; they'd be drifting away before she'd have time to explain, and 'loneliness' would be laughed at. Everyone is lonely these days. She'd have to think of an original reason for rescue. She thought of Jack. She liked Jack. He was decent. Yet he was worried about being followed. But – she felt a surge of satisfaction at the logic of her thought – wasn't being followed better than not being followed? Better than being so invisible that not even a man in a big coat could be bothered to tail you.

The yellow washing machine shuddered then revved up into spin cycle, an activity which never failed to make her jump. She sat down on the bench and opened her notebook. She hadn't written anything since her conversation with Mr. Harcourt in the pub. He'd worried her. Not when he suggested she move to another launderette. No, it was when he'd glanced at the leaflets in her bag and gave her a funny look.

She was wondering if he would be angry if he caught her back in *her* launderette, when the latch on the door clicked and in walked *big back*.

She saw him before he had a chance to turn round and see her, so Eve leant further back into her corner and watched. She watched his tweed jacket rise up and his bum crack reveal itself as he bent forward to open his bag and stuff his clothes into the machine. Bare backs make you vulnerable, she thought. When people have seen the delicate skin at the top of your waistband you have a little power over them. In fact, when people have seen your dirty clothes under the harsh lights of the launderette they have some power over you too. She felt a nub of something rise in her chest as she noted the man's faded boxer shorts and filthy socks tossed into the machine. Vests, shirts, handkerchiefs, every garment made her more intimate with him. And intimacy gave her confidence.

"That shirt looks like silk,' she said, emerging from behind the dryer.

The man turned. "You what?"

"Silk. It has to be washed by hand."

He straightened up and looked at her, a shirt limp in his hand. "What's that got to do with you?"

"I lost a silk shirt to the heat once. It came out like a doll's."

"A doll's what?"

Eve felt her voice shrink. "Shirt."

The man's expression was hard to read. Would he kill her there and then? Would he stuff her into the big dryer and set it to high? Then she remembered the bare skin at the base of his back. "Let me show you the label." It was her kindest voice, the one she saved for girls with abusive stepfathers. She stepped towards him and gently took the shirt from his hand. "Dry clean only," she said, pointing to the label. The man squinted at the inside of the collar. The gesture set off a little squirt of delight in Eve; he wore glasses.

"You mean I can't stick it in with the rest?" he said.

"Exactly." Eve's thoughts were on the leaflet in her bag, *Understanding Washing Codes*. Everything had a leaflet. Even old-fashioned clothes had a couple of pages on how to press velvet and rinse out brocade.

The man chucked the shirt back into his bag, pulled a copy of the *Daily Mail* off the bench and sat down. Just sat. No 'thank you.' No 'that's really kind of you.'

Eve lowered herself down beside him. Keep at least six inches between yourself and any man, her mother had always warned. The advice had held her in good stead for the previous fifty years but now, settling down beside this man, five inches felt right. After all, even killers needed help with their washing labels; even killers might need the warmth of a sympathetic ear. She glanced at the headlines over his shoulder. Then she said something she shouldn't have.

CHAPTER
22

I had no idea there were so many different types: big ones, small ones, round ones, long ones. It was a cold Wednesday evening in my flat when I typed *sound mirror* into my search engine, expecting to be presented with an obscure website untouched for a decade, yet clinging to the hope that I might find out more about the fate of the war-time eavesdroppers. But no, the websites were numerous, extremely detailed and all resounding with boffin-like love. They talked of bearings, graduated scales and counterpoised arms, but no mention of the fate of the hapless Lydd listeners.

Sound mirrors, it transpired, dotted the English coast from Durham to Kent, and round the underbelly of England as far as Selsey Bill. Concave giants tipped up towards the sky again and again. I loved that angle, the angle of reception. There was hope in that angle. Hope and expectation.

Raymond Watt had been vague during parts of his tale. Did I imagine evasive? He said names, he relayed events, but what had he actually said? What was his story *really* about?

The old man had started life as a listener, he told me as much. He described the devastation of temporary blindness at six years old, but then his story skipped forward to the darkest days of the war when the south coast was threatened nightly by German bombers and he'd spent week after week in front of the mirror, not daring to turn, not daring to stop. With a specially made stethoscope plugged in his ears he'd trawled the mirror's surface, seeking the loudest spot – the spot of greatest danger. Finally, he'd read the bearings and altitudes of his foe and relayed them to the control room by telephone.

And in spite of the wind constantly shoving his body and the blackness of the sky, he'd had to make a decision. Every night he had to record the location of the sound and decide who, in the vast dark hinterland of southern England, would live. And who would die.

I checked my watch and pulled on my coat. The stairs down to my building entrance sounded unnaturally loud as I descended so I tiptoed across the final treads before opening the door and entering the street. Dusk falls early in October and I felt a stab of melancholy as I looked up at the tree on the corner, its leaves crinkled and brown, hanging on ageing threads. I turned the corner and walked along Kendall Road, a broad street where the trees grew larger, the buildings taller and the eaves projected shadows onto the bedroom windows. I pressed the button on the traffic light and was watching a woman stretching out her arms inside the house opposite when – bang!

I instinctively slapped my hand over my eyes and waited, my ears tautening, my heart pumping, the traffic lights beeping. I formed a slit in my fingers and peeped through and saw: the street with bins, the cars with empty insides, the trees with leaves. Feeling foolish I dropped my hand to my sides but still did not move. I scanned the street, along the rooftops, across the faces of the buildings, between the trees, down onto the pavement, past the parking meters, the manhole covers, the lamp columns, until I saw it.

A black lump lay on the pavement. A discarded glove? A dead bird? A blob of melted tar? I waited a moment longer, then edged my way towards it. The lump took shape as I grew closer – a small furry back, a leather limb at a broken angle. I knelt down to see.

When I arrived at the surgery my ophthalmologist was seated at his desk with his fingertips resting on his keyboard. "Looking good, Mr. Harcourt."

I smiled. I'd practiced saying *ophthalmologist* in the bath the previous night and now I felt embarrassed to see him again. I'd tried learning to spell the interminable word too, but never reached the second 'O.' "Thanks. I feel good."

"Take a seat." He went over to a small sink and began to wash his hands.

A model of a giant eye sat on the end of his desk. I looked at it. It looked at me. In a moment of panic I recalled my post-op instructions. Had I had a head bath? I couldn't remember. Had I washed the eye shield and glasses every day with soap and water? Bugger. Had I? It was all such a distant memory. Then I remembered the more obscure instructions. *Do not play with children. Do not lift heavy objects. Do not take snuff.* I realised I'd need to cover up the fact that I'd mopped my eyes with a grubby handkerchief at one point – a heinous crime in the sterile, glares and haloes world of the eye surgeon.

The doctor returned to the desk and sat down opposite me. "Any problems?"

I was certain I hadn't taken snuff. "No."

"Excellent." He picked up a small torch, switched it on and shone it in my eye. "Look at my face."

Looking is harder than listening. Listening can be anonymous. I tried not to peer straight into his eyes; I focused on his nostril hairs, an assortment of whites and greys and blacks.

"Peripheral vision looks good. Hang on … don't have a cat, do you?"

"No."

"Cat's hair under the top lid."

I shuddered. "Is that a problem?"

"Animal fur and incisions aren't the best bedfellows. I'll get it out."
His hand hardly seemed to touch my eye so fast was the movement.

"Thank you. And ... I have a question."

"Fire away."

"Is it possible that I could have been hit by an animal?"

"What sort of animal?"

I shifted in my seat. "I know it sounds a bit mad, but could it
have been a bat?"

The doctor unfolded his hands from his lap. "A bat?"

"Yes, I was wondering if–"

"Most unlikely. Bats' navigation systems are superb. Virtually
infallible."

"Virtually?"

"Well, yes. The only way they'd collide with a human is if they
were sick or dying or if ... their navigation was somehow ... thrown
off. Now Mr. Harcourt, any itching?"

"Not much."

"You're healing up very fast. Eyeballs are a tad dry, though."

I wasn't sure if that was a good thing or not. "Thanks."

"I'll get you some more moisturising drops. I'll be back in a
minute."

Left alone with the giant eye, I felt nervous. It stared at me. I
stared at it. It had an accusing look to it. No, I definitely hadn't lifted
any heavy objects, I felt certain. The doctor was taking a long time.

I glanced at the papers on his desk, and then I looked at the books
on his shelf, avoiding the eye. Finally I picked up the stethoscope lying
beside his computer. Such an odd instrument, I held it in my hand, not
guilty, not worried, fully prepared to look the eye in the eye.

I slung it round my neck, all doctorly and professional. Then I
placed the buds into my ears. They fitted rather nicely. I inspected
the listening piece. It wasn't rough and concave like the sound mirror

but smooth and flat. I placed it down on the doctor's desk. Silence. I placed it on my knee. More silence. Then, under the steady gaze of the eye I placed it on my chest. I'd never heard the inside of myself before. I'd always imagined calm in there, a tranquil environment of organs working in unison and blood quietly flowing. So I was unprepared for what I heard. A booming *thump, thump, whoosh*. Then a pause.

4:30 pm Friday 4th November

Tottenham Court Road Tube Station.
Old man: Smelt rotten down there.
Young man: What do you mean 'rotten.'
Old man: Mouldy. Something rotting on the train. You didn't mind me coming round with you, did you?
Young man: No.
Old man: Sure?
Young man: Yes, sure. But … you needn't have bothered.
Old man: Why not?
Young man: He wasn't there.
Old man: Wasn't he?
Young man: Not today anyway.
Old man: Okay. Not today–
Young man: Hold on a second. Can you hear that noise?
Old man: What noise?
Young man: A sort of….
Old man: Sort of what?
Young man: A hum … just a minute … a low frequency hum.
Old man: No.
Young man: Listen harder. It's there. In the distance.
Old man: Nope. Nothing. It must be inside.
Young man: Inside what?
Old man: Inside your ears.

STANLEY was the first patient to enter the dentist's waiting room. The staff seemed unprepared for the arrival of customers and he felt a little narked by the smell of early morning chlorine rising from the damp floor. He'd grown tired of the Job Centre. Everyone was either sad or boisterous (never both) and he'd begun to feel beaten up by the whole thing. Also, eavesdropping amongst the lost and dispirited had become increasingly difficult as he'd got known by the regulars, young lads with paint on their trousers and aftershave on the backs of their necks who insisted on pulling their chairs close to his and wanting to know what his problem was when he refused to impart the wisdom of his age.

He quickly set up camp in the corner of the waiting room with a copy of *National Geographic* on his lap and set to work on an article about the recreation of woolly mammoths in Outer Mongolia.

"You're too early," said the receptionist.

"That's okay. I'll catch up on my reading." He winked in the direction of the woman behind the reception counter and returned to details of the *legendary creatures with long hair and short woolly undercoats*. He was puzzling over the shape of mammoth molars when he heard other people come into the room. He didn't look up.

"How's your Fred since he's been in the old people's home?" said a voice nearby.

"Oh, he's really settled in now and I visit regularly," replied another voice – deeper, rougher, ex-smoker.

"That's good. My Reggie went in permanently a few weeks ago, and now he wants to come back home.

"Oh, yes?"

"But I've burnt his slippers."

With his finger perched on a photo of an enormous tusk Stanley looked sideways. As predicted he saw two elderly women, matching handbags clutched tightly to their chests. But there was a third person in the room. A child. Alone.

Stanley dropped his gaze back down and studied a map of *Distribution in the last glacial period.*

"So what are you going to do?"

"About what?"

"The slippers?"

Stanley looked up again. The child was watching him. She wasn't shy, not like he'd been at that age; she didn't even have the expression of a child. He wasn't good at guessing age; the girl had the body of a child but the eyes of a woman. He opened the magazine to a double page spread of the mammoth, turned it round and held it out towards her. She smiled. Her teeth were perfect, white and ultra-straight and he wondered, why was *she* there? Was she there on false pretenses too?

"Mr. Stipple, I've checked our diary and I can't see any record of your appointment this morning."

He didn't like the receptionist's tone one bit. "Oh, really?"

The woman glanced at the magazine on his lap. "Yes, really. Would you like to book one?"

Stanley rubbed his gum in the way he had seen cocaine addicts do it on the telly. "Yes. I'll come tomorrow at eight o'clock."

"Nothing until next week," said the woman – cruelly, he felt.

"Don't worry, I'll come by just in case. In case of a cancellation."

He didn't look at the girl when he left the room, but he knew she was watching him.

Beryl was in a strop when Stanley got home. Not the usual. Not just the grumpy neck and hunched shoulders but a complete black mood of accusing eyes and sideward glances that rendered unspoken things said. He made a cup of tea then changed his mind and left it steeping on the kitchen top while he went upstairs to the bathroom. He pulled his lower lip down roughly and peered into the mirror. The inside of his mouth was shiny and pink as bubblegum but his teeth, oh my, his teeth, they were like pieces of broken brick pulled up from the soil. Not at all like her teeth; *they* had been spotless.

"We're giving up caffeine," Stanley announced to Beryl on returning to the kitchen. "We've got to get our teeth in better shape." He peered into the cage. Beryl was grinding her beak on the cuttle-fish, back and forth, back and forth. "I'm going to the chemist's to get some supplies."

Beryl didn't answer.

That was the day he started his new routine. Every morning he'd begin with the normal clean, the pea of toothpaste on the soft brush like everyone else up and down the land, followed by a sprinkling of water and the gentle up and down strokes. Then the deep clean would begin, the hard brush dipped in bleach, all finished off with a gener-ous helping of salt rubbed round his gums. He was cultivating top quality gums – the envy of the street, the sort of gums that provided the backdrop to top quality words. And it didn't really matter that his gums bled – they were new to such cleanliness – and it didn't really matter that he had blood on his pillow every now and then. What mattered was that he could pull back his lips and show the world that there was more to this old codger than they first thought. Next he would purge his ears too. Yes, that was long overdue.

CHAPTER

23

I dreamt Jack wore a military uniform. I dreamt I brushed Missy's hair. I dreamt I put Stanley in a drawer and closed it.

We had agreed a weekly meeting schedule – time enough to get out and about and listen to a statistically relevant sample, yet I found myself wishing time would move faster, that Friday would come sooner.

Stanley was holding court by the time I arrived for our fifth meeting, tipping his chair right back and talking about getting some customised T-shirts made up. Violet had a glazed look on her face, a look that could not be shattered even when he waved the sketch for his design in front of her face.

"What are you getting T-shirts made for, Stanley?" I said.

He frowned in a smiling way, and then he turned to Violet who filled in the missing word with all the enthusiasm of a teenager at a pension plan briefing. "Us."

"What do you mean *us*?"

"We," she said, as if by explanation.

Stanley took this as a cue to give the full story, not just the gist, but the extensive backstory involving his grandnephew's art class and the hen party he'd seen from the top of the bus.

"He means we get matching clobber with an *E* on the front," said Violet, briefly dragging her attention away from the half moon on her thumb that she was exposing with pokes from a vicious-looking tool.

Stanley smiled. "Yours has a bigger *E* than ours … as you're the boss."

"Stanley," I said, struggling to keep condescension out of my voice, "the main idea is that people don't notice us. We merge into the crowd. We disappear."

"It's not for work," he said. "It's for … you know, get-togethers."

Now I was the idiot child, pinned beneath Stanley's stare. "Whose get-togethers?" I said.

His look was of a mother who realised her child had been humiliated. "Ours," he said gently.

Ours. The word seemed to mark the air.

"Stanley's having a buffet at his house."

It was Eve who spoke; she had eye make-up on for the first time I noticed, thin black lines that seemed to have landed randomly on the edge of her eyelids. I looked away and was instantly embroiled in judgmental imaginings of Stanley's buffet: fish paste sandwiches, defrosted sausage rolls, tinned mandarins with evaporated milk.

"I thought I'd make a curry," he said happily.

"But Stanley, why would we need matching T-shirts for a buffet at your house?" I said.

Stanley looked astonished. "To show we are family, of course."

"It's a nice idea, Stanley," I straightened my papers, "… great idea, but can we start our reports and think about this later."

"Maybe we could go over the details in the pub after work?" he said.

"Um …"

"I'll pencil in the 15th, okay?"

" … Okay," I looked towards the end of the table. "Jack, can you begin?"

Jack didn't like to begin. He opened his notebook slowly and looked back at me with nervous eyes.

"Go ahead," I said, forever the kindly uncle.

"I haven't got much– "

"Don't worry, just read us what's there."

He stared down at his notebook. "Every word is a goblin."

"Jack, can you speak up a tad," I said. "It's noisy in here today."

"Every word is a goblin." Jack's voice sounded different at a higher volume.

"Did they say anything else?"

"No. That's all they had to say."

"Jack," said Stanley. "Were you finding it hard to listen? You know, to concentrate?"

"A bit." Jack's voice was low.

"The bloke in the crowd," continued Stanley, "he wasn't there when I came round with you, was he?"

"No." Jack pressed the spine of his notebook flat. "But he's back."

I felt Stanley's eyes on me. His irises were saying something, but I can't read irises. "Jack, are you sure you want to continue with the job? You don't have to if–"

"Yes! Yes, Mr. Harcourt, I do. I'll get more next time, I promise."

I smiled. "Quantity isn't important, Jack. It's the content that I care about and … " I glanced down at my notes; "'every word is a goblin' … you can't beat that for … for … "

"Shall I start my report?" said Eve, her hand resting lightly on Jack's shoulder.

"Yes, Eve, yes do."

Her hand dropped towards the bag leaning against her chair, and then returned to her notebook. "I noted down a conversation I heard in the launderette between a man and a woman."

"Were they together?" asked Missy.

"No. They don't know each other."

Stanley's eyes sparkled with interest. "So, why were they talking?"

Eve frowned. "I don't know."

"What did they say?" I asked.

"Shall I just read?"

"Yes, just read."

"Shall I set the scene?"

I nodded. "Please set the scene."

"The man was reading the newspaper and the woman looked over his shoulder."

"Smart chat-up move," said Stanley.

Eve's cheeks flushed pink.

"Stanley, just let her speak, " I said.

Eve held up her notebook in front of her face, the words were hard to catch. "Woman in a blue dress–"

"Long or short–?"

"Schhh! Stanley," I said. "Pleeeese let her speak."

"A woman in a blue dress said … 'Have you ever killed a man?'"

"Fuck!" I glanced round the group "Sorry. *So* sorry everyone. Eve, did she really say that?"

She looked me calmly in the eye. "Why would I lie?"

I was slow in forming my next question. Questions demand answers, but I was scared of the answer. "What did the man reply?"

It was Jack who interrupted this time. Jack never interrupted. "Eve, did these people know you were listening to their conversation?"

"Oh, no." She smiled. " I was hidden. I was behind the big drier. No one goes back there. Only me."

"What did the man say," said Violet. Her nails rested on the table.

Eve looked back down at her notebook. "The man said, 'Yeah, sweetheart, every … effing day.'"

I forced something out of my mouth. "He was joking, right?"

Eve smiled. "Of course … well, I think so. But Mr. Harcourt, should we … be interpreting meaning?

" I … maybe … sometimes."

"Did he really say 'effing'?" asked Stanley.

Eve's cheeks deepened to red. "Not exactly. There was actually an F and a U and a C and a K."

Stanley glanced in my direction but did not utter.

Bloody hell, me again. "We should write the exact words, Eve. Okay?"

Eve performed the most perfunctory nod I had ever seen.

"So what happened next?" asked Violet.

Eve continued to read. "The woman in the blue dress said, 'I could help you with your laundry, if you like.' Then the man said, 'Oh yeah, I do a lot of laundering.'"

"Wait! Eve," I said. "Did he say, laun*drying* or laund*ering?*" I glanced at Stanley, my most learned of allies.

"Does it matter?" Eve looked down at her notes. "'Laundering,' I think."

Stanley whistled. "Sounds like a bit of a tangle."

"What do you mean?" said Eve.

"You know, two different meanings."

"Are there?"

"Yes," I said. "Laundrying is washing your clothes, kind of, laundering is…. it's sort of, disguising or … recycling your stolen stuff."

Eve picked up her pencil, licked the end and crossed out a word on the page. Next she wrote a new one in its place. She smiled brightly.

"Eve," I asked. "What did you just do?"

Her smiled brightened further. "I made a mistake. I've corrected it."

"So did he need any?" asked Violet.

Eve frowned. "Any what?"

"Help."

"He didn't actually say. But he certainly *did*." She looked straight at me. "My interpretation."

"Eve, I have to be honest," I adjusted my tone, "I'm concerned that you are overhearing a conversation such as this one."

"Me too," added Stanley.

"You did change launderettes, didn't you?" I said.

"Yes."

"Why did Eve need to change launderettes?" said Jack.

"The last one was a bit dodgy," I said, sensing a problem with my choice of adjective as it arrived in the sentence.

"*All* launderettes down the Cally Road are a bit dodgy," said Stanley.

Nobody spoke. A shout from the street entered the room, a scrap over a parking space.

"Talking of dodgy," said Stanley, "have you been down those Camden toilets again, Missy?" He looked around for approval.

"It's not *that* dodgy," she said, "but I think it's the place where people show themselves up ... the most."

Someone sniffed.

"Did you hear anything interesting?" I said, feeling a nerve twist in my stomach.

She frowned. "They were talking about their bodies."

"What sort of bodies?" asked Eve. Her cheeks had cooled and a look of authority had settled on her face.

Missy's voice mixed indignation and uncertainty. "Fat sort of bodies."

"What did they say?" Violet pulled her chair closer to the table.

"They were ashamed."

"How did you know they were ashamed?" asked Eve, her pencil poised between her fingers.

"She said so."

"So only *one* of them was ashamed," said Violet.

Missy blinked fast. 'Yes. Only one. But she was *very* ashamed."

"Why?' asked Jack, looking genuinely puzzled.

"'Because she had cellu ... cellulite. That's why."

Out of the corner of my eye I glimpsed Violet's hand high on her arm. "Did they say anything particularly insightful about their ... cellulite?"

Missy glanced down at her notes. "Not really. Just that it was … let me check … 'all over the place.'"

I felt drained. Only nine thirty in the morning, yet my neck ached and my eyes were watering. I dabbed them with my handkerchief and blinked rapidly. I wondered if this was all I was ever going to get from the eavesdroppers. Snippets of minor importance, conversations we could already predict. It was obvious women were going to talk about their bodies in a Ladies' toilet. I could just imagine the look on Wilson's face as I gave him my findings. Sir, I have discovered that women discuss their body shape in toilets and people talk about coffee in cafes.

"*Is* it a bit iffy down there?" persisted Jack.

"Sorry, what did you say?" I said, returning to the moment.

"Is it a bit iffy down in those Camden bogs?"

I couldn't read his look. "I don't–"

"You don't go there at night do you, dear?" said Eve.

Missy smiled. "Oh, no. I'd never go down there at night."

"Missy loves daylight," I said.

She smiled again.

"You alright, Bill?"

"Yeah, I was just thinking."

"'Bout what?"

"Oh, you know, the gang."

"Getting a bit out of hand, are they?"

I sighed. "I don't know, James. They're a bit … all over the place."

"That's the whole point isn't it?"

"Yeah … well … I suppose so."

"Got a loose cannon, have you?"

I sighed again. "I feel like I've got a whole room of loose cannons."

"How d'ya mean?"

"Nothing concrete, just a bit of a feeling that things aren't quite right."

James sighed. "Spit it out, Bill."

"Well, Jack thinks he's being followed."

"Oh yeah? Who by?"

"I don't know. I really don't think he is. He's scared of everything, hangs on the edges of the meeting, never says much. But that's not my main worry."

"What's your main worry?"

"It's Eve. You know, she's the one who works at the Citizen's Advice Bureau. The one with the ginger hair."

"Guinea?"

"Yeah, Guinea. She's been hearing some dicey stuff in the launderette, you know, petty thieves and that."

James tilted his head to one side. "Is she discrete?"

"Oh, yes. She's probably the most discrete."

"Sounds like she's going to really hear *something*."

"Yeah. I ... hope so."

I clicked on my mouse and opened a new page in *Word*. I was glad to be in my office. The sight of James now trying to cut his nails with a pair of blunt scissors made me feel relaxed, so I set to work typing up the minutes of the meeting. It occurred to me that whoever invented the method for writing minutes must have been a sadist. Apart from the tedium of the meaningless *preambles* and the banality of the *additional comments* section, I always felt pressured by the *action required* column. What the hell to write here? *Arrange next meeting* was considered lame by the higher administrative tiers while *write minutes* was a joke that hadn't been funny even the first time.

"By the way, how are you going to collate all the data?" asked James, tidying a thumbnail with his teeth.

"God knows. I'm trying to categorise it into themes right now."

"What have you got there?"

I glanced at my notes. *Curry, murder, cellulite.* "There was talk of a woman's weight."

James snorted. "That's illuminating. Wilson's going to love that. Hey, you could write a self-help manual."

I dispatched a look across the room. "You may joke, but I think I might be starting to sense something interesting out there."

"Like what?"

"I'm not sure yet … I'm working on it."

"Are those eavesdroppers really earning their keep? It's going to reflect badly on us if you spend all this money on them and they come up with nothing."

"They're working very hard; they're professional; they want to hear."

"I'm surprised they've got so much energy. Some of them are really old, aren't they?"

"Not *that* old, although I suppose they might be finding it rather a long day, but I can't let them stop now."

"Maybe it's time you burnt their slippers." He grinned.

"James, where did you–"

The phone rang. It was Wilson.

MISSY always felt guilty relieving her bladder. It seemed like an insult to her place of work, rather like releasing wind in one of their meetings, something she dreaded, but she'd been *in position* for over three hours so was on the verge of giving in. She pulled up her pelvic floor and looked down at the back of her hands. Such smooth hands. The blue light of the toilet had ironed out the veins and removed all the freckles from her skin. She was tracing her finger across her knuckle when she heard voices outside the door. Women. Two. The voices stopped and she waited, waited, waited until she couldn't wait any more – urine trickled into the toilet.

"Oi! Who's in there?"

She held her breath.

"Who is it?"

"Nobody."

"Get out here."

Missy pulled up her knickers, let her dress drop to her knees, rushed her notebook and pencil into her bag and opened the door. Two girls barred her way. One had a cold sore on her upper lip.

"Were you listening to us?"

"No."

"Bet you were!" The taller girl moved towards her and pinched Missy's arm. "Little spy. Bet you're gonna put us on the Internet."

"No ... really, I'm not."

"So what you doing creeping about down here at this time of night? Are you a prostitute?"

"No."

"What are you then?"

Missy squeezed out a smile. "Just a girl."

They both laughed. The breasts on the larger girl shook; a strand of hair settled into her cleavage.

"Are you looking at my tits?" said the larger girl.

"No. I was just leaving."

Missy turned to go but as she reached the bottom step she felt someone yank the back of her hood.

"Didn't your mummy ever tell you to wash your hands?"

Missy didn't reply. She twisted free and she ran. She tore up the steps, up into the cold air of the High Street. She dashed across the road and didn't stop running until she was inside the Tube station, through the ticket barrier, and onto the escalators. Then her life slowed. Her heart slowed. She drifted down past the advertisements on the wall, past the passengers coming up on the other side. Only then did she have time to sniff the disinfectant on her sleeve and adjust her bag on her shoulder. And only then did she become aware of the feeling in her chest, the desire to get back down beneath the ground as soon as possible and look at her naked skin in the cold blue light.

CHAPTER

24

Sunday the 13ᵗʰ of November was a cold day. I knew I'd be standing around so I put on a pair of thick socks and my old school scarf, which was the only one left after my mother had purged my wardrobe in a malevolent fit of orderliness.

I pictured the scene that awaited me as I rode the Tube to Charing Cross: the quiet huddles of people shuffling their way down Whitehall, the flanks of police horses in high-vis coats, but I was unprepared for the queue. Turning into Horse Guards Avenue I stopped with such abruptness that the person walking behind bumped into me.

"Watch it, mate!"

"Sorry," I said, annoyed with myself for apologising when the fault was clearly equally spread. But more annoying was that now we had spoken and had had bodily contact, I was connected to this stranger. I felt compelled to nod as he let loose his opinions on the state of the buses these days and went through all the details of an unfortunate incident with the driver when he'd tried to pay with a Scottish five pound note.

"What are we queuing up for?" I asked, hoping to swing the conversation towards a topic of some usefulness.

He looked at me blankly. "What d'ya mean?"

"The queue. Why are we standing in a queue in the middle of a London street?"

He looked me up and down. What did he make of my comfortable coat and corduroy trousers, I wondered. He was dressed in a leather jacket airbrushed with poppies. Biker veteran, James would have labelled him.

"Not been here before?"

"No."

"It's security. We're a prime target."

Not feeling particularly prime, I stretched my neck up and looked towards the front of the queue – past the old ladies in wheelchairs, beyond the clutch of teenagers in orange anoraks – until I saw the cause of the delay. "Christ, there's a metal detector up there!"

"Keep it down, mate. They'll haul you in if you make a fuss."

I looked closely at my companion's face for the first time. One eye was bloodshot and he had a scar on his nose. "You mean we have to go through metal detectors just to walk down the street?"

"This ain't your average street."

"No, but … is it like this every year?"

"Every year."

I looked at my queuing companion with new respect. He seemed to have a knowledge of city life that was far superior to mine. I checked my watch. Ten forty. Only twenty minutes to go.

We shuffled forward; I felt a trickle of guilt as I passed through the metal detector and was released into Whitehall. There were thick crowds of people here all trying ingenious ways to elevate themselves: sitting on walls, standing on little plastic stools and clinging to niches in buildings. A small boy had inserted his head through an iron railing, but his mother was showing no sign of concern, so I sauntered by without a second glance. Finally, I squeezed myself onto the bottom of a flight of steps with what seemed like fifty other people and checked my watch. Ten forty-five.

For some reason I found myself thinking of Eisenstein's dodge in *Battleship Potemkin,* of allowing one sailor to turn his head when the dead mutineers were carried by. What sort of people come to the Cenotaph on Remembrance Sunday, I wondered. Old soldiers for sure – berets and caps bobbed everywhere – and military families, dad in a blazer, mum in a sensible coat, little Jimmy wanting some crisps, but who were the others? Who were the ordinary-looking people who surrounded me, fingering their service sheets and checking their mobile phones? Why was *I* here?

Surely nothing more than a whim had made me pull on my coat, leave the house without any breakfast and board the Tube to the most ceremonial part of London, but now, looking round, seeing the sad faces, the sad, bent necks, I wondered if something else had brought me to this street on this day, for this moment.

As I looked again at my watch, someone nudged my arm; I smelt leather and there he was again.

"Watcha, mate."

"Oh, hello." My queuing companion was now sharing twelve inches of step with me.

He turned his head. "This is Kiera, my girlfriend."

I took her in quickly, a big woman hanging onto his arm. She had on a leather jacket with *Lest We Forget* stitched across her front. "Hello, Kiera," I said, hurriedly making eye contact as I realised I had been reading her chest. But before she could reply a gun salute tore down the street, slamming into the buildings, detonating in my ears.

"Fucking hell!" said Kiera. She slapped her hand across her mouth.

"Schh," A voice behind me, breath on the back of my neck.

"It's nearly eleven o'clock," said another voice, a few steps higher up.

And then I saw them – an extended family of Gurkhas threading their way towards us. The men were tweaking the bands in their hats and the Gurkha grandmas were chatting in an unrecognizable tongue, oblivious to the rigid crowd. It wasn't until they reached the bottom of my steps that they paused, looked round bewildered, and then smartly closed their mouths as eleven o'clock arrived and the golden tones of Big Ben began their march down the street.

Two minutes in silence is not a long time, but as I stood on the steps, surrounded by hundreds of people, it seemed as if we were frozen; no limbs moved, no eyes blinked

I closed my eyes, sifting out the silence of the crowd. At first there was nothing, absolutely nothing, then my ears sharpened, my whole body became taut, and the tiny bones of my ear moved as the hammer struck the anvil. Minute sounds had arrived in the street: the gentle rustle of the plane trees above our heads, the *tap tap* of loose rope on a flagpole, the zip on a Gurkha grandma's handbag being pulled shut. And then I heard something else.

Wilson was in a good mood when I finally made it to his office. He looked up as soon as I entered the room and smiled. Yes, smiled. Not a malevolent grin but a real human greeting, full of well-meaning teeth. I'd been quite successful at postponing the meeting up until that point, what with a check-up at the eye hospital and a leaking toilet in my flat demanding attention. However after his emailed requests to see me had been bumped up to 'urgent' and Jean had ominously mouthed something across the street as I left work the previous day, I decided I had to 'face the music,' as James liked to categorise it. But the procrastination had not been entirely in vain. It had given me time to collect in the eavesdroppers' notebooks – a traumatic event akin to removing sweets from a child – and see what we had. At first I wasn't sure what we had. There were the descriptions of course. I'd never requested settings or details of clothes but all of the eavesdroppers included them. Jack frequently referred to the 'small, pale scout' he'd seen on the train while Eve described with great affection the 'man with the large singing mouth,' who frequented the launderette. Then there was the slapstick. Missy noted how 'the man's folding stool collapsed,' and Stanley had described in capital letters the man who had 'actually, yes really,' (underlined) slipped on a banana skin. Finally there were the miniature scenes so beloved of Jack. 'One of them just stares, combs her hair and backchats,' impressed me more than I'd like to admit. Even Stanley wrote of the 'ground slippery with rain and orange peel.' But it was Violet's final line that surprised me the most. 'I admit I thought London had gone crazy and felt annoyed with the world.' Not a quote overheard from someone else but, it seemed, a thought from within. How bitter and bereft they'd been when I collected the books, but now I began to understand why it was so hard to let them go.

But with my meeting with Wilson looming I tried to ignore the stories brewing in those pages and attempted to see a pattern, an under-current slowly rising to the surface.

"What have you got for me?" said my boss.

I sat on the chair on the other side of Wilson's desk and placed the notebooks down.

"What are those?" His smile had drooped, his voice an octave lower.

"It's the data."

Wilson studied me for a moment. It was as if he was trying to make sense of the situation just by gazing at my mouth. He picked up the closest notebook and flicked through it. Never had the turn of a page sounded so threatening, "Where's the report?" he said. "Where's the overview? The description of methods ... where is your summary of the findings to date?"

Such archaic terms. In my new world of notebooks and erasers and pencilling in I'd as good as forgotten the templates, the tried and tested methods of social research. "We haven't got to that stage yet."

"What stage *have* you got to?"

"We're still at the rough data stage. There's been no crunching of numbers, nothing's been ... digitised ... yet."

"I see." He glanced at the calendar on the wall. "But there must be something you can tell me about what the public is saying."

"They're saying …" I inhaled, "they're talking about sex … and drugs and … rock and roll."

Wilson stared. "William. This isn't a joke. This project is costing me a lot of money. I need to get some results. I need to know how your so-called eavesdroppers are performing."

"It's not a performance."

"Oh? What is it?"

"It's more of a calling."

"A calling? Are they nuns?"

"I'm sorry. I know it sounds strange but they're really getting into it. They do a lot more hours than we pay them for and–"

"Why do they do a lot more hours than we pay them for?"

"Because they love it."

"They're not going to be demanding overtime are they?"

"No! They're very happy. They love what they're doing, for them it's just life carrying on."

"Life carrying on. I see." He tapped his thumbnail on the desk. "So there's nothing to be concerned about?"

"Nothing."

"Nothing concrete to report?"

"Not yet."

"And you're going to digitise them?"

"Yes. I'm going to digitise them."

JACK counted forty-three poppies in all. The wearers seemed oblivious to the cardboard flowers planted in their buttonholes and merely turned the pages of their newspapers or gazed at the Tube maps lining the walls as if they were seeing them for the first time. But to Jack the flowers shouted blood red, to remember. You must remember.

He had chosen his clothes carefully that morning. First the shirt – white, ironed crisp to the touch – then black jeans, brown shoes (the only proper footwear he owned) and a jacket that he'd wiped with a damp cloth. He thought about the hours ahead of him as he poked his finger into his empty buttonhole. He thought about the place to which he was going.

Eavesdropping on the Tube was dense and intense, so many people squashed together under the ground, so much noise, all rattles and bumps, but recently he'd grown tired of the noise, he'd got worn out by the constant sounds of the crowd. He wanted the silence of the crowd. He wanted to know what *that* silence sounded like.

A poppy wearer sat down next to him. Jack felt an urge to lean in and smell the cardboard flower fixed to the lapel. Then he felt an even stronger desire to ask, 'Why do you wear that?' But Jack didn't like to speak to strangers. He tried to limit the number of people to whom he must speak: his mother, his sister and the three work colleagues who shared his cramped workspace. And now the eavesdroppers. In the presence of this new group in his life he must speak. Not only speak, he must share. It wasn't as hard as he'd imagined. He'd said a few things at meetings. He'd even begun to hear a casual ease brewing in his remarks – Jack the wry commentator, Jack the lad.

The train grew steadily more crowded as it passed through each station, *Monument ... Canon Street ... Mansion House ... Blackfriars ... Temple ... Embankment.* Fuller and fuller until the bloodless intercom announced "Westminster." The train emptied as a block of bodies surged to get off, sweeping Jack with it, across the gap, onto the platform. Then up the steps he went, following the obedient backs, up, up into the street level world of sorrow and emptiness and guilt. So much guilt. He followed the sad snake of people as it crawled up Horse Guards Avenue and twisted round the corner into Whitehall. The snake halted and compacted into itself as it came to a barrier.

Jack had been expecting, almost wanting, the checkpoint, but he was unprepared for the policeman's hands in his pockets. Yet that was nothing compared to what came next. He felt his entire body solidify as the man ran his hands down his inner thigh, perfunctory at first, then lingering at the back of his knees.

"You'll do, mate. Go through."

Jack had trouble getting the zip of his jacket done up with cold-stiffened fingers but a moment later it was done, his gloves returned to his hands and his hat pulled down over his ears. So many people, it was hard to walk in a straight line and he dodged left and right, right and left. He glanced behind; a woman smiled. Why had she smiled? Was she going to put her hands into his pockets too? He fingered the zip of his jacket and pushed further into the throng.

A small boy had inserted his head into a gap in a railing and his mother was pressing his ears back as she tried to ease him back out.

"Can I help?" Jack said.

"No," she snapped, giving the child a painful-looking tug.

Jack walked on. He glimpsed the top of the Cenotaph over the heads of the crowd – the stone wreath, *The Glorious Dead* etched into the stone. Glorious. What glorious things were here? Or there? Then over the tops of people's heads he spied the bishops coming, with their silver crooks held high, and golden crosses, and skirts flapping in the breeze, dragging their god into the godless street. He fought to suppress his anger, poor dead memories wrapped up in the skirts of the bishops. Then he spotted the politicians lining up: heads bowed, new haircuts, new hats, new suits of remembrance, their only fear the fear of the crowd.

People all around him were making themselves higher, balanced on walls and stretched up onto their toes whenever a new sound entered the confined space, a hint of something about to happen. But he didn't want to be higher; Jack wanted to stay low. He squeezed himself between a tree and an empty pram. He looked down at the bare sheet, with the blanket pushed to the bottom, then surveyed the scene around him. It was all backs and sleeves and elbows. He closed his eyes and listened. People were talking round him, but he couldn't hear what anyone was saying, just a murmur of words mixed together into the high notes of expectation. And all the time the old soldiers were marching past, brave necks, brave elbows, brave legs covered by blankets in wheelchairs as they rolled by. An endless line of brave elbows; Jack bit his thumbnail and sniffed. Something was in the air.

Jack looked at the people around him, up on their toes, necks stretched, mouths ajar. Then he saw the face of a baby through a slit in the crowd. He looked away, and then he looked up, briefly comforted by the sky, before scanning the buildings lining the street – high windows, high window ledges, places to get a good view, places for snipers to rest a rifle.

A cannon fired. He jumped. A clock began to strike, one, two, three ... the people around him were getting into position ... four, five, six ... the baby was slipped into its pram, its eyes watching ... seven, eight, nine ... a man straightened his back and pushed out his chest ... ten, eleven.

Then an invisible cloth seemed to drop down on the crowd; it held them all together in stiff silence, a silence so taut that Jack could hardly breathe. The baby stared. Why was it staring? Why wouldn't it close its eyes and sleep in the silence, the jagged, crushing silence that seemed to squeeze fingers round Jack's throat.

Jack closed his eyes again and listened; the leaves in the tree grated against each other, a rope flayed a flagpole, a handbag was wrenched open. That was the moment he had no choice. He slowly opened his mouth, sucked breath into his lungs and shouted. A giant, booming voice echoed down the length of the street. *His* voice.

The crowd remained silent and still. But the baby, the staring baby, turned its head and looked straight at him. A string of saliva dripped from its lips. Then sound erupted, men's voices, women's voices, voices, voices. Then the voices had words.

"What fucker said that? Him! Yeah, him. That bloke there! It was him, there. Right there! The little shit! Him? Yeah, him there. Him. It was him! The skinny fucker. There."

Jack returned to his body.

"Him! Get him! Yeah, geddim!"

Jack began to run, shoving a path through the crowd. The pram shuddered as he tore by, but he didn't look back. He didn't. He didn't. He ran. The baby bawled, the crowd bawled, still he ran, chased down the street by the weaving people, all shouting, dribbling, bawling.

Then it stopped. A white glove, a black sleeve, a polished cuf- flink – weight on his shoulder. Jack paused. The crowd paused, held at bay by the hand on the shoulder. Jack was aware only of the weight of fingers and the black eyes of the crowd. And so aware of his breath; it laboured in his chest, slowly, so slowly, in, out, in ... out....

The back window of the police car framed Jack's last glimpse of his pursuers. They stretched their necks to see him; their eyes bulged. No sound, but he didn't need sound to hear. He could read lips. He knew the mouth shapes of hate.

Jack closed his eyes, leant his head on the window and felt his muscles relax, succumbing to a warm and deep sense of calm. The back seat of the police car was comfortable, the upholstery soft to touch. The scent of lavender drifted from the air freshener dangling from the front mirror. Yet he didn't dwell on the present. He didn't dwell on what lay ahead. He dwelled on the recent past. A voice had soared down the street. His.

CHAPTER

25

Jean wore heels. She always wore heels, but that day she seemed to have chosen the pair with the most dramatic altitude which meant that as her feet brought her legs to the door of my office I could hear a little gap in her footsteps, not the sound of evenly spaced limbs but the broken rhythm of ankles out of sync. She didn't like me. Jean. She'd whispered as much into Sammy's ear at the Christmas party before last. She'd whispered I had a big head. I'd laughed when Sammy told me five minutes later, but then I'd spent the rest of the day worrying over her meaning.

She usually approached me with a ready-made comment, but that day as she materialised in the doorway she remained silent.

"Looking for me?" I said.

She tottered towards me and placed a newspaper down on my desk. I stared down at it. "What's this?"

"Bottom right corner." She stabbed her finger at a short article entitled, *'Johnny 'O' gets night in the clink.'*

I was briefly distracted by the length of her nails, then started to read. Before I'd reached the second sentence, she was tapping a finger at the bottom of the page.

"There…! Not there…. That's one of your … your people isn't it?"

I scanned the new set of words. More than scanned, speed-read, the words running into each other.

"He was at the Cenotaph on Sunday," said Jean. "He waited until the two-minute silence, and then, the bloody sod, he shouted out." She brought her face close to mine as if I was hard of hearing. "He shouted out some crap."

I met her eye. I smelt her accusing perfume. "What did he shout out?"

Jean dug her longest fingernail into the sentence. She drew in air from the room. "Why … all … this … hypocrisy?" She seemed to have rehearsed. She seemed to own the question.

"You mean that person–"

"Yes. It was him."

"Shit! I didn't…."

"What?"

"I didn't know it was him."

"He *is* one of yours, isn't he?"

I felt like a parent whose child had bitten a teacher. "Was it really *him* during the silence?"

"Yes."

I looked back down at the article and read the final paragraph.

' … The man had to be rescued from the crowd by the police. He was charged with a public disorder offence at Paddington Police Station, but was released with a caution.'

"Little creep," said Jean. "He should get time for this. It looked like butter wouldn't melt in his mouth, but no, he has to go and disrespect us."

"Us?"

"Oh, come on. You know what I'm talking about. He should be sent out to Afghanistan, see what it's like. Then he won't go shouting. And look at his face. Smiling like a silly goat."

I looked closely at the photo. Jack's face was half-hidden by a man's elbow. The face, yes, the face looked silly and frightened. But there was also a bit of a smile. Strange and twisted. Was it a smile of fear? Or – I peered closer – was it a smile of triumph?

I waited until evening before I plucked up the courage to go to Jack's flat. I lingered at the exit to the Tube station, reading a discarded copy of the *Evening Standard* for several minutes before I felt confident enough to walk down the street and approach Jack's building. It had the look of a council block that had been sold off, and I hesitated again, wondering how to find his door. There was a confusing array of buzzers labelled with peeling names, but Jack's was typed in a fresh font. I pressed. As I waited I turned the question over in my mind once more. Should I tell him that *I* was there too? Should I mention that I too had heard his voice in the temporarily sacred street? But then, my pragmatic side argued, I'd have to explain what I was doing opposite the Cenotaph on Remembrance Sunday.

I wondered if I'd got him out of bed when he answered the door, but no, he reassured me, he'd been writing, an activity that always left him rumpled and creased and sometimes a little dirty.

He lived in the smallest flat I had ever been in – surely illegal I thought as we squeezed up the stairs. Surely the human body *must* require more room in which to breathe. I wondered about carbon monoxide levels as he moved aside to let me into the room.

"Jack," I said. I was hardly out of my coat; the sofa hadn't had time to warm up beneath my legs. "I saw your face on the front of yesterday's *Evening Standard*."

His smile sagged. "Do you mind if I have a cigarette?"

"It's your house."

"Do you want one?"

"Yes." I didn't smoke. I'd hadn't held a cigarette in my hand since I was sixteen years old when I'd blown instead of sucked. I'd never tried a roll-up and began to regret my answer as I watched him take some Rizlas out and pinch some tobacco out of a small tin. The rolling was skillful, finished off with a quick flash of his tongue as he sealed the join.

"Here you go."

"Thanks."

He set to work on the second one. My fag lay limp in my fingers.

"Light?" he said.

"No, thanks."

He leant back in his chair. Smoke is silent, but I was profoundly aware of the gentle *put, put* from his lips.

I shifted my centre of gravity forward. "Jack, what were you thinking?"

He drew on his cigarette and looked at me full in the face. "I wasn't thinking." He inhaled again. "But ... I don't regret it."

I watched the smoke pour from his mouth. It curled round once then drifted slowly upwards. "Jack, I ... okay, I won't ask any more. I'll try to ... understand."

"Will you?"

I looked down at the table – a ream of papers lay there, the corners dog-eared and grubby. "Is that your play?"

He drew more smoke into his lungs. "Not yet, but it might be, one day."

He looked older than I remembered. Or younger.

"What's it about?" I said.

He tapped his cigarette onto a saucer. "I can't say."

"Ah, I imagine it's secret. Have to be careful of plagiarism."

"It's not that. *I* don't know what it's about."

"Oh. Well, good luck with it."

"Thank you."

I laid the unlit cigarette on the table. "Thanks for that."

"You're welcome."

"See you at the next meeting."

He nodded.

I felt tired as I walked back down the stairs to the street. I had wanted to know what had possessed him to break such a sacred silence. But when the time came I didn't want to know. Some things are meant to be private. Who was I to ask? Who was I to listen?

I walked slowly. I walked forwards, watching the Tube station grow bigger, then I walked backwards, watching Jack's building get smaller and smaller. I turned, walked, turned, walked, trying to memorise the route from different directions, forwards and backwards, then backwards and forwards. Then my journey was interrupted; something darted out from beneath the eaves of a nearby house, and then disappeared into the darkness. I paused, my hand on my forehead, and looked up at the sky, the clouds grey on a black background. And then I was back in the *other* street. My mind rolled my thoughts backwards: the blood on my face, the pain in my eyeball, the fur on my cheek, the body slicing through the air, the creature clinging to the eaves.

JACK opened his sock drawer and pulled out the newspaper. The time spent in his pocket had left creases in the headline, lines on his face. He scanned the sentence, scared of its letters, terrified of its blackness on the page.

'Unknown man breaks silence at Unknown Soldier's tomb.'

He'd found the newspaper on an empty seat as soon as he got onto the Tube after leaving the police station. It had been left open on the editorial page where he'd read a gushing piece on London's new bike lanes before he'd flicked back to the front page. And there, amongst the photographs of briskly marching veterans and shivering royalty he saw his own pale face, a face in a crowd, head tipped back, mouth contorted. Only three stops between Green Park and Oxford Circus, yet it seemed like ten. An inexplicable wait at Victoria, a rustle of papers at Embankment as a clutch of new arrivals settled down with their free news, and all the time the fear of recognition, the matching of a face to a face. But none of his fellow travellers had looked in his direction. Not one had noticed how damp was his brow or that hands trembled in their midst.

He'd heard Mr. Harcourt approaching his flat. Each step told him the weight of the body, the wear on the heels, the tightness of the shoelaces. Even the amount of pressure on the doorbell told him it was Bill Harcourt's finger. Jack knew he would be coming, he just hadn't known when.

Jack half wished his employer *had* asked him more questions. He needed the question to answer the question. He'd gone to the Cenotaph to see. And hear. Nowhere in the city would there be a silence like that, one filled with people. After so much time on the Tube he'd begun to crave silence, just so as he could hear. He wanted to hear the city without sound. He imagined, in a scenario in his head, that when the people stopped talking, the traffic stopped moving and the machines stopped running, that he might hear something. Something he hadn't heard before – the sound of the background. He lived in the background. It was his world. He wanted to hear *his* noise. But he didn't recognise *his* noise when the moment came. And when the silence started he had to fill it.

Jack went into the kitchen and turned off his fridge. He closed all the windows and switched off the heating. He took off his watch and put it beneath his pillow. Then he removed the battery from his alarm clock and put it on the bedside table. Finally, he sat down at his computer, closed his eyes and began to type.

[*Enter man*]
Younger man: Do you mind if I have a cigarette?
Older man: It's your house.
Younger man: Do you want one?
Older man: Yes.
Younger man: Here you go.

Older man: Thanks.

Younger man: Light?

Older man: No, thanks.

Younger man: I don't regret it.

Older man: You should! You bloody well should! It's a fucking
disgrace.

Younger man: I don't regret it.

 [*Exit man*]

CHAPTER

26

The bus was crowded when I jumped on so I headed for the stairs, grabbing the handrail as we shuddered round a corner. I heaved myself upstairs, sat down and established my territory. I was the man at the top of the Clapham omnibus. I was he: the reasonable man, the regular male who leant neither this way nor that, who spoke neither loudly nor softly. I represented the average; my life ran bang on the line.

Then I noticed my immediate world – two men in front of me were whispering, but my ears got to work, separating the pauses from the clauses.

"He's trying."

"I know he's trying."

"He's trying very hard."

"I know."

"Too hard."

"I don't like it."

"I don't like it, either."

"He's seen the ears."

"Yeah, whopping great ears."

The first man laughed. "Whopping great ears. Flapping."

I stared at the nape of the neck in front of me, recently scratched, so close I could touch it.

"Hey, it's our stop!" The neck skin shook with the words.

"Yeah. Let's go."

The two men staggered to the stairwell, gripping the backs of seats as they went. I pulled out my notebook and dabbed some words onto the page. *Whopping great ears. Flapping.*

By the time I reached the end of Stanley's street I thought I had managed to suppress all my prejudices concerning his lifestyle. That was before I turned the corner and saw the brown pebbledash bungalow with the concrete garden and yes, there it was, a garden gnome with horribly yellow teeth. "Shit," I muttered under my breath. "Be nice. Just be nice."

The eavesdroppers had all arrived before me. I realised this as an aproned Stanley ushered me inside and the sound of laughter washed into the hallway. I hung up my coat and wondered how I was going to tread the delicate line between boss at work and boss at a buffet. Stanley was in an impossibly good mood. I flinched as he buffered my shoulder with a warm oven mitt before disappearing into what I could only suppose was the kitchen. I was left stranded, alone in the lounge doorway.

"Hi, everyone." I waved.

"Hi!" Jack jumped up, crossed the room and shook my hand. "How are you?"

"Hungry," I said.

They were all well ahead of me in the alcohol stakes; that was obvious from the noise level – even Eve's cheeks were pink – so I hurried to the table I'd spotted in the corner of the room and ripped the ring from a can of beer. My fears regarding assimilation were quickly assuaged as I realised the booze had dispensed with the need for any sort of reintroduction of myself in a new environment. I was one of them, one part of a tipsy crowd.

I sat on the sofa and observed the scene. Next to me, Jack, in torn jeans, was demolishing a glass of red wine. Missy wore a skirt made of sacking and Eve was in a flat-chested dress that clung to her knees when she moved. Violet, drunk, was the most elaborately dressed, shimmering in leather trousers and a shiny top.

"Hello, Bill." she said, "Wanna listen to what I got to say?"

Something forced primness into my reply. "No, Violet. Not now."

"I'm going to…." began Missy, sitting cross-legged on the floor beside my feet. "I'm going to eavesdrop on the eavesdroppers." She smiled at the curtains.

"Jack!' bellowed Violet. "Tell Bill who you saw on the Tube."

"Who did you see on the Tube, Jack?" I said.

Jack glugged a swig of wine.

Violet smiled. "No one."

The room went quiet; Eve hiccupped; the sound of frying wafted from the kitchen.

Jack swallowed another mouthful of wine and smiled, teeth tinged purple. "It was really noticeable." He looked in my direction. "The absence. It was just me."

"Apart from all the others," said Violet, still smiling.

Jack grinned. The pull of the muscles altered his face. "Yes, me and all the others. But not *him*."

"Let's have a toast." Eve, flushed and unsteady, held up her glass as if she'd never adopted such a pose before.

"To absence," said Violet.

"The return of glorious absence!" said Jack.

I wasn't sure what was happening, but I raised my beer and hugged the eavesdroppers, one by one – and they hugged me.

"Does everyone like sultanas in their curry?" Stanley stood in the doorway to the lounge, a tea towel flung over his shoulder. "Oh, hugs! What'd I miss?"

No one answered; momentarily we just existed.

"Alright, does anyone *not* like sultanas in their curry?"

Still no one spoke.

He tutted to the air then disappeared back through the doorway, his back scolding us as he went.

I stood up and headed towards the kitchen. "Can I come in?"

"Be my guest!" Stanley ushered me into the room, a hot oven glove brushing my arm.

Objects were on display: a pan of simmering water, smashed garlic, ginger peelings, but there on the end of the counter, surrounded by scattered seed was a bird in a cage.

Stanley flounced his hand in a circle. "Beryl, meet Mr. Harcourt. Mr. Harcourt, meet Beryl."

"Ah, so this is Beryl." A blue and yellow budgerigar looked at me – smaller than I'd imagined. "Stanley, she alright?"

He turned quickly. "What do you mean?"

"Just noticing that bald bit there on her front. Is it meant to be like that?"

"What ba – oh, yes. That's all right. That's seasonal." He turned down the gas on the stove. "Jack okay?"

I glanced at the kitchen door. "Didn't you hear, he said that bloke on the Tube's gone."

Stanley grinned. "If he was ever there."

"Yeah, yeah. What a relief."

"Let's go back in. I have a surprise for you. You and all."

We returned to a scene of quiet sipping. Stanley gesticulated for me to sit. "Close your eyes, everyone."

I closed my eyes and succumbed to only sounds: a sniff, a hiccup, the sound of a body being rearranged on a sofa. Then a plastic bag, a hand inside and finally, something soft placed on a surface, cotton or maybe wool.

"You can look now."

Stanley stood on the rug in front of us. He was squeezed into a tight white T-shirt over his sweater, large letters stretched across his chest. *The Eavesdroppers*. He turned round – *nothing gets past us*.

My eyes watered: mustn't scratch.

"Came up a bit small, but what do you think?" he said.

Jack was the first. "They're great! Where's mine?"

Stanley touched a pile of T-shirts that hung over the arm of the sofa. "They're all here. One size only, I'm afraid."

I adjusted the scaffolding on my smile and from the comfort of my chair observed the rush. They formed an orderly queue beside Stanley, looking happily at their T-shirts as he handed them out. My corneas were bothering me as I watched them pull their new clothes over their heads then wrench them down over assorted chests. Suddenly everyone was the same shape, white bags of distorted writing, flesh squeezed in unlikely places.

"Here's yours, Mr. B."

Shit, the *E* was bigger than the others. "Thank you, Stanley."

They all watched as I stood up, raised my arms and gingerly slipped the T-shirt over my head, keeping the neck well away from eyes. I could hardly breathe, but I dragged it down, over my stomach, over my hips, until it brushed my knees.

I turned and looked at them, all the faces smiling and flushed. Then I turned slowly round so they could read my back. They laughed; I laughed. How we all laughed.

The scent of cumin was still lingering in my nose when I arrived home just after midnight. The heating had already gone off but my head was too busy for sleep, so I pulled a blanket off the sofa, dragged my chair up to the window and looked at the street. The moon was out; grey clouds rushed by; the building site slept.

I wasn't sure if I was up for another curry buffet. Stanley had tried to arrange a second gathering, forcing a diary out of Eve's handbag and making a great fuss about the importance of *pencilling* something in. I wasn't certain if I was ready for that – the idea that events involving me littered other people's calendars, unconfirmed, yet real enough to create bothersome guilt. But it wasn't the enforced camaraderie that was bothering me now. It was something else.

I'd walked back to the station with Jack after the meal. He was chatty, describing a website he'd designed at work, but when I brought up the subject of eavesdropping, in an abstract, general sort of way, he paused.

"Everything's okay now, isn't it, Jack?" I said.

"I'm not being followed any more, if that's what you mean. I'm not of any interest, not for now."

Rekindled worry is the worst type. "What do you mean?"

"Just that."

We walked on. I hated that, just walking along in silence, just the sound of our shoes on the pavement and dogs barking from far off windows. I watched his back for a long time after we said our goodbyes. Enough time to wonder – were all the eavesdroppers changing? Were they becoming something different, something I couldn't understand?

A noise from the street brought me back to the present. A corner of tarpaulin on the building opposite flapped in the wind. Everything else on the site was silent, tools stowed, engines off.

I looked up at the top of the building. It had three storeys now; I could no longer see the sun set on the top of Primrose Hill.

VIOLET leant against the big tree. The night bus had been full when it arrived at her stop but she'd charmed her way on with puppy dog eyes and slid into Lexington Street on a high not even the cold dispel. Most of the house numbers were hidden in dark porches but number 9 was nailed to the front gate. All brass and shine, 'Over here,' it said. So over there she'd staggered, heels sinking into the grass on the verge, a feeling she was beginning to enjoy. The tree seemed to fit her back and she leant into it, not caring that the bark was rough and spiders might sleep there.

She thought about the man's voice, so firm yet with a minute tremble hiding inside certain letters – how the *l* in the word table quivered, the *f* in coffee shook. How she loved vulnerability in a man. She didn't care what he looked like. She didn't want to know. Beauty is on the inside, after all. She smiled to herself. His beauty had revealed itself to her in the sound of his voice, in his charmingly mistimed words.

She tried to imagine what he would see if he looked out of his bedroom window right then. What man could resist a nymph resting on a tree outside his window at three in the morning? She'd always been good at draping herself gracefully. She should have been a model. But as she looked ahead the curtains were drawn and all she could hear was a low hum somewhere in the air and the creak of the trunk as it leant further towards the ground.

CHAPTER
27

After fretting over thoughts of digitisation I was nervous about calling another group meeting and I spent the days following my conversation with Wilson flicking through my diary, biting my nails – a new habit James had infected me with – and forgetting to eat lunch. I even picked up a heavy object: a large box of paper beneath the photocopier no one else could be bothered to move.

I didn't want to digitise the data. The analogue nature of my project was becoming increasingly precious to me, and in a fit of pique I bought a paper diary from the stationer's and wrote all my appointments in it with a pen. It was one of the things that I really liked about the eavesdroppers' work: the human ears, the real notebooks, the pencils, the pencil sharpeners, the erasers. They all gave it a human dimension to which I found myself increasingly drawn. Not a thought I'd let loose near James, but one that sat quietly inside my head.

Despite a pleading phone call from Missy asking for her notebook back and a rude email from Violet, I hung onto them for several days. I read them in the office; I read them at home; I read them in my bed. I even took one to the park and read it beneath the rays of the sun, but apart from learning some of the lines off by heart – *he loves me, he bought me burgers and chips* – I couldn't see any rhythms. I couldn't see one distinct pattern forming. 'Just read between the lines,' James kept telling me from the comfort of his chair. But how? The lines were clear but the 'between' refused to present itself. The notion struck me, not for the first time, that perhaps James was right – perhaps there was nothing out there beyond the mundane and meaningless, nothing beyond what we already knew.

I closed the notebooks, pushed them to the corner of my desk and turned on my computer. I clicked on my search engine. An advert for an Alzheimer's cure popped up at the side of the screen. I looked at the door to my office. I stared at the keyhole. It looked the same as it always did.

Missy's empty chair worried me. She'd been the most desperate to retrieve her notebook and after I'd placed them into the clamouring hands of the other eavesdroppers, I felt nervous, so very nervous, about the one left lying on the table. 'Probably got that vomiting bug,' Eve had said after we'd waited for ten minutes, filling the time listening to a long and filthy joke Stanley had overheard on the bus on his way to the meeting. But I couldn't help but fret that an empty chair meant a problem.

I cleared my throat. "I declare our seventh meeting open."

I was hopeless at bringing people to order. I had tested out various methods: letting out an abrupt, 'right, everyone,' or glaring schoolmaster-like around the table, but now I was trying out formality.

"Shouldn't we call her?' Jack said.

"Missy?"

"Yeah."

"She ... she hasn't got a phone."

Violet looked genuinely upset. "No phone? Is that true?"

"Yes. She called me from a phone box on the first day."

"Do you know where she lives?" asked Stanley.

I thought of the human resources folder. "Jean will know. Do you think we should go round there?"

"That vomiting bug is contagious," said Eve.

Jack was on his feet. "We should go. Just to make sure."

"Hold on," I said, "we can't just turn up unannounced."

"But you said there's no way to announce ourselves," said Jack. He picked up his notebook. "I'm going."

"Me too." Violet gathered her notebook and pencil and stuffed them into her handbag.

"I'll meet you in the entrance," said Eve. "I'm just going to wash my hands."

Jean was watching a film of chihuahuas dressed in elf suits on *YouTube* when we all barged into her office. I felt a surge of new respect, but she misread my expression and in her panic pressed the pause button so as we gathered round the desk her face was framed by a frozen tableau of green jackets and eager noses. But no one commented. We all just waited while Jean fished out Missy's address and gave us a look that said, 'please go.'

Missy lived in a 1930s block of flats, the kind which had once been the epitome of suburban living but now had grass growing in its gutters and broken curtain rails in its windows. The air seemed to have left our sails as we waited for her to answer the bell but returned when we heard a small voice on the intercom. "Hello everyone."

"It's us," said Stanley, leaning in to speak.

"I know."

"Can we come in?"

The intercom, the object of all our attention, suddenly seemed an idiotic thing. "Missy . . . ?" Stanley said.

Violet swayed. "She's not going to let us in."

"She's probably tidying up," said Eve.

Stanley pressed the bell again and leant in closer. "No need to tidy up, Missy."

Jack squeezed in between us and spoke into the box. "Missy, are you okay?"

The door opened. Missy wore a dressing gown and slippers. "Hello … everyone."

She didn't smile exactly, just pulled up her lips at the corners.

"We were worried about you, Missy." Stanley had assumed the tone of an elderly community nurse.

"Do you want to come in?"

"Is that, okay?" Jack asked.

She nodded. "Of course, come on up."

Missy seemed unfamiliar with the turn of the stairs and the slow ascent to her flat allowed me to get a sense of the place. The stairwell reminded me of my first rented flat, dust lining the edge of the carpet, thumbprints on the walls.

"Nice place you've got here," Stanley said, as we entered her flat.

A small snort escaped Violet's nose.

Missy's flat was what an estate agent would have called compact. The living room was tiny and the floorboards had an expectation of rugs, but there were no rugs. I sat on the only armchair while the eaves-droppers lined themselves up on the sofa, a tight squeeze that made me wonder if they would ever be able to extricate themselves. Missy sat on the floor and tightened the dressing gown at the waist.

"Sorry to barge in,' I began, "but, we were a bit concerned when you didn't come to the meeting."

"I didn't feel well."

"Maybe you could call me next time?" I said.

Eve pulled a handkerchief from her sleeve and held it in her hand. "You haven't picked something up down in those toilets, have you?"

"No, no, I just felt tired."

"Those your miniatures?" said Stanley, attempting to extricate himself from the sofa, then deciding against it.

She glanced at the mantelpiece and then smiled. "Yes. Yes, there they are."

"I'd have a closer look if I could get out up," said Stanley, still wriggling.

Missy seemed unnaturally still. "They don't bear close inspection. It wasn't a good casting. Best seen at a distance."

The sofa seemed unnaturally still.

"So. How's life down in the bowels of the earth?" Stanley beamed and sank back into the sofa

"A rich seam," observed Jack from the far end.

"It's going okay." Missy held her hand up to push her hair off her face. Her arms were freckled, but it was hard to see all the freckles because of the bandage.

'You okay, Missy?" I said.

"Yes. Why?" She slipped her arm beneath her back.

"Just that I saw your bandage."

"Oh, that. Silly me. I stroked a cat in the street and he didn't like it."

"Never stroke a cat in the street," said Eve. "It's not infected, is it?"

"No. It's fine. Just a cat that didn't like to be stroked."

EVE knew *Word* but she didn't know *InDesign*. She wasn't even sure what desktop publishing meant but every time she googled 'make your own leaflets' she got sent down the same path. And that was after she'd clicked her way through the rows of print shops offering her deals on leaflets by the thousand. But she didn't need a thousand. She only needed one.

She was proud of her computer skills. At risk of being stranded on the shore of middle age she had agreed to be sent by her employers on a course entitled *Computing for the Over-40s*. To her way of thinking the title alone was telling and for a woman of sixty-two years of age, comforting. Even those twenty years her junior must be struggling to connect finger to cursor, and maybe, just maybe, there were other people out there who also didn't know what a cookie was.

Feeling dispirited, she drafted out her leaflet in *Word*. No need to involve anyone else, she thought. She could print it out herself and stick it on the back of a piece of card to show it was professional. It took about two hours, what with all the corrections and all the copying and pasting, but by the end it looked good. It looked really good.

Turn garments inside out to wash and dry.

Separate contrasting colours.

Wash at the temperature shown on the label.

Do not iron, rub, twist or wring

Wash woollens by hand in warm water.

Dry flat.

Eve sat down in her usual spot on the bench. She wore a flowery skirt, which, she only noticed when she sat down, rode above her knee when she was seated. She went through the motions: she slipped her hand into her bag and felt inside. She patted the back of her hair, wondering if any grey had crept back. She pulled her skirt down over her knees. She was calm; she was decent; she was ready. An hour passed before a shout from the street made her jump.

"Let me in!"

Eve turned towards the door. A foul face was at the window, the mouth an elongated 'O'; an armful of dripping sheets was soaking a tweeded arm.

"Open this fucking door!"

Eve scuttled to the door and pulled it open, but before she could speak someone barged past her – a woman.

"You're too late," the woman said. "We're closing in five minutes and – what the hell have you got there?"

"Sheets! My fucking sheets."

The woman straightened her back. "You can't bring them in here. Not dripping like that, you'll soak my floor. You're too late." She closed the door and locked it. Then she turned around and walked to the back of the launderette on dictatorial heels.

But Eve's feet had put down roots. She watched helplessly as the man turned to go and a revengeful back took shape out on the street – his head sunk into shoulders, his arms clenched. Then the man turned and accusing eyes, familiar accusing eyes, locked onto her face.

Eve inched her way back to the bench, sat down and fingered the leaflet in her bag. She smiled.

CHAPTER

28

'Why can't I see? It's the bandage, dear. Over your eyes.'

It had been several weeks since I'd thought of my hospital bed. My bed at home was the same length as that one had been, same width too, but my duvet was not scant and worn but thick and warm and the smell of my room was my own. I reached onto the floor, picked up a discarded sock and placed it over my eyes. It smelt of my feet but it felt like the hospital bandage, cutting me off from my surroundings. Missy had a bandage.

I threw the sock back onto the floor and tried to sleep. But images of surgical dressings kept coming into my mind. They wrapped my face; they wrapped Missy's arm. Finally, I got up and made myself a bowl of cornflakes in the kitchen. Still unable to sleep, I pulled on a sweatshirt and a pair of shoes and went down into the street.

The street sounded different when I stepped outside into the night. The building site opposite, normally characterised by the whine of power tools and the irritating beep of reversing trucks – God's tool of torture – was quiet, and I could hear a bird singing a misjudged evensong. I couldn't see it but I could still hear it, tweeting its incomprehensible message to whoever cared to hear. A blackbird, I knew it from my childhood bird-listening days. Then I heard another sound. I couldn't identify it at first. Was it wheels? Badly oiled wheels? I imagined a large pram, the sort I slept in as a baby. A man came into view. He was pulling a suitcase on wheels. But the wheels were broken and the case bumped across bumps in the pavement. He walked past me, seemingly oblivious to the racket he was making, *clackety clack, clackety clack, clackety, clackety*. Someone was going somewhere. Someone was leaving.

I watched his back until he disappeared from view - then a lull in the air. Then another sound - I looked towards the other end of the street and saw a man and a woman talking at the corner, far in the distance.

"You sound like death," he said.

"I know. Part of me died yesterday."

"I think–"

"What? Bill. What's the matter?"

I put my finger to my lips and got out of my chair.

"Bill, what the–"

"Schh!"

I tiptoed towards the office door, trying to keep my bones quiet. I opened it. "Got y–" Outside – nothing. Just the corridor: beige carpet, fluorescent light, air.

James was looking at me when I turned round to speak. "You know, I could have sworn I heard someone out there."

"Bill," said James. "You've been spending too much time with eavesdroppers."

"Aren't we all eavesdroppers?" I said, returning to my seat.

"If you mean listening at keyholes, no."

I glared at the door. "Are you sure you didn't hear something out there?"

"Positive."

I glared again. "Soddit. It doesn't even have a proper hole."

"Exactly," said James. "Hey, Bill, why don't you go home and get an early night. You look wrecked."

I checked my watch. "Yeah, maybe I will." I gathered my stuff and put on my coat. "See you."

James had an oddly expressionless shape to his face. "Yeah, see you tomorrow."

I went out into the corridor and closed the door behind me. So quiet out there, just the beige carpet and fluorescent light and air, and the smell of myself. I pressed my ear against the closed door; the wood gently hummed with the sound of James' voice.

MISSY removed the lightbulb from the cardboard package, carefully, very carefully, and then held it aloft in her right hand as she levered herself up onto the stool. She unscrewed the red bulb and replaced it with the blue. She jumped down and switched on the light. Blue – everything blue: blue walls, blue sofa, blue shoes and blue shadows. She lay on the floor, stretched out her legs and held up her arms and looked at the back of her hands. No bulging veins, no signs of misuse, just perfect fingers attached to a blemish-free wrist. She touched the bandage on her arm then stroked the back of her hand. It was easier to think in the cool blue light. It was easier to think inside a perfect body.

She thought of the eavesdroppers. They had knocked on her door so loudly the day she'd missed the meeting, it had taken a few seconds to compose, to switch to herself. It was like a party, the way they'd sat on her sofa and sipped orange juice, so much so she'd forgotten to show them her real glasses, the multipacks so useful if catering for large numbers. She'd gone out the next day and bought an eighteen-pack set of tumblers from the Pound Shop on the Caledonian Road and found three quartz ashtrays at the Salvation Army shop and a second-hand fondue set that didn't need much cleaning. Now she was ready for unexpected guests. And when she didn't have guests she could have a party of her own.

The entrance to the underground toilets was surrounded by the abandoned parts of a market stall when she arrived, stacked milk crates and tarpaulin held together with clamps, and she wondered at the trader who would leave so many wares in the street unattended. She rummaged through a bucket of flowers on the verge of death, and then walked down the steps. Even before she reached the toilet floor she felt goose pimples pop up on her arms. But no one was down there, just a grey mop leaning against the wall and the newspaper open on the day attendant's table.

Missy went into the first cubicle, put down the toilet seat and sat down. It was cold but she'd bought an extra sweater so she pulled it on, placed her elbows on her knees and rested her jaw in her hands. Such was her pose. The cold statue, waiting for words to enter her ears.

She *could* have listened somewhere else. Violet sipped espresso in cosy coffee bars while Eve huddled against a warm drier on chilly days. But many things about this room drew her underground: the quiet, the dankness, the dark square of the attendant's window.

The air above ground was always crowded, a constant cacophony of competing sounds testing her ears, which long ago had learned to catagorise, to separate the shrill shriek of her house mother from the slumped and sodden sounds of her house father. Underground rooms held cold, clear sounds, one after the other. And cold ears are sharper ears.

A noise coming down the steps broke her reverie. Kitten heels: half a size too big. Then the shoes were on the floor; then the shoes were outside her door.

"I know you're in there."

CHAPTER

29

"Where's Eve?"

"Haven't seen her." Stanley's reply was spokesmanlike.

I glanced at my phone beneath the table. No messages. "Okay, I expect she's missed her bus, let's get started, we can't wait any longer. Can everyone get their notebooks out, please?"

Yes, Sir," said Stanley.

I wasn't imagining it; his eyes were definitely twinkling. They contrasted sharply with the dull irises in the faces of the others.

"So, who would like to go first?" Had a pin dropped onto the meeting room floor at that moment you would have heard it. "Anyone?"

Stanley flicked his lips back and forth, half confessant, half monkey. His teeth were whiter than I remembered.

He cleared his throat. "The general consensus in the dentist's waiting room is that orthodontic success is directly related to the size of one's mouth."

I was truly astonished by the nature of this remark and did a surreptitious survey of the mouths round the table. 'What's better, little or big?"

"Big, of course. More work space."

"More space for his equipment," added Jack, helpfully.

"What equipment?" Missy said. She wore a hairy sweater; it looked itchy.

"Scrapers, sluicers, filers and fillers," replied Stanley.

"Stanley," I said, "did you hear anyone talk about anything … significant? Politics or–"

"Or someone planning a murder," said Violet.

Jack giggled. I'd never heard Jack giggle before.

Stanley commanded the pause in the room. He now had a cocktail stick in his mouth and he rolled it between his lips, the point darting back and forth like a sharp little fish. "No. Nothing political. No murders. Just lots of talk of mouths." He looked around the table.

"So what else were they talking about, Stanley?" I said.

He smiled – a flash of teeth followed by a slacking of lips. "To be honest, I wasn't really listening."

"Why weren't you listening, Stanley?" Funny how nervous I felt.

"I was distracted."

"By what?" Violet asked.

"I saw a lovely little girl."

I gazed at him. 'Lovely little girl' was not a phrase that could be easily said about young girls by elderly men who weren't their grandfathers.

"Did she look scared?" Missy enquired.

I flinched. "Why would she–?"

"I was *always* scared at the dentist," she added.

"Not scared … more … hopeful," said Stanley.

"You didn't talk to her, did you?" A memory rose up in my head. The memory of the day in the shopping centre years earlier when I'd found a lost child and taken her by the hand and led her towards the manager's office and bumped into her mother and heard the accusation.

"No."

"Men can't talk to little girls any more," said Violet. "Not *old* men, anyway."

Stanley gazed sadly down at his notebook.

"Did you listen to her mother?" Eve enquired.

"Her mother wasn't there. But the little girl … she *was* lovely. She had lovely teeth."

We all looked at him. Gathered together.

"Can I give my report now?" said Violet.

"Oh … yes. Yes, do." I realised I was picking at the skin down the side of my thumb as Violet began her presentation. The cafe had been busy she told us and she had sorted her *overheards* into categories listed in alphabetical order. Buttons and their annoying habit of coming off was followed by neglected children, then the state of Sunday night telly, but all the time I was thinking of Stanley and his little girl. He seemed harmless enough – no, he was a great bloke. The lovely little girl probably thought he was a lovely bloke. He had a budgie, after all. He could cook curry.

"Are you listening?" Violet was leaning across the desk. I hadn't noticed before how low her voice was.

"Yes, sorry. Carry on."

But then, before she had a chance to proceed, everything changed.

No one had heard her coming. None of us were ready for what happened next. The door opened. Everyone turned to look towards it.

"Eve!' exclaimed Missy.

Whitehall was deserted by the time I left the office. I never knew streets in central London could be so deserted, but on this evening the entire pavement was visible and I watched an empty bag of crisps dance back and forth across the road without being flattened by passing traffic. Yet on the fringe of the street there were people: a homeless man wrapped in a nylon sleeping bag and reading a novel by the street light, and a maid sweeping some embassy steps with a broken dustpan and brush.

I sat down on the steps of the Cenotaph, rested my head in my hands and took my eyes off the city. I didn't have children, I'd never even considered what it would be like to have that amount of responsibility, but at that moment I felt like a parent who had failed. Something was terribly wrong with the eavesdroppers. Stanley had noticed a little girl; he'd mentioned her; he'd thought about her. And Eve. Her arrival at the meeting had caused Stanley's cocktail stick to fall from his mouth.

She was different. Her skin was different, caked with orange make-up and her hair was a rich, unnamable colour, auburn verging on auburgine. She appeared to be wearing false eyelashes that had become unstuck at the corners and they batted up and down like the skeletal wings of a dead bird. And when she spoke, her voice shook. I'd wanted to rush back to my desk, dig out a bar of chocolate and chew quietly, alone, just me and the Internet. But no, I had to face this new and disturbing development.

In the early days of the group *someone else* would have come to my aid: Violet would have summarised the situation neatly and efficiently, Stanley would have charmed out a solution and Eve, yes Eve, she would have known what to do when faced with such a transformation. But it wasn't the Eve I knew who stood in the doorway.

I'd offered her a seat and even through my shock I noticed she moved differently, bringing her body down onto the chair with great delicacy and holding her neck in a way that seemed to say, 'don't say a thing.' But I felt reassured when she rummaged in her bag in a familiar way and soon even Stanley stopped giving her sideways glances. We proceeded with the meeting. It seemed too difficult to ask. Even Violet, connoisseur of makeovers, had refrained from comment, and we'd concluded our reports in a show of normality, closing our notebooks, waving our departure and heading down the stairs in quietly chatting groups.

A sound returned my attention to the street. A pigeon had landed on the edge of the Cenotaph steps, one foot a stump. But he ignored

his useless limb, pecking on a stale crisp and going about his life as if
nothing ailed him. My stomach flexed as a single muscle. I felt nauseous.
Something was terribly wrong with the eavesdroppers.

Ladies Toilets Camden High St.1 am.
Angry girl: You're late.
Shy girl: I'm sorry.
Angry girl: Give me the money.
Sound of a bag being opened.
Scared girl: Here you are.
Angry girl: What the hell's that?
Scared girl: It's all I have.
Angry girl: Look, little miss watery eyes, I need more than this.
Scared girl: I'm sorry.
Angry girl: I don't want 'sorry.' I want money. When am I gonna
    get it?
Scared girl: When I get paid.
Angry girl: When the fuck's that?
Scared girl: Next week.
Angry girl: How am I supposed to survive until next week …? I
    said, how am I going to survive until next week?
Scared girl: I don't know.
Angry girl: What's your name?
Scared girl: Jane.
Angry girl: Jane! It's not fucking Jane.
Scared girl: It's … Missy.
Angry girl: Oh *come* on. Little Miss Missy?
Scared girl: Yes.
Angry girl: Hey, Jane.
Scared girl: Yes?
Angry girl: You better be here tomorrow with the money or else
    I'll be inviting myself to your place for a cup of tea.
Scared girl: I'll be here.

Angry girl: You will.
Scared girl: I will.

STANLEY had never known Beryl to be so soft. He stroked her head, back and forth, back and forth, and decided he was happy. He'd spent the afternoon going round the big chemist's up on Weatherton Street. He was in heaven in there, what with the expanding floss, the transparent blue gels and the coloured packs of interdental picks. How he loved his little mouth mirror with its ergonomic grip and shiny face. These days he dreamt of mint and woke up smelling of cloves. He'd even added a shake of toothpowder to his soup, which gave it a delicious tang and made his teeth feel fresh all day

Earlier that morning he'd made his third appointment in three weeks at the surgery. The receptionist was against him of course. She had no idea of the revitalising power of clean enamel, but the dentist had understood. Yes, that man knew when a filling was needed. No qualms, no 'ifs,' no 'buts,' just a professional, 'let's not take any chances with that dark shadow Mr. Stipple' that left Stanley with an even whiter smile on his face.

He put his face to Beryl's bars, smelling the metal. Even though the area beneath her was crunchy with droppings and a feather was loose in her back, she looked like a beautiful queen in a gilded cage. "I have something to tell you, Beryl," he said.

Beryl didn't like preambles; she was a stickler for direct, concise language, but on this occasion he couldn't get the words out without a little build-up. "So, I was in the dentist the other day, you know the place where they repair your teeth and I saw ... someone."

Beryl twisted her head and began preening the feathers on her wing.

"Didn't you hear what I said? I saw someone I liked the look of."

She paused and gazed at him: a cold, grey stare.

"But she won't replace you, darling. She won't ever replace you."

Beryl shivered, then stared at him. A cold, grey, judgemental stare.

"Bugger you, Beryl," he said.

He went out into the garage, rummaged in a drawer and brought his hammer back into the kitchen. Then he wrenched Beryl's half-pecked cuttlefish out of the cage, rinsed it under the tap and began to break it up, five pieces, then eight, then twenty. But his wrists began to ache so he returned to the garage, came back with a drill and held it to the cuttlefish. Beryl's shoulders stiffened; she pecked at the bars of the cage, *crabety crab, crabety crab.* The drill whined; Beryl pecked *crabety crab, crabety crab.* Stanley found the pestle and mortar and drowned out Beryl's noise with a grating and grinding that went on and on and on. At last the perfect texture. Stanley licked his finger, dipped it into the powder and massaged his inflamed gums.

Stuff Beryl, he thought. She had no idea what pleasure he had.

He looked back at her. He didn't say it, but he thought it. *I don't love you any more.*

CHAPTER
30

I ordered tea but what turned up was a dark, coffee-like brew, tarry to the taste and already staining the inside of the mug. The cafe at Dungeness beach was frayed all over – sad old tablecloths and tired curtains, and each time someone opened the door a breeze swept round my ankles. Still, I liked it. No complicated choices of beverage, no line-up of fancies, just tea or coffee, sandwich or cake.

The people, and there were people, seemed content with their lot: the sea – always over there – the wild cabbage growing on the shingle and the long, swaying washing lines all heavy with jeans and shirts and wiped-down motorbike covers. People's hair seemed permanently windswept – a comb in a pocket, a hairband waiting on a wrist. I liked the place, and strangely, felt it liked me.

Although the idea had dropped into my head quickly it had taken time to arrange the meeting with Raymond Watt. It's hard to rush the Royal Mail, I discovered. The post office queue is a slovenly beast, threaded with customers with complicated requests and by the time I'd reached the front to buy a stamp I was ready to snap. Then I'd waited. I hadn't watched for the postman from the window so much since I fell in love with my French pen friend at thirteen years old, but finally an envelope with the familiar writing, once so derided, fell onto my doormat.

By the time the old man finally arrived my plate was covered in crumbs and I was wiping cake grease off my fingers with a napkin. He sat down on the chair opposite me in the same way my dad would have, cautiously, as if expecting a practical joke to befall him. We looked at each other. The usual pleasantries that stagger out in social situations such as this seemed redundant and I found myself observing, by way of introduction, without even an attempt at a greeting, that the government's new bedroom tax was wildly unfair.

He viewed me coldly. "I have no interest in bedrooms."

I reorganised the cutlery on my plate in an effort to occupy the ensuing and interminably long hiatus. "I…."

"Has it begun?" he said, his face the grimmest of masks.

A cup rattled on a saucer. "Yes. It *has* begun. That's why I'm here."

He sighed, a slight release of air through his nose that left him looking kinder. "What's happened?"

I ran through the eavesdroppers in my head: Stanley at the dentist, Eve in the launderette, Missy in the toilet, Violet in the cafe, Jack going round and round beneath the streets of London. But now that I had to say it out loud it was hard to get it right. What *had* happened? "Some of them are in trouble."

A brow lined on the other side of the table. "What kind of trouble?"

"It's hard to put my finger on it exactly, it's not all of them, but they seem to be taking it all a bit too seriously."

"Listening is a serious job."

"I know that, it's just that I think it's beginning to affect them." I took a vigorous sip of my tea.

"Go on."

"They're having some … problems." He didn't reply; I tried to read his thought. "Serious problems."

He held my eye. "Are any of them being followed yet?"

"How the hell did you know about that?"

"Have they started following other people yet?"

"No! Wait, you mean stalking? No, nothing like that that has happened, but one of them, one of the women–"

"You have women?"

"Er … well, yes. I have three women."

"And you let them go out alone?"

"Yes, but … in public places."

"In daylight?"

"Oh, yes. Always in daylight."

"So what's happened to one of the women?"

"One of them has a bandage on her arm. A cat … scratched it. And one of them overheard a conversation between … sort of … criminals."

He glanced across the room, leant towards me and lowered his voice to a whisper. "Mr. Harcourt. You must be frank with me." He glanced across the room again. "Are they all still alive?"

I struggled across the shingle, feet like lead, my shoes sucked down into the stones, then up and free again, crunching, crunching, crunching, then down. The wind scraped my hair off my forehead; the ducks flew up into the air with splashes of water, silent wings and feet hanging down loose.

I slogged past the first sound mirror and on towards the long wall beyond, so long, so hard to reach with feet in the shingle. *The long wall*. Such a plain name for an object so forbidding. Rather than being round and sitting on a pedestal like its brother this sound mirror touched the ground and curved in a long, gentle arc.

I stood at one end of the wall. Something made me want to measure it, so I paced its length – sixty paces that I almost lost count of – then I pressed my chest against the seaward side and looked up. At least forty feet of concrete towered above me. Then I stretched out my arms and spread-eagled myself against it. The wind rushed past my ears. I could hear my own breath. I could feel my heart thumping in my chest. And I could hear the hum of the concrete. Could the mirror still hear after all these years? What was it listening to? Was it listening to me?

I gazed out to sea. Someone had died. Someone had listened so hard that it had ended their life. 'How?' I'd pressed the old man. But 'how' was locked away somewhere, in his mind, in a file, in a long forgotten drawer. He couldn't say. He wouldn't say. It had been Raymond's responsibility to close their ears, to cut them off. But the ears kept on flapping. 'But how *did* you stop it?' had been my most insistent question. 'Your responsibility' was all he'd said. 'Your responsibility.'

Bloody responsibility; I hated it. Bloody, bloody responsibility. I looked at my watch. Thirty minutes until the last train. I had to get back to London.

Someone had died.

VIOLET had taken the skin off her heels from walking. But even the ruin of her seventh pair of stilettos was nothing compared to the feeling of elation she had got from the chase. She'd allowed herself to call it that. Her previous life, of waiting to be sought out by men, was now over. She was now the seeker. More than that, she was the pursuer, the bloodhound that sniffed and followed and never gave up. But bloodhounds need food and for now she was back in the all-night cafe, chomping on a bacon sandwich laced with ketchup, planning her next move.

Her first night beneath *his* tree had been hard. The damp in the air had made her colder than she'd ever been and a man had shouted 'great arse' out of a passing car, but it had been worth it. She'd caught glimpses of life inside the house. His life. Not once, but three times. His shoulder had glanced the window. Heartbeat up. His hand had pulled the curtain and his silhouette had seemed to open the door and sniff the air, as if detecting a new scent in the garden. She'd sensed that final action coming, so she'd moved quickly behind the tree and observed undetected. She'd always been good at stealth. She should have been a detective. She *was* a detective. How she enjoyed the details she was collecting. She knew more about this man than she knew about her own mother.

A clatter of plates brought Violet back to the present. She wiped the remains of her bread round the edge of the plate and put the reddened dough into her mouth. She glanced at her watch. Time to go back. Her vigil awaited her.

A couple of shouty teenagers were occupying the end of his street when she turned the corner, but when they saw her they linked arms and disappeared into the dark. She walked up the road, her heels tapping on the pavement, her trousers softly chafing between her thighs. Lights were on in an upstairs room. She adjusted the clasp at the back of her bra and leant against the tree. She *was* the tree, leaning and listening, absorbing the sounds around her. It was surprising how many noises gathered beneath her leafy canopy. Then a new sound took shelter close to her ear and for just a fraction of a second, she thought she could hear what was being said inside the house.

CHAPTER

31

My message took an eternity to write. I'd never learnt to text on my phone with thumbs. The movement reminded me too much of the stunted flippers of a baby seal, so my typing was usually one-fingered and slow and the message evaded me for several minutes. The spellcheck repeatedly replaced 'tomorrow' with *timorous* and 'Violet' with *bio,* but finally the urgent call to convene was out in cyberspace.

Stanley, Jack, Violet, Eve. I'm calling an urgent meeting tomorrow afternoon at 3 o'clock. At my flat. Not the office. At my flat. Please let me know if you can make it. I need you to confirm. Please confirm you can come. Bill H.

The train back to London was soporific, stopping at every station, dragging its wheels over a vibrating track. I imagined my message lodged inside their mobiles, waiting to be opened and read. I regretted my use of the word 'urgent' only after I'd pressed *send*. They'd worry. Missy would wring anxiety from her handkerchief and Jack would purse his lips into a very straight line.

The bins at Victoria Station were overflowing when I arrived, yet I could only find a small jam-stained scrap of paper to write Missy a note. My pencil was stubby but had enough lead to write: *Missy. We have an urgent meeting at 3 o'clock tomorrow. Please be there. At my flat. You have the address. Kind regards. Bill Harcourt.*

I was relieved to see that Missy's lights were all out when I reached her building. It seemed odd that a twenty-something woman would be in bed so early, but it suited my intent of sliding the note into her postbox unnoticed. Please let her find it, I thought as I slipped back into the dark street. Please.

"Say that again!"

"I'm going to cancel the eavesdropping project."

"But, Bill, you're only two months in!"

'I know. But it's … going wrong."

"What's going wrong?" said James. "I know there were teething problems but I thought they were getting really good at it."

"They *are* getting good at it. But they're also getting in more … trouble."

James stood up and closed the office door. "What sort of trouble? Is Jack still being followed by that geezer?"

I ran my hand through my hair. "No, no, it's not that … God, James, it's so messed up. They're all doing crazy stuff."

James bit his lip. "Go on."

Where to start? The deluded version or the real version? The deluded version was easy to live with. I took a deep breath "Eve turned up the other day looking all done up … all … like a … a prostitute. Missy has fucking bandages all up her arm and Stanley…."

James shifted in his seat. "And Stanley…."

" … Stanley seems to have fallen in love with a child."

"Oh God."

"Yeah."

"He hasn't–"

"No! No, I'm sure he ... hasn't. It's all in his mind."

"Sure?"

"Pretty sure."

"Have you told–"

"No. I haven't told Wilson."

He leant back in his chair. "How did Missy get the bandages?"

"I don't know!"

"No need to shout."

"Sorry."

"Did you even ask her?"

"She said it was a cat."

"Huh?"

"She said a cat scratched her."

James frowned. "I can't take all this in. Did you say Eve looked like a prostitute?"

I laughed, just for a second. Then I explained. Not every shameful detail but what I could bear to retell. He listened diligently, nodding and smiling kindly, and then winced before pointing out that it probably *wasn't* the whole story (how did he suddenly get so clever?) but only my side of it. Before I had a chance to challenge this statement he spoke again. "What about Violet?"

"What do you mean?"

"Did she get into any trouble?"

Violet. I took a minute to trawl through all our encounters in my head.

"Well? " James insisted. "Did she show any sign of problems?"

"She ... never really changed. She's been pretty consistent throughout."

James cocked his head to one side. "Bill."

"Yes."

"Just thinking ... in all this, you left someone else off the list of names. Someone important."

"Oh, yeah? Who?"

"You."

I didn't let the word, this 'you' word sink in. I just let it slide down the outside of my body. "James … there's something else I haven't told you."

"Go on."

"I went to see that bloke again."

I waited.

"Can I assume you mean the man down at Lydd?" he said.

"Yes."

He shifted his shoulders into an uncomfortable-looking shape. "What did he say?"

"He was a bit peculiar."

"In what way?"

"He told me one of the original eavesdroppers, you know the ones who operated the sound mirrors during the war, that they'd … well, one of them, they'd … sort of died."

"Died? How?"

"He wouldn't say exactly, he got a bit cagey."

"He must have said something!"

I felt vaguely queasy. "'Careless talk costs lives.' That's what he said."

James stared at me across the empty space of the office.

It had seemed wrong to have the final meeting in the office. There would be an expectation that everything was alright. Also, I didn't want to risk an encounter with Wilson in the corridor – the grizzled look, the demand for an update – so I'd invited them all to my flat. But I hadn't counted on the excitement it would cause. Violet emailed me back quickly and told me she was going out to buy a new dress, an announcement I didn't have the guts to reply to, while Stanley promised the re-emergence of his Teddy Boy suit not worn since his days as a spiv down The Old Kent Road in the 1950s.

I remained in my armchair after the bell rang, facing the door. But the inside of my body couldn't stay still. It squeezed sweat to the surface; it forced extra blood through my heart and it stabbed a miniscule pain into one of my eyelids. My ears sought out some reassuring sounds but all I could hear was the rumble of my neighbour's washing machine, the patter of rain on the roof and in the distance, the bite of a drill into wood. I got up and let them into the building.

A moment later feet sounded on the stairs. "Come in, come in," I said, opening the door.

To my surprise they were all there at once, pecking order intact – Violet and Stanley at the front, Eve and Missy behind them, yet Jack, back-of-the-bunch Jack, wasn't at the rear, but standing to one side looking straight at me, a relaxed smile on his face.

Not questioning how they'd managed to choreograph the simultaneous arrival, I ushered them into my flat. They were damp from the rain and I suppressed an urge to get out a towel and rub them all down like dogs. I'd set out some nibbles – nuts and raisins and cheese biscuits – and before I'd had time to take their coats they were digging in.

"Can I take everyone's coats?" I said, peeved that being the host meant I had to haul a bundle of damp garments out into the hall and force them onto the overloaded coat tree. I glanced back into the living room as I tried to ram Stanley's trench coat over my jacket. Violet sat straight-backed on a stool; she was rubbing something white and creamy into the back of her hand. She looked all right. She looked the same as the day I had first set eyes on her.

The snacks were three-quarters gone by the time I returned to the room, so I grabbed a handful of the remaining almonds, the over-salted detritus, and by way of reward sat down in the most comfortable chair. "Can everyone find a seat, please," I said.

"Shall I begin?" asked Eve, settling herself on the sofa and flicking through her notebook.

"No, Eve. *I'll* begin."

I don't know if there was something in the tone of my voice, but that was the moment they seemed to understand something was different. Their faces looked paler than their necks. Their mouths hung.

"I have something important to say. You five...." I waved my hand across them, "are a quintet of natural listeners with ears as sharp as razors and–"

"You're going to end it, aren't you."

It was Jack who'd spoken. He sat a little crookedly in his chair and for a second I felt nervous of him. I looked down; the almonds looked pathetic in my hand. "Yes. I'm going to end it," I said. A clock ticked somewhere.

"You can't!" Missy's voice was the squeak of a creature.

Stanley stood up; I had a new view of his nostrils. "No. You *can't* end it."

"I have to," I said.

"Why exactly do you *have* to? " asked Eve, all reasonableness and calm.

I took a deep breath and consulted my mental notes. "Listen carefully, everyone. The project was set up to try and find out what the general public was talking about. I was looking for something that other researchers hadn't found. But it appears that I was wrong. There isn't ... anything out there."

"But there is!" said Eve. "We just haven't found it yet."

I examined my hands folded round my knees, but the reply wasn't there.

"Giving up a bit easily, aren't you, Bill?" Stanley had a new tone in his voice.

"I've given this a lot of thought. It's not a rash decision."

Violet snorted. No one spoke. I wondered if they were rehearsing something, polishing a group tirade.

I began a few limp sentences. "I really appreciate the work you've all done. We did make some progress and–"

But it wasn't a sentence that halted the words in my mouth. It was something else. A new sound had entered the room. A sob – deep in the back of a throat.

On a bench outside 21 Chart Street, Shoreditch, London. 3.30pm.

Young man: We've never been alone together without him.

Older woman: Say that again. I can't hear you over that hammering.

Young man: I said, we've never been alone together without him.

Old man: Never.

Young man: Anyone want a cigarette?

Old man: We don't smoke.

Young man: Not even a bit?

Loud woman: I might start.

Older woman: You *won't*.

Young woman: *I* won't.

Old man: He didn't have to do it.

Old woman: Of course he didn't have to do it.

Young woman: Weren't we any good?

Old man: Of course, we were good. We were bloody brilliant. Oh, no. He's the one who's in the wrong.

Loud woman: There's something else. Something he's not telling us. I mean it's not as if we did anything bad, is it.

Old man: *I* definitely didn't do anything bad.

Old woman: I didn't do anything bad … wrong either, but….

Loud woman: But what?

Old woman: I might have got lost.

Old man: I thought you knew London like the back of your hand?

Old woman: I meant I could have lost my moral compass.

Loud woman: Jesus!

Old woman: Oh, no. I'm not religious–

Old man: We know you're not religious. You might have been though.

Old woman: I don't understand.

Loud woman: You know what? We should carry on. Just us.

Young woman: Just us?

Old man: No!

Loud woman: Why the big 'no'?

Old man: What would we do with our notes? All the data?

Loud woman: There is no data, according to him upstairs.

Old man: So … does that mean there's no need to go on then?

Young woman: Couldn't we keep in touch? I really like you … all.

Old man: I like you all too. But we don't need to do any more listening to like each other.

Loud woman: Don't we?

EVE entered the launderette and walked straight up to the man on the bench. "Hello. I have something to give you."

The man glanced up from his newspaper. "Who are you?"

"I'm … well, we spoke the other day."

"What about?"

"I helped you with that shirt. That delicate one."

The man turned his whole body and looked at her. Eve hadn't been looked at like that before. She slipped her hand into her bag and pulled out the leaflet. "I thought this might help with your woollens, when you're hand-washing at home."

She didn't usually smile when she gave out her leaflets. It might appear condescending or worse flirtatious; she liked to keep things professional, but this man looked like he needed a little cheering up. And this was a very special leaflet. Made just for him.

He didn't smile back. "What else have you got in that bag?"

"Nothing."

"Sure?" He snatched her bag out of her hand, turned it upside down and began flinging the contents onto the floor, leaflet after leaflet: *tax fraud, benefit fraud, senior debt, Internet fraud, student debt.*

"What's all this fucking crap?" The man kicked the pile then picked up a leaflet, *Getting the most from your benefits.* He opened the first page and then turned to her with a look of genuine fear on his face. "What *are* you?"

"I'm ... well, I'm...."

But the man wasn't listening. He now had his hand in her pocket. He wrenched out her notebook. "What the fuck's this?"

Eve's tongue had dried. 'Could I have that back, please?"

"No." He opened a page at random.

The man was a slow reader. So slow there was time for Eve to think he might hear her heart so violent was the thump in her chest. He traced the first three sentences with his finger, paused, and then traced again. He slapped the book shut and shoved it into his pocket. "Come outside."

The beat inside Eve's ribs was hurting now, but somehow she forced life into her trembling legs and trailed the man out of the launderette, three paces behind, then five, then eight.

"Get 'ere!" he said, before turning his back to her and striding on.

She scuttled behind, her ankles painful. She scanned the street, left to right, right to left. Where were the people? she thought. Why was there no one here?

The man strode down the street for a few yards then stopped beneath the shadow of an awning. She paused behind him, feeling the enclosure, hardly able to draw air into her terrified lungs.

"Are you with the police?" he demanded.

"No."

He smiled – a rotten, sickly grin that oozed out of his face. "So what are these notes?" He held out her notebook.

A survivalist slipped into her clothes. "I just like listening."

He gripped her wrist. His hand felt like a huge warm bunch of bananas. But tight. "I'm not an idiot. You were spying on me, weren't you."

"No, I … meant no harm. I like listening to people stalking – I mean talking. I like people."

"Yeah? I *don't* like people." His face moved closer to hers. "And *nobody* likes a fucking eavesdropper."

It was at that moment Eve remembered the words of her self-defence teacher years earlier; they punched their way into her head – 'Go for the nose. If all else fails, go for the nose.' She'd cringed at the time. The idea of ramming two fingers into a stranger's nostrils, the gristle, the cold touch of moist snot, was more than she could bear. She'd practiced the shin slide instead. But it was a nose not a shin that was bearing down on her, so she did it. Just like her teacher told her, with conviction and intent and with the benefit of recently sharpened ladies' nails.

"Fuck!"

Eve paused on the street corner, arranged her scarf around her neck and adjusted her brooch so it was straight. After that she went into the pub on the next street and washed her hands in the toilet sink. Finally she returned to the launderette, gathered her leaflets up from the floor, (brushing off the occasional footprint) and then walked down the street and waited at the bus stop. She was fingering the notebook, safe in her pocket, as the bus appeared on the horizon.

CHAPTER

32

We did make some progress and.... We did make some progress and.... We did make some progress and....

They'd taken turns to dab at the tears streaming down Missy's face and they remained in my living room even after I began loudly washing up, refusing to go home. I was scared they'd still be there by the time I had wiped every part of the kitchen counter three times, but when I peeped back into the room it was empty. Just a hint of damp donkey in the air and a scattering of salt spilt on the table. I sat on a chair, just sat.

My shoes sounded more like slippers a little later as I trailed through my flat going through the motions, closing the blinds, throwing a ball of paper into the bin, then switching off the toilet light. I sat on a chair and stared at a grey square on the wall where someone had tested a new paint colour a decade earlier, before picking the eavesdropper file up off the table and opening it. So much had happened since I'd first read the application forms yet the paper looked fresh and still smelt like the inside of the stationary cupboard. I read every detail – the first names, the surnames, the middle names, the postcodes, the dates of birth, the genders and the array of signatures, each unique: sprawling, uptight, unstable, shaky, reckless. My injured eye watered, I couldn't stop it; I couldn't stop it; my good eye watered too.

MISSY's nose was blocked and her eyes itchy, but she ignored them as she slipped her key into her keyhole and entered her flat on soundless feet. She looked across the living room, past the sofa, along the floorboards, halfway up the wall. *They* were waiting for her.

She approached the mantelpiece. The family hadn't moved – same straight-backed father, same yellow-haired mother and same expressionless child, her eyes badly painted, her head out of scale with her neck. Dust was there too, veiling the tiny plastic chicken beside the father's elbow, the knives and forks, the three plates touching the outstretched fingertips. Missy ground her teeth and sniffed, ground and sniffed. Then with over-sized fingers she lifted the child from its chair and sat it gently down on the mother's lap.

CHAPTER

33

A whole day passed before I plucked up the courage to tell Wilson what I'd done.

I knew this moment, the *great confession* as James christened it, had to come. My eyes were itching as I hovered outside Wilson's door, so I scratched them, both of them, with nails and for a long time. Done.

The door opened. "What are you doing hovering about out there? Come in."

Wilson wore his usual suit, the one with white stitching, but he also had on a wide orange tie. I could not take my watering eyes off it.

"Thanks," I said, sliding into the room.

"Take a seat, William. You alright?"

"Yes, thank you." My vision cleared and I felt myself to be in his space, perching rather than lounging, grimacing rather than smiling. It struck me – applying for a job, losing a job – we do the same things: smile inanely, agree with everything that is said, and dredge up manners that make us look like automatons.

"So to what do I owe this pleasure?"

"It's over," I said.

"What's over?" he replied, his voice uncharacteristically firm.

I thought he was joking, but no, he had his hands on his desk in a managerial way. His features were arranged just so.

"I've abandoned the eavesdropper project."

Abandoned. The word was hardly out of my mouth before I realised how poor a choice it was.

Wilson narrowed his eyes in the way, which for a man so benign, was chilling. "Abandoned?"

"Yes. There were problems."

"What sort of problems?"

"The data … it wasn't quantifiable."

"I see." He looked normal, his eyes blank, mouth a bit shifty. "So it was all for nothing – the training, the money?"

I nodded and looked down at the table. "It just wasn't a good idea."

"And what about the people. Did they go willingly?"

I held his eye. "Yes. Of course."

He looked at me for so long I found myself counting the moles on his nose. "I'll have to find you a new project," he said. "Something a little more … conventional."

I smiled. I nodded. The sound of a distant plane entered the room.

Lies. Lies. Lies caused cold sores; cold sores caused lies. I sat alone in my office and rubbed Herpesan onto my upper lip. The eavesdropper project was over. The file would be closed, documents shredded and the notebooks archived in the dusty room with the locked door in the basement. I opened Violet's notebook and read.

No. 27 bus. 3 pm
Boy: What happens when a star explodes?
Girl: What?
Boy: Do you know what happens when a star explodes?
Girl: No.
Boy: The world moves away.

Girl: What do you mean?

Boy: The stars are holding us in place.

Girl: What's your favourite place?

Boy: Scotland and Ukraine. Ukraine is so big there is a bridge to
it.

Girl: Is there a bridge to London?

Boy: Yes, there's lots of bridges to London.

I closed the book again and stared into space. It was *my* property
in a way, or the firm's at least, but with Violet gone it seemed personal,
a diary halted in mid-sentence. She had personalised hers with doodles
and hearts, plus it had an aroma, a musky scent that I'd last smelt on my
collar as a sixteen-year-old behind a shed on a caravan site in Hastings.

The eavesdroppers hadn't wanted to relinquish their notebooks
at the end of our final meeting, but I'd insisted. You've bloody *got* to,
I'd growled as their faces fell and their fingers tightened. Eventually
they'd given in and I'd returned all the books to my desk drawer, and
turned the key.

I pulled a sheaf of papers from my in tray. Wilson's hallmark ver-
biage littered the top sheet – *the company appreciates … a resumption
of duties … assist Mr. Gingold with …* and I felt shitty as I turned off
my computer, put on my coat and left the building. I couldn't face the
Tube so I walked along the Embankment, crossed Hungerford Bridge,
strolled along the Southbank then doubled back across Westminster
Bridge and started the long walk through the royal parks to the eggshell
blue houses of South Kensington.

I liked it there; I wanted to live there, but I didn't stop, I walked on
for another half hour, treating the city as a country walk – shrivelled
berries in the hedges, leaves in the puddles – until I came to the cheap
end of Fulham Road. Here I walked more slowly, gazing at my reflection in each shop window: off licence, betting shop, hardware store,
launderette. My reflection and I stopped together; I looked through
my face into the launderette.

A woman sat alone on a bench. She looked directly at me, her face as raw as a smacked bum. Not Eve. Thank God, not Eve.

JACK flicked through the pages of his new play. *Pages* – tens of them. In some sections the words had lost their shape, collapsing into circles of no meaning and mixed with slack letters lying down on the line as if they had died. But in others the words sat up straight, bolt and ready to go. He'd been up half the night working on it. He had a plot; he had characters; he felt he had touched the poetic part of the play, the elusive *other*. He even had a title: *Didn't See it Coming*.

He'd almost forgotten the joy of writing. Yet the grubby bundle of papers was the proof scattered in front of him; he hadn't dreamt it, he'd written lines and every day, every minute he could go and check. They were there on the page. Once written, they were always there.

But he was tired. Tired and sad. He closed his manuscript, sipped from a glass of water and gazed into space. He missed his listening notebook. It usually rested on the corner of the table, but now that corner was bare. Mr. Harcourt had gathered them up at the last meeting like a priest collecting bibles at the end of a sermon, but Jack had held it together. His features hadn't cracked; his eyes hadn't filled with tears. Even his voice, usually the part of his body most likely to let him down, had held steady. But now he was wavering.

He picked up his bank statement that lay open on the table. He'd taken three months unpaid leave to be part of the project and now here he was, unemployed for a month, soon to be very broke. He'd wanted to ask about money at the meeting, not long after the terrible moment when Mr. Harcourt had detonated his grenade, but in the outbreak of anguish which followed, it had seemed churlish to mention something as mundane as paying the gas bill.

Jack went over to what he called *The Cupboard*. Here, in extreme order lay the tools of his trade: empty notebooks, erasers still in their wrappers, pencil sharpeners, coloured pencils. He picked out a small notebook with a grey cover and then found a 2B pencil, its lead as sharp as a pin. Finally, he put on his coat, checked he had his Tube pass, slipped the book and pencil into his pocket and left the building.

CHAPTER

34

I left work early the next day, tired of reading through Sammy Gringold's tedious statistical analysis. Jean had given me an odd look as I passed her office and I glimpsed Wilson out of the corner of my eye as I brushed the coffee machine, and as I left the building I wondered briefly if I'd get into trouble, but no, I didn't care.

With my hands stuffed into my pockets I walked towards Covent Garden – land of scented soap shops and overpriced cappuccino. Yet on that day the air wasn't filled with the perfume of lavender and vanilla but with the smell of a laundry somewhere close by. I paused outside the back entrance of a hotel and breathed slowly in, imagining the suds chugging and sheets spinning.

I set off towards Covent Garden Tube Station at a brisk rate, took the Piccadilly Line until I reached the enamel-striped station at Holloway Road. Before I knew it I was standing outside Eve's launderette, not daring to turn round and look in, such was the weight of premonition straddling my shoulders. I felt heat on my back from the interior as the door was opened, then closed. Opened then closed. Opened.

"Mr. Harcourt."

The voice I knew well. The clothes dredged up a memory of a time before, but the face, oh God, the face. "Eve! Is that you?"

The face smiled. A line of pus squeezed out from a fold of skin. "Yes."

"What ... bloody hell, what happened?" I touched her arm, held my hand there.

The smile withered. "Let's go somewhere else ... can we? And I'll ... tell you."

"Yes. Yes, let's go."

Somewhere else was a greasy spoon halfway up the Holloway Road. Eve seemed unsure at first about entering, but it started to rain so we went inside and found a table in the corner.

"I hardly recognised you," I said.

She squeezed out another smile. "I hardly recognise myself."

I waited for some elaboration, but it didn't come. Eve fingered the menu.

"Cup of tea?" I said.

"Yes. Thank you."

I got up and ordered from the counter. I watched steam rise from a teapot then turned round to look at Eve. Eve was gone.

"Eve...." I yelled at the door. "Eve!" I rushed over and picked up my coat – "Cancel the tea, sorry," – and ran out of the cafe. Rain rushed into my eyes, up into my nostrils; the street blurred as I scanned it. Then I spotted her in the distance.

She'd got quite far. A man, reeling from being recently knocked into, indicated her direction with a furious shake of his eyebrows. I scampered across the wet pavement. "Eve!" I bellowed. "Eeeve!"

She *had* to stop. She had to show her bruised face again and tell me what happened. I ran and caught her up and lay my hand on her arm. "Eve, please wait."

Her cheeks were soaked when she turned round to face me. Rain or tears, the colour is the same.

"I'm sorry," she said. "I don't know why I was so stupid. I–"

"Eve," I said. "Let's go to my place. We can talk there."

"Alright," she said in a voice that was dead.

We took the Tube in silence. I wanted a chance to think but it was hard not to listen to a man in a bedraggled and pungent Afghan coat giving the carriage his loud opinion on Londoners – "Even in moments of great excitement the people of London are thinking of their homes as the centre of their lives."

It was a teasing point, but I avoided dwelling on it by watching the woman opposite me who was looking for something lost in her bag, pocket after pocket, zip after zip.

"People of London are scarcely human," continued the bard. "They should be kept as far out of London as possible…."

I read the Tube map. I counted the stations between Epping and Ealing Broadway; I examined the skin on the edge of my thumb. Anything. Anything to avoid looking at Eve's poor punched face. But the memory was there. Engraved into my mind like an inscription on a trophy.

Eve wouldn't take off her coat when we arrived at my flat, but she accepted a cup of tea, which she sipped painfully, perched on the edge of my sofa like a pigeon on a damp ledge.

I sat opposite her and I took her hand in mine "Eve," I said. "What on earth happened?"

The train shot through the tunnel; it roared between the embankments, over the viaduct, between the fields with cows. I had bought a cheap Saturday return at London Bridge and was now leaning back in my seat, watching the Kent Stations flash past the window, reading the names, not reading the names, reading the names. My heart, an organ to which I didn't usually pay much attention, was racing too, a disconcerting thumping, which, if I let myself think it, hurt. I'd never felt such an urgent feeling to *be* somewhere. To just *get* there, for God's sake. And in all the rush, the breathy panic of hailing a taxi, the desperate fumbling to get the money out of my wallet, I had forgotten the most important thing. I had not told *him* I was coming.

I got off the train at Lydd. The platform was still deserted and, unable to get a signal on my phone, I unfolded the map I'd sketched on the back of a serviette, and headed in the direction of the house. The oppressive flatness to the place I'd felt on my first visit was upon me. Flatness and sadness. Something about the stretches of yellow grass, and the light, an eerie mould of green and grey, gave me a funny, nervous feeling. Signs marked my route. Not traffic signs but fish signs, fixed to every surface that would take a nail: jellied eels, whelks, dressed crabs, local lobsters and fresh bait, all for sale. Who was buying these salty wares remained a mystery as I walked down the empty street, but I kept going, past a small rowing boat beached on the pavement, past an obscenely thin concrete fence until I reached number 21 Battery Road.

This home didn't want visitors. The grass in the front garden had turned to straw and only a handful of mournful daisies struggled through cracks in the tarmac drive. The house was a beige pebbledash bungalow, with lace-curtained windows and lichen growing on its roof. The only spot of colour was a blue gas canister that sat mournfully by the front door. Dust rose from the grass as approached the house and pressed the bell. No one answered and I waited, just me and the canister and the dead grass and the big mouldy sky.

I licked the sore on my lip, trying to decide if it would be worth going back to the cafe. But glancing at my watch I realised it was almost five o'clock so I turned round and headed towards Lydd's one and only pub.

It was easy to find The Britannia Inn; the smell of fish and chips led the way and five minutes later I was walking across the forecourt and feeling even more unease as I glanced up at the St. George's flag that flapped so disapprovingly at me. The empty flowerpots marking the entrance made me want to call my mother and ask what they meant. Funny how the cracked little pots felt more threatening than the nuclear power station that squatted broodily on the horizon. I crossed the threshold and sidled up to the bar, a welcoming collection of pump handles, liquor on a shelf at the back, red cash register, everything red, ice bucket, beer mats and a poster that read *No Fokker Comes Close*. I sat on a red velvet stool, ordered a pint of *Bishop's Finger* and remembered the reason for my frightened heart.

Eve's story the night before had been breathy, but to the point. Words meant moving muscles and moving muscles meant pain so I asked her to keep it simple. It *was* simple. So simple it could be boiled down to three words: *launderette, man, punch*. The man had needed help on the domestic front. Of course he did, I'd agreed, everyone needs a bit of help on the domestic front from time to time. And then, she said, 'I think I went too far.' Everyone goes a bit far sometimes, I'd replied, tightening my mug in my fingers. Then her sore face muscles seemed to loosen and she told me the whole grubby story. The man hadn't appreciated her leaflet on getting limescale off his taps. And Eve hadn't appreciated that alcohol and limescale advice don't mix and only noticed the smell on his breath after it was too late. But, no, it wasn't as bad as it looked she'd kept saying and no, she hadn't told the police. I took her home after she'd drunk three cups of tea, only just resisting the urge to lead her across the road, and I lingered outside her house for over an hour, watching her window and feeling like a complete shit. Once home I spent a further two hours thinking, agonising, wondering what the hell to do. And, on top of the anxiety about Eve there was another worry beginning to gnaw at me. Perhaps Eve wasn't the only eavesdropper still at work.

The bartender had the knack of looking at my face while wiping the glass in his hand with a tea towel; there was something a little pervy in the way he rubbed.

Loth to speak, I spoke. "So, what's the story behind those big concrete things up by the gravel pits?" I said.

Forget thirty-four, I was yet to reach twelve years of age beneath the weight of his gaze. "What big concrete things?"

"Those sound mirrors. You must have–"

"Never heard of them."

He continued to polish the glass. I took a swig of my drink; too late I noticed lipstick on the rim as I put it back down on the bar.

"Want a top up?" he said.

"No thanks."

The man slapped what to me seemed an overly wet cloth across my part of the bar, but as he turned back to the pumps I thought of something. "Don't know a bloke called Raymond Watt do you? He loves round here – I mean *lives* round here."

"Never heard of him." The man reached up and pulled a fresh glass from the rack above the bar. "Not many blokes with a name like that loving round here."

"Right." There weren't many people I couldn't read, but this man, not a morsel. "I'll be off then."

"I'll listen out for him."

"Pardon?"

"That Watt bloke. I'll listen out for him."

"Yeah, right … I don't actually live round here … but, thanks."

The path was rougher than I remembered and even though I'd worn what my mother called 'sturdies' the pebbles felt greasy beneath my feet. I slipped a couple of times and once fell over completely, feeling foolish in spite of being alone. A duck watched me though. From the safety of a reedy enclave he looked at me as if I had something important to say.

"Watcha, mate," I said. "Bet you've seen some stuff."

The duck didn't reply, he just dipped his beak into the water and shook a slimy looking bundle of weed down his throat.

I walked up to the first mirror, hovered in its shadow then strolled towards the long wall. The long listening mirror seemed bigger than I remembered and recent spalling had left little piles of concrete chips at its feet. I stood at one end with my back to it, my spine pressed against its face. I closed my eyes. I could hear the wind and I could hear the sound of the reeds rubbing together. I also fancied I heard the sound of an aeroplane coming but I didn't, just the wind and the grass. Everything seemed simple here, but my life wasn't simple. It was complicated and I was in trouble. *We* were in trouble. I wanted someone to blame. I urgently needed an unwitting patsy at whom I could point my now shaky finger and say, *he* did it. But I couldn't. The unholy mess was all my fault.

As I opened my eyes I noticed a flash of red out of the corner of my eye. A woman, no, a couple, stood by the water at the far end of the long listening wall a couple of hundred yards away. Their backs were towards me. They seemed to be looking at something in the water. Then the man turned to the woman and whispered in her ear. "I'll never smile again," he said.

EVE took a bottle of antiseptic out of the bathroom cupboard. Then she picked up a piece of cotton wool, dropped some liquid on to it and dabbed her face. It hurt. Of course it hurt, her mother always said antiseptic *had* to hurt. Otherwise it wasn't working. She held her breath and dabbed again. It was hard not to cry. Tear salt was an antiseptic too, but it stung her skin. How it stung.

She went into her bedroom, sat on the bed and thought about Mr. Harcourt. He hadn't been cross with her. No, he'd held her hand and looked deep into her eyes. He'd stared hard at her puffed-up old face. His shoulder had even touched hers. She was the one who'd got cross. In spite of the sting in her face she had told him not to tell anyone what had happened. In return she was never to go to the launderette ever again.

She smoothed her hand across her eiderdown, the sound of her mother's hand, tucking her in. The silence of the room seemed to beat in her ears. But there was no silence. As she squeezed her eyelids shut she absorbed the sounds moving in the room: the rustle of pleats unfolding on her knee, a whistle of air within the hairs of her nose, and the hum of the fridge through the wall. And another hum, lower, further away. She couldn't remember if it had always been there.

She stood up and went along the landing into her box room. It was cold in there, always left unheated to save on the heating bill. There were more boxes than she remembered, stacked on shelves from floor to ceiling and the labels, she noticed for the first time, looked shabby. The piles of out-of-date leaflets, crisp with cold, suddenly overwhelmed her, *tax, eviction, debt, domestic abuse, mental illness, redundancy, marriage guidance, pensions, benefits, personal injury.* She sat on the chair by the door and more salt stung her face. Something for every person's dilemma, but nothing for her.

CHAPTER

35

Victoria Station looked bashed up by the time I got off the train – bins overflowed with coffee-stained cups and weary commuters were perched on every horizontal: benches, tops of suitcases, the hard bases of roof columns. The flowers at the florists were closed and there was a sense that something had happened, something that had dirtied the floor and left a faint whiff of the office in the air. The concourse was still pockmarked with stragglers and their possessions: suitcases on wheels, magazines in plastic bags, hands in pockets, hands holding newspapers. A clump of bodies parted effortlessly as a lone commuter stopped to think, tweaked his chin, rubbed his neck and then moved on again. Anybody would have been able to tell I was a Londoner the way I navigated the platform so easily, nipping through the space behind the coffee cart, shortcutting, trimming my route, walking as the crow would fly. I rushed down into the Tube station, *clackety clack, clackety clack,* and sank into a seat, warm in the tunnel, relaxed in my body, yet busy in my mind. I couldn't find Raymond. I couldn't find Raymond. I had to find the eavesdroppers.

The street lamps were out when I reached the front of my building and I cursed the keyhole as I tried to insert my key. Once inside I went over to the window and looked out. The building opposite sat hunched. It was wrapped in sheeting, all over sheeting, yet somehow seemed different, like a monster that had changed position in the night. Still in my coat, I went back down the stairs, opened the front door and walked over to the building site. But *site* wasn't the right word any more. The building had almost filled its plot – I realised this as I paced round the back of it. Even the slivers of remaining ground were filled with bits of unfinished building: concrete columns with rebar poking out and internal brickwork with rough mortar joints. And wheelbarrows. Everywhere there were wheelbarrows. But still, however many positions I tried in the street, I couldn't see the shape or full extent of it.

"Oi, you!"

I turned to see a man approaching. His eyes were fixed on me and he was rolling up a coat sleeve in a parody of annoyance.

"What are you doing here?" he said as he reached me.

"Looking."

"What are you looking *at*?"

I disliked the *duh* that James insisted on using in times of blinding obviousness, but it seemed to be bubbling up from my throat. "Du … building."

He placed his feet more firmly on the pavement. "At eleven o'clock at night?"

I pointed towards my window. "I live opposite."

Even in the low light I could see his lips tighten. "We don't like people looking at night."

"Who are we?" I said.

He cleared his throat. "My employers."

"Who *are* your employers?"

"It's a con … conglomerate."

"No name then?"

He cleared his throat. "It's a security company. We do security."

I glanced at his jacket. It could have graced the shoulders of a bailiff or a debt collector with a dubious resume. "Seriously, what is the name of the company?"

'I can't divulge."

Divulge. Coming from this man's mouth the word sounded faintly obscene. "I see."

He cleared his throat yet again. "You need to move on."

I sighed and moved on. I couldn't be bothered to be bolshie, but I felt annoyed. I crossed the road, my feet slapping the ground in a way that said 'in my own time' and then stopped at the entrance to my building and looked back. The man had gone. The building looked black, blacker than the night sky behind it. I closed my eyes and listened. A sound came towards me. The *hum*. Louder than usual, right inside my head. Starting to get on my nerves. I put my hands over my ears. The hum carried on.

I was uncertain what time I opened my eyes the next morning. I felt it was early but the light in the room was the bright white of daybreak. I left my bed bad-tempered, troubled by the vague necessity of having to get dressed and brush my teeth, and I showered to the tunes of the radio but didn't sing-along. I skipped breakfast, drank a glass of water, pulled on my coat and went down to the street.

I remembered the pleasure my rounds had given me only a few weeks earlier, the little buds of pride I'd felt as I observed the eavesdroppers at work, the thrill of imagining what they might discover. Now I was the spoilsport policeman, the saddo who no longer encouraged my team with sound bites and rousing spiels but checked that they were no longer at work.

Violet first. The windows of the cafe were steamed up when I arrived. I tried to peer in but all I could see were vague outlines and occasional movement as the shapes wriggled, grew and then shrunk.

But suddenly, just as I was wondering if I dared go inside, the palm of a small hand appeared in front of my face and wiped a circle in the condensation. I stepped back and waited, but nothing appeared in the opening so I stepped forward and looked in. Violet sat at a table in the corner of the room. Just an innocent coffee, surely? Then I looked down at her hand and saw a pencil held between her fingers. Shit. Shit. Shit.

In spite of the weights accumulating in my stomach I rushed round the rest of the eavesdropping haunts at high speed, springing onto the bus as it left the stop, cursing the smallness of the steps as I scuttled down into the Tube.

The launderette windows were even more steamed up than the cafe, but what looked like the work of a large body had wiped a hole in the condensation and I could see Eve clearly, sitting in that signature listening pose of hers. I didn't go in, just plodded back to the Tube and travelled the circle line, imagining every now and then I'd caught a whiff of Jack, until I reached Stanley's neck of the woods. Here I concealed myself in the alcove of a block of flats and watched the door to the dentist for over three hours until I saw Stanley turn the corner. He straightened his tie at the door and went inside with the apprehensive air of someone on a blind date. I didn't even bother making an attempt on the Ladies toilet in Camden Town. I knew what I would find. I didn't know what I would find.

I was standing adrift in the street, thinking things couldn't get any worse, when my phone vibrated in my pocket.

Never in all my dreams, never in all my boyhood fantasies of being the leader of a gang had I imagined I would be going out late at night at the age of thirty-four in order to threaten a girl. James came with me. His face dripped misgiving but he was there, trotting by my side in what I could only imagine was his gangster outfit: jeans, bomber jacket and scuffed-up shoes. He'd swept his hair back in a strange and greasy way and I'd felt nervous when he joined me at the exit to Camden Town Tube.

We'd planned our strategy in the pub the night before. After her phone call and tearful plea for help Missy had seemed frightened at the sight of James at my elbow. But I'd explained the reason for his presence, and after a few minutes, between gulps of lager and lime, she'd told us what we didn't want to hear. Guilt prickled in my chest as she pulled up her sleeve and revealed a fresh bandage, whiter than before.

'It's just one girl,' she'd told us. 'But I need you to help me … to make her go away. Please make her go away.'

James had looked increasingly anxious as we hatched our plan. Missy would point out the girl from behind the safety of a scarf and James and I, the toughs that we were, would speak to her. Neither of us mentioned the elephant in the room, and only when the smell of dung became too great did I acknowledge the fact inside my head. We were scared too.

Yet after forty-five minutes of loitering in front of a mobile phone shop with a mind-numbingly dull window display my fear had begun to dissipate. I was even beginning to think that stakeouts were tiring, overrated things when Missy hissed, "It's her!"

She could have been someone's forgettable niece so unremarkable was the young woman who walked towards the entrance to the ladies toilets. No leather jacket, no sharp rings on her fingers, just a nondescript coat and sensible shoes.

"Are you sure it's her?" I whispered into Missy's ear.

"I'm certain," she said. " Be careful, please."

I looked back at the shoes, then at James' pale face. "Okay, matey. Let's do this."

We crossed the road quickly, bulking up our shoulders as we closed in.

"Miss," I said.

"Yeah, Miss," James repeated.

The woman turned, and there, surrounded by a circle of mousy hair, I saw the expression that had so terrified Missy.

"What?"

"I need … we need to talk to you for a moment. Please." I'd decided I was going to start pleasantly, appeal to her nicer side.

"Fuck off."

She started to walk away.

"Just a minute!" James laid his hand on her arm. We had discussed this in the pub. We wouldn't touch her, under *no* circumstances would we touch her.

"Geddoff me!"

James snatched back his hand as if he'd been bitten. "Sorry, I didn't mean…."

I puffed out my chest, lowered my voice and put frightening spaces between my words. "Leave Missy alone."

The woman stopped and stared. "Little Miss Missy?" she said.

My turn to reply; I lowered my voice further; my eyes watered. "I'm serious, just leave Missy alone and we'll forget we ever met you."

"She was listening to me, snooping little snitch. She deserves what she gets."

"Ah, yes," I said. "Eavesdropping. It's frightening, isn't it."

The girl frowned. "What do you mean?"

"Eavesdroppers get hold of peoples' secrets."

"What has she told you?"

"Only what I need to know." Such suavity, I hardly recognised myself.

"Yeah," smooched James.

I'd forgotten he was there – just the creak of a jacket.

"Who *are* you?" asked the girl.

"I'm the eavesdropper."

Up until then the title had been gentle, a lazy, relaxed word that suggested one lay back and waited for words to float into one's ears. But somehow I'd injected it with menace. I think I might even have shown my teeth as I enunciated the 'e.'

Years seemed to drop from the woman; she pushed her hair behind her ears; she licked the sore resting on her lip. "Alright," she said, "I'll let her go."

I didn't reply – just looked. "But tell her," she glanced across the street, "tell her not to come down any more."

"Down to the toilet, you mean?" asked James, looking relieved to be making a contribution.

The years poured back. "Yeah, down to the toilet."

"I'll tell her." Now a master of the clipped retort I managed to end my sentence there.

Suppressing an instinct to bid her farewell I turned and walked briskly away, my gaze fixed on the phone shop, praying that James was with me. I smelt damp leather.

"Bloody hell, what happened?" said James through his teeth.

"Don't speak," I replied, through even tighter incisors.

We walked fast, but with dignity, leaving the toilet behind us and crossing the street on our own terms.

Like a rapidly rising moon Missy's face appeared out of the gloom of a side street. "What happened?"

"Sorted," announced James happily.

"She won't bother you again, Missy," I said, definitely taller. "But you mustn't go down into those toilets again. Ever."

"Okay." The moon waxed, then waned. "Thank you."

"Thank *him*," said James, deflecting her gratitude in my direction. "Bill's the one who ... who did it."

My voice remained loud. I bade James and Missy farewell using unnecessary decibels; I boomed out my order when I picked up a coffee on my way home and I yelled 'Good evening' to my neighbour on the stairs so loudly that she backed up against the wall. Only when I was telling myself that I fancied a late-night bowl of cereal did my voice lower and my chest regain its regular profile. Over the crunch of cornflakes I went over the details of the encounter in my mind: the sore, the smell of leather, the taut circle of Missy's face.

Then I lay on my bed fully dressed. 'Sorted' James had said. Everything sorted out. But it wasn't. The eavesdroppers were still roaming the streets of London, pen and notebook in hand. I'd started something that had taken on a life of its own. It had to stop. *I* had to stop it.

I didn't know how.

STANLEY had a toothache. It was one of those big molars at the back, which had ground its way through fifty years of pork chops and gristle and bacon skin, but now was prone to flaking and exposed nerves. He'd tried to stem the creaking pain with antiseptic swilled round his gums and even embarked on a week of one-sided chewing, but still it throbbed and stabbed and bothered his every thought. The receptionist at the dentist's had been unduly surly when he made the appointment, but she'd grudgingly found him a spot and now he sat in his usual chair. Waiting.

He'd regretted telling the others about the girl. They'd got it all wrong. He thought they'd be proud of him for looking outwards instead of in. But no, they'd ticked him off like a schoolboy who had looked up a girl's skirt. Beryl had disapproved too. She hadn't gone near her new cuttlefish for a whole day and even the Christmas edition of the Lonely Hearts ads slipped beneath her feet had failed to bring her out of her sulk.

With his eyes on the *National Geographic* his ears went to work. He could hear all the sounds of the room: the squeak of the reception-ist's chair (he hoped it was uncomfortable), the tap of her keyboard and the rhythmic breathing through diseased lungs of the only other occupant of the room. He knew the sound of diseased lungs; after forty years of smoking he had them himself. Then his ears expanded their range, beyond the walls, beyond the garden and out into the street, from where he heard a new sound. The murderous drone of a chainsaw, cutting down a tree.

Stanley could taste blood in his saliva as he flicked through the magazine. Someone had drawn a moustache above the mammoth's reconstructed lips since he'd last been there, which made him feel sad. He was so busy trying to rub the whiskers off with his thumb that he didn't notice someone had come into the waiting room, until they coughed. A child's cough. And there she was. Hardly more than ten years old, she sat on the chair like a miniature woman. Alone.

The girl looked blandly in his direction then winced as the high-pitched whine of the chainsaw pierced the room. This was the moment Stanley had been waiting for. He pulled back his lips and smiled the pearliest, healthiest and most hygienic of smiles. She didn't smile back; she looked out of the window.

He studied the small silver bag on her lap. What was inside, he wondered. Her bus fare? A tiny doll perhaps? He didn't have to wait long to find out. Small fingers pulled the zip and delved inside. He could hear the contents rubbing against one another other as she rummaged. She paused and Stanley stopped breathing as the girl pulled out a small, glass bird. Its body was transparent but the head was yellow and the wings blue.

Stanley rose from his seat slowly. He walked over to where the girl was sitting and sat down beside her. "That's a pretty bird," he said.

"His name's Bobby." The girl looked at Stanley's eyebrows.

Stanley held out his hand. "Can I hold him?"

The girl met his eye then placed the bird gently down on Stanley's outstretched palm. It weighed nothing. Legless and smooth, it lay on its side as if mortally wounded.

"That's a *very* pretty bird," he said.

The girl smiled up into his face.

"I have a bird in my house," he continued.

"What's his name?"

"Beryl. He's a *she*."

The girl touched her cheeks. "Bobby could be her boyfriend."

"Yes." Stanley glanced round the now empty waiting room, then at the vacant reception desk. "Would you like to meet her?"

She touched her cheeks again. "Yes!"

Stanley took a deep breath. "Would your mother bring you?"

The girl shook her head. "She works."

"Can you remember things?" Stanley asked.

"*What* things?" The girl's hands were back on her lap.

"Names and things?"

"Yes, silly."

"I live at 12 Barnet's Lane. Come whenever you like. Just knock on the door. And bring Bobby."

The girl took the bird out of Stanley's hand and slipped it back into the silver bag.

Stanley glanced round the room again. No one was there but he, the girl, and the bird. No one was listening. No one would hear his belting heart.

CHAPTER

36

In spite of the worry that now tugged at my insides, I brushed my teeth, drank tea, nibbled a piece of toast and went to work early next day. If my blood flowed faster then the hands of the clock moved more slowly and the morning dragged with the weight of my thoughts. Although not hungry I took an early lunch and left the office just before midday. I liked to think I knew London inside out, but occasionally I was drawn down one of the many alleys that cut through the city where my mental map would dissolve and my bearings be lost. I wanted to be lost. I needed to find solace in a place full of strangers.

I knew I'd be late back to the office but I kept on walking, enjoying the unfamiliarity of London's secret arteries and as I popped out into the bright light of Ludgate Hill I saw the dome of St. Paul's rising from the end of the street and felt the bulky happiness of being a Londoner.

I walked up the steps of the cathedral, feeling a shiver in my back. It was an effort, lifting my feet up the high steps, each stone smoothed by thousands of earlier feet, yet I glided easily through the massive doors into the most imposing, no, the most sacred church in all of London. I could be tempted by this, I thought as I gazed up at the central dome. The grandeur seemed to pull me in further, lead me down the aisle and offer me a seat close to the altar. But the dripping smile of a wide-skirted clergywoman, eager to assist and smelling of wax, was enough to persuade me back onto my feet and I walked in the direction of another set of stairs at the side of the main aisle, not made of stone, but crafted in wood.

A sign on the wall gave stark warning to the feebler members of the congregation. *Two hundred and fifty-seven steps up to the Whispering Gallery.*

It was hard to picture the effort involved: the calculation of height, the ache in the legs, but I went up, up and up, then up some more. And not just me; the sound of a weary person shadowed my every step, breathing heavily, gasping out a 'holy shit' as we paused on each landing, me hoping it would be the last.

Then I heard another sound, deeper in the void behind me. Childish voices drifted up from below, "I'm tired." "These steps are too big." "Can we have lunch up there?"

Then a teacher's voice, projectile, out of breath. "Kids, you're going to love this place. But you have to whisper."

I walked faster. I passed a locked door, then another, and then another. Finally, with the steps behind me and my heart beating heavily in my neck, I entered the Whispering Gallery – a vast circular room with a hole in the centre of the floor that dropped down to the main space below. I peeped over the railing that circled the void and saw black and white tiles dotted with tops of heads, whole people reduced to bald spots and partings and thick, optimistic comb-overs.

The gallery was empty, just me and the people painted on the huge domed ceiling, all dressed in robes, lots of folds in their robes, all sitting at the feet of the painted orator. Listening. And behind the orator a horse reared, its mane thrown up, the inside of its mouth purple. There seemed to be something coming straight out the horse's mouth.

I sat on the curved bench that lined the entire room, sat at the feet of the orator. I saw no one. I heard no one, and as I looked up thoughts of a god began to preoccupy me. The misty light trapped in the top of the dome could have been *his* doing. The painted men in robes were listening to someone; *I* was listening, my head tipped back, not caring that my mouth hung open.

I sat up straight as the children filed into the other side of gallery, their small faces blurred by distance across the vast space of the room. Voices seeped out from behind the locked doors, "sit," "sit," "sit."

The dome coughed.

Then a whisper in my ears, "hello, hello, hello, hello, hello." More children entered, "sit" "sit." "Johnny, just sit."

Then the long whisper, "schh … schh … schh.…"

I put my ear to the wall.

"This is beautiful," said the wall.

I pressed my ear closer.

"It's boring," said the wall. "I want to go to the shop."

Then I heard a new noise, the muffled voice of a sermon starting far below me, 257 steps further down. I stood up and looked over the railing. So much was being said but I could only hear one repeated word that floated up towards me, "Jesus, Jesus, Jesus." *Jesus wept.*

I looked up at the ceiling men in robes. Was it them speaking? Or the orator with his big muscular arms, or the horse, its lips pulled back.

More children filed into the gallery with their teacher, "sit, sit, sit, schh … schh …" spreading along the long wall, more and more. Conversations were everywhere: behind the locked doors, inside the wall, inside my head. "Sit, sit, schh, schh.…"

Suddenly, I couldn't stand it: the dome, the void, the painted robes, the inside of the horse's mouth, the locked doors, the children – the low, insistent whispers.

I put my hands over my ears; I drew in a breath and opened my mouth wide. "Stop! Stop talking! I don't want to hear any more! Stop!"

The line of children turned to face me. I could hear someone crying behind me, crying inside the wall.

The wall spoke. "Jesus wept."

It was hard to run down the stairs. The shallow steps, so kind on the way up, were hard to judge on the descent and twice I nearly fell, first clutching at the handle of one of the locked doors then grabbing the elbow of an upcoming woman who swayed like a swooning statue. "Sorry! So sorry."

I rushed back up the aisle, through the great doors and down into the square outside the cathedral. But here the noise of the world seemed even louder, people everywhere, chatting, laughing, arguing, getting the last word. I couldn't turn the sound down. I rushed on, past everyone and everything, my ears chased by the loudest words, those of a street preacher clutching a handful of leaflets. "Jesus! Remember Jesus."

Jesus wept.

I rushed back towards the office, primed to swerve around anyone who crossed my path. And many people did. A tangled mob of bewildered tourists stopped me crossing the road as I strode down The Strand, then a taxi driver nearly ran over my toes as it mounted the kerb to drop off its ride. A large party of pensioners collecting their luggage from the side of a coach was my final obstacle, and in spite of my plummeting mood I was forced to stop and smile as they spilled across the pavement in a chaotic spectacle of Zimmer frames, handbags and suitcases on wheels.

An elderly man leant against the coach, his mouth crinkled like the peel of a dried-up orange. He was mouthing something, drowned out by the drone of the traffic.

I turned my ear in his direction.

"Listen," he wailed. "Will someone listen to me?"

I stared at the grid of wrinkles on his cheeks, felt phlegm form in my throat, and rushed on.

Wilson's office was empty as I drifted by in a coat of nonchalance. I slipped into my office and started an afternoon of fake business.

"You all right?" said James.

"Yeah."

"You sure you're alright?"

"Yeah."

"What are you doing?"

"Oh, you know. Stuff."

I tidied my desk, James observed me, and then I typed random letters of the alphabet on a blank page. I studied it after, noting that two combinations kept cropping up by themselves: *self* and *skew*. Finally, I let myself pause, sat back in my chair and thought of St. Paul's: the painted ceiling, the painted horse, the purple painted mouth. It had seemed that something was coming straight from the horse's mouth. I turned the phrase over in my mouth in silence. Straight from the horse's mouth.

I flung open my drawer, dragged out some paper, grabbed a pen and started to write.

VIOLET had never touched *his* grass before. She waited until the last light went out in the upstairs bedroom then tiptoed across the front garden and lay down against the side of the house. Grass was her mattress, and ivy, crisp with frost, was her pillow. She shivered several times before she relaxed, feeling separated from the world. She looked up. The underside of the eaves was dark against the luminous night sky, but she could see drips of rainwater on the edge of the roof. She wanted one to drop onto her face, a cold drip that had been hanging there, waiting for the moment. But the drop didn't move; it clung to the eaves. Violet put her hand into her pocket and pulled out her phone. She dialled. She didn't speak. She listened.

"Hello? Hello? Hello. . . . Who is this? I know you're there. I can hear you breathing. . . . For God's sake! *Say* who it is or stop calling me.... I know you're there.... Bloody coward. I can hear you, you know. I can hear you breathing. I can hear you."

CHAPTER
37

They were late, all of them. I sat alone in the meeting room, my ears tuned to the direction of the corridor, straining, willing, sifting, but no sound came.

Fog had shrouded London that morning and during my walk to the Tube I had understood why the word *fog* always got itself entangled with the word *blanket*. Muffled birds, muffled cars, muffled conversations, all seemed to be wrapped in wool. I could almost see passers-by pulling stray hairs from their mouths. The office had seemed quieter too and I found myself tiptoeing up to the room upstairs. I'd had to tell Wilson something of course. A 'final debriefing' had sounded lame even as it left my mouth, but he seemed to accept it. As I picked up a packet of saccharine and squeezed the granules one by one, I wondered if the eavesdroppers had stood me up, preferring to hatch a mini gunpowder plot, huddled round the table in Stanley's kitchen.

"Good morning, Mr. Harcourt."

I looked up. And there, yes, right there, in the meeting room with the polished table and broken phone and trolley packed with cups, stood the old man from Lydd.

"Mr. Watt! You got my letter. I thought you weren't–"

"Of course I got your letter." He moved into the room soundlessly, pulled out a chair and sat down.

"I'm so glad to see you."

His cheeks were shiny, as if painted with a ceramic glaze. "Why? Your letter was rather short on detail."

"I...." Simplicity was all I needed. And truth. "I need your help."

He didn't reply. He just stared at my mouth as though I had sworn. "I can't help you," he said. "I told you that before."

My mind hunted for something to say: words, phrases, sentences ... anything. When the words finally emerged they were tainted with sulk. "Then why did you come, Mr. Watt?"

Before he could reply voices began rumbling down the corridor – the sound of assorted sole types on wood. The door opened and five eavesdroppers entered the room, a great tumbling gang.

"Sorry, sorry, sorry, Mr. B." Stanley was raucous and dribbling and loud, so loud, and flushed in the face. "Shall we shit ... sit down? So happy to be back!" A faded eavesdropper T-shirt peeped out from the innards of his coat.

The others followed: Jack in a black jacket, Missy in a tie-dye dress and long hairy cardigan, Eve in a beige coat and white knitted gloves and Violet in a violet suit, entirely violet.

I glimpsed Watt's expression as I stood up and ushered them into their chairs. They seemed oddly unfamiliar with the room, unable to decide who should sit beside whom. When they eventually settled, an empty chair remained either side of the old man.

We sat. We all waited in complete silence. But there is never silence. We knew that. An ambulance siren wailed somewhere far away, still we sat.

I cleared my throat. "I'd like to introduce Mr. Watt, he's...." I paused. I was starting a speech I'd had no time to prepare, a great oration, a sweeping explanation that showed them how it was "... from Lydd."

The eavesdroppers slumped in their seats; Eve absent-mindedly fingered the bruise fading on her face. It looked normal, part of her.

The old man took a breath, placed his hands on the table and spoke. "You're probably wondering who I am and why I'm here."

I sensed heads nodding out of the corner of my eye.

"The reason I am here is that I was once like you. I was once an eavesdropper." He looked round the table: his forefinger lifted slightly as if he was counting something we couldn't see. "Mr. Harcourt invited me here today."

All eyes swivelled in my direction.

"I haven't been to London for thirty years," he continued, "but I felt compelled to come. I know what has happened here. What happened here has happened before. Over seventy years ago in a place called Lydd." He looked round the table, pausing at each face. "I know you have been suffering. Eavesdropping changes your life. It changes you. I know."

Fake silence descended again. Together we listened to someone in the next room drain water from the water cooler, *glug, glug, glug, glop.*

"What are we doing here?" asked Jack. "Our project is over."

With the onus thrown back so suddenly onto me I almost failed to catch it. "I ... we...."

"It's never over," said Watt. He began struggling to his feet.

"You're not going are you?" I knocked my pen off the desk – loud, so loud.

"I need to visit the toilet," he said.

"Do you need a hand? I...."

"No, thank you. I'll finish what I have to say when I get back."

"Third on the left," said Violet.

As the door closed it was Jack who spoke. "What's going on?"

"We're in ... trouble," I said.

Violet placed her hands on the table in the same way as the old man. Her spans looked big. "Who's in trouble?"

"All of us," someone said.

Silence. Then more silence. Then even more silence that filled the room and hurt my ears. I couldn't get enough air into my lungs to speak.

"Who *is* that man?" said Eve.

"Schh! He's coming back," whispered Missy.

Watt entered the room slowly, and resumed his position in the friendless chair at the top of the table. He looked around without expectation.

"Find it okay?" said Stanley.

The old man nodded. "I need to tell you a story."

We settled into our chairs, remnants of our childhood selves, all except Violet who sat bolt upright and stared straight ahead.

"I've been watching you," he began. "From the moment the advertisement for eavesdroppers blew into my garden and landed on the grass I've been watching you in my mind."

Missy's chair creaked.

"The original eavesdropper project began at Lydd in 1939. We used sound mirrors–"

"What are they?" said Stanley.

The man hesitated. "Sound mirrors were enormous concrete discs designed to listen for the German planes crossing the channel. We were a team. A close group of highly trained listeners and our job was to give warning of impending attack. To save lives. And we did. We saved thousands of lives, But…."

A pair of heels rubbed together beneath the table.

" … but … these warnings came at a cost. The eavesdroppers suffered … how they suffered. Five young, spirited men changed into five … five frightened shells of their former selves."

A pause inserted itself into the room.

"One snooped on his wife and lost her, one had a mental breakdown, one gentle soul was blinded in a fight, one gave away national secrets and was court martialled.

Missy's hands moved slowly to her cheeks. She held them there.

"Then finally, one of the eavesdroppers, the best, killed a man." He looked straight at me. "Jamie was my brother."

Brother. All the time the old man had been talking of a brother, shared DNA, shared mother, everything shared. "What ... happened?" I said.

"Jamie heard something he shouldn't have."

"What did he hear?"

"He overheard a man talking about a woman. The man ... the talking man, he had raped a woman – a woman with red hair and pale blue eyes. Just like my brother's wife – red hair, pale blue eyes."

"And then what happened?" I said.

"Jamie killed the man. Jamie went to court. Jamie, my brother, was shot by a firing squad."

Pure silence – at last. So intense, it was as if the world had halted on its axis. I became aware of the tiniest of sounds, a whoosh, a pulse in my ears.

"Our project is over," said Jack.

"It's never over," said the old man again. He glanced in my direction then gripped the sides of his chair and hauled himself to his feet.

"Are you leaving?" I said.

He pulled on his coat, walked across to the door and turned. "Yes. I have nothing else to say. Please take this as a warning. Listen to me. Don't listen any more."

I jumped up. "Let me–"

"No. I won't let you." Before anyone could move he walked nimbly though the door and shut it firmly behind him.

I slumped back in my chair and my ears slowly emptied of sound.

"Shit," said Jack.

I examined the perfect roundness of a coffee ring on the table.

Stanley sighed. "Of course, we all knew it."

"Knew what?" asked Eve quietly.

"That the listening had got to us."

"It didn't get to me," Violet said.

Stanley oozed understanding. "You maybe didn't know it, Vi, but it did."

"What shall we do now?" said Eve.

I looked at Eve. Silence again – my ears throbbed with the weight of it. I couldn't meet anyone's eye: I just stared out of the window and listened – *glug, glug, glug, glop*.

Outside 29 Craven Street. London. 5 pm.

Older woman: Awful.

Old man: You mean –

Older woman: Yes, I mean those men. Dead, and killed and … and….

Loud woman: Broken.

Young man: Who *was* that man?

Old man: Dunno. Do you think it was true? What he said?

Loud woman: *I* think it was true.

Young man: Anyone want a cigarette?

Old man: We don't smoke.

Young man: Not even a bit?

Loud woman: I'll have one.

Older woman: You won't.

Young woman: She will.

Old man: He didn't have to do it.

Young man: Do what?

Old man: Blame it on us.

Young woman: He didn't blame it on us! He stopped it.

Young man: Yeah, glad he stopped it.

Young woman: Yes, I'm so glad he stopped it.

EVE arrived at the stationer's. It was empty and she surveyed the shelves at a leisurely pace. No shop within a shop for her. This place was dedicated: a small empire of pens, nibs, inks, watermarked paper and notebooks. It smelt of books. It sounded like a library.

"Can I help you?"

Eve looked at the shop assistant's face, a woman of the grey-eyed type. "Yes. I'm looking for a notebook."

"Ah!" The woman's eyes brightened. "My area of expertise. Come this way."

With a feathery wave of her hand the woman swept Eve along to the other side of the shop. "Daily use, special occasions or gift?" she said, as they paused at a shelf.

"Daily use … that is special."

"Oh.…"

Eve didn't want to be mean, but she did want to be precise. She felt no sympathy as she watched the woman struggle for a reply.

"Well … it depends a bit on your budget."

"I don't have a budget."

The woman searched her face. "Well. *I* like this one." She picked a notebook off the shelf.

"I like that one too." Eve took the leather-bound book and sniffed its cover.

"May I ask what you are going to use it for?" asked the woman.

"Making a record."

"Oh. A record of what might I enquire?"

"Life."

"I see.…"

CHAPTER

38

I promise. I promise I won't. Pale, wide-eyed and sad, every eavesdropper had spouted the easily articulated verb at the end of the meeting. Missy was shocked and tearful – I promise I won't go to the toilet any more. Stanley was martyrous – I promise not to go to the dentist ever again, and Eve, bruised and buffeted Eve, crossed her heart and hoped to die. Jack had looked me straight in the eye, 'No. I won't take notes on the Tube again. I promise.' I had no need to extract assurances from Violet. She was the only eavesdropper to have kept her listening at a distance, yet her eyes shone with such innocence I felt a reborn bite of worry inside.

I tried out a promise on my mother - I'll call you, I will. But when the next day came it was easy, so easy to not. Useless, empty, treacherous word.

Feeling a new weight in my shoulders I toured every eavesdropper site one more time. The launderette was empty, the dentist's waiting room contained just two people, a surly receptionist and a fearful-looking teenager, and the toilets beneath the street in Camden Town were locked and bolted and a paper bag being blown down the street bore a curious resemblance to tumbleweed. Finally, I walked back along Whitehall and peered through the gates of Downing Street. The same policeman stared back at me. Same gun at his hip, same gum in his mouth.

Everything was going to be all right. It was over. Finished. I would be able to lay my head on my pillow and sleep all night. I'd heard the words; I'd seen their lips move. I promise.

MISSY wasn't ready for the knock at the door when it came. On a dry day she could hear footsteps from the street, but not that day. The sharp tap forced her right out of her skin. She tiptoed to the window and peeped out. A top of a head was visible. How happy she was to see the top of *that* head: the comfort of the parting, the pleasure of early hints of baldness. She rushed down the stairs and opened the door. "Mr. Harcourt!"

"Missy, that was fast. You look … happy."

"I am … happy to see you."

"Would you mind if I come inside for a moment."

"Of course not, come up."

She rushed ahead and opened the door to her flat. This time she was ready.

"Wow! You've had a party!"

Missy saw admiration in his eyes. "Yes – a bit of a riot."

He took off his coat, laid it over the arm of the sofa and sat down. "This blue light's cool."

"Yes, isn't it."

His lips formed into a ghastly smile. "We look like aliens," he said.

She laughed. "Everything looks different in blue light."

He tilted his head. "Everything?"

"Everything that matters."

Mr. Harcourt sat down on the sofa. Missy sat on the chair opposite him and studied his discomfort. "Is everything okay?"

He sighed. "I just wanted to make sure that you were alright."

"What do you mean?"

"Well … you know."

She didn't know. She did. "I'm fine."

He smiled. "Your teeth look blue!"

"Ha! Yours too."

He glanced round the room. "Where do your friends live, Missy? Around here?"

"My friends … oh, all over."

Mr. Harcourt looked at her. She wondered how well his eyes focused. He leant forward in a gesture that suggested he might take her hand.

"There's nothing wrong with being someone else," he said.

She sucked in a silent breath. Her instinct was to deny, summon a loud, 'You've got me all wrong,' but she couldn't. She gazed into his face – patient, bloodshot eyes. She thought of the cans of stale beer, the fag ends squashed into ashtrays, the stain on the sofa. She thought of her party shoes, scuffed at the toes. "Will you help me clear up?" she said.

He smiled a blue smile. "Sure."

She opened every kitchen cupboard and scanned the insides. Then she flapped air into a bin bag, stretched its skin over the back of a chair where its large black mouth drooped open, and they set to work. The box of plastic wine glasses dropped willingly out of her hands and the paper plates fitted into the bag as if it had been made for them. Serviettes, novelty ice-cubes, unopened packets of cocktail umbrellas made the bag bulge and she gritted her teeth as she forced the top shut.

"That it?" he said.

"That's it."

"I should go."

"Yes."

He picked up his coat, opened the door and turned to look at her. "I won't bother you again."

"Mr. Harcourt."

"Yes?"

"A lot happened," she said.

A blue smile appeared on his face. "Yeah. A lot happened."

Missy rinsed the final glass beneath the tap. Alone, yet the smell of Bill Harcourt remained in the room. She sat on the kitchen chair and leafed through her feelings: sad in the way she'd felt when she'd thrown out her school uniform, happy in the hope that emptying her cupboards would be enough. Her rubbish would be collected, the bag taken to an unknown place. Only one thing remained in the fridge, a jar of fisherman's maggots. She took them out, untied the knot and emptied them onto a plate. Fifteen minutes later they were warm and moving, oozing life, squirming with joy, or squirming with despair. She went downstairs and emptied them out onto the grass.

She came back upstairs, washed and dried her hands, then she approached the mantelpiece and looked into the mother's eyes – plastic blue and plastic white. She picked the child off the mother's lap and placed her back down on her chair.

Finally, she pulled the stool to the middle of the room and with a tea towel over her hands removed the blue bulb. Then she screwed in the red one. She switched it on. She stepped down off the stool and lay down on the floor in the middle of her lounge. The smell of beer still lingered on her skin but she ignored it. She closed her eyes; she relaxed her muscles; she angled her ears and listened. It was 8 o'clock. Grandma O'Malley would be coming up the stairs any minute.

CHAPTER

39

Violet wasn't in the cafe when I arrived. A whim had taken me there, but I checked the tables with all the stealth of a double agent, ordered a coffee, sat down and tried to be Violet. I was tall; I was thin. I was confident; I wasn't worried by passing things. But it was tiring sitting up straight so I let my shoulders sag and sipped my coffee, a double cappuccino with a heart of chocolate stencilled on the foam.

I was lucky I could still afford a double. Wilson hadn't fired me. Much to my bewilderment he'd let things go. I'd had to endure a lecture that had wandered off the subject of the mismanagement of company funds and on to the question of how to fix the printer on his desk and I'd felt wrung out by the time he'd finished with me. But, I'd held on to my job.

Something caught my eye on the other side of the cafe. A man was sitting alone at a table in the corner. He had a cup like mine at his elbow and a bag slung over the back of his chair. But what really caught my attention was his hand, writing in a notebook, with a pencil.

No problem. Just a bloke with a notebook. He must be writing a shopping list, a to-do list; he's writing a play, he's writing a novel; he's writing down an important thought he's just had.

I was overcome with feelings. Nosiness? Suspicion? Jealousy? Surely he was just a bloke trying to write his shopping list in peace: bread, butter, milk, peas. Mustn't forget the peas.

I stood up and sidled across the room, picked up a sachet of sugar from the counter, cast a trusting eye. "Alright, mate?"

The man looked up. "Sure.... You?"

I smiled "Terrific. Thanks for asking."

He was watching my back as I put on my coat, I could feel it. He was still watching my back as I left the cafe. Why shouldn't he? He was just a bloke writing his shopping list: bread, butter, milk, peas.

JACK had his ticket ready as he stepped off the Tube. He held his left hand at the precise angle for passing through the barrier in the most efficient way. But the barrier was open: he hesitated.

"Go on through, for fuck's sake," said a voice from behind.

Jack felt a knuckle in the small of his back. He stepped forward and continued up the steps without looking back until he emerged onto the street and was enveloped by the calm of Whitehall with its sleeping policemen, gently ticking taxis and soothing orange tarmac.

He kept to the edge of the dark street, his shoulder brushing the rough façades of embassies, while keeping his gaze down on the pavement, skimming his feet over the fag ends and the circles of gum, all flattened by endless soles in a hurry. This was the place. The sacred place that remembered war and forgot the reasons why. He trembled as his feet trod the ground. He paused by the Cenotaph and looked up. The blackness of the sky blurred the outline of the stone.

He walked on, slipped beneath an awning and waited, half-hidden from the street. He heard a muffled sound and turning his head noticed a group of people at the far end of the shop front, huddled together, just a cluster of shoulders and backs of necks. He looked up at the war memorial. Stripped of the yearning crowd it seemed so alone, stranded on the traffic island, getting in the way. Then, an excited voice cut into his thoughts and he turned his attention back to the huddled group. His second more lingering glance took in the detail: five people dressed as clowns – white-painted faces, bulbous red noses. One wore an enormous pair of glasses. And hats, they all wore bowlers pulled comically down over their ears. Jack trimmed his gaze and looked back at the street, so quiet, so still. The chatter of excited voices drew his attention back once more to the end of the awning. Voices brimmed, but the language was not one he knew. The words were fast, stalling at the back of their throats, pauses forced between the words. A luminous white face looked his way.

Jack turned back to the Cenotaph. Moonlight white. Unbearably white. Then Jack's ears were pulled back beneath the awning once more by the utterance of a single word. "Shakespeare." Tossed in with the glottal stops and glides of the foreign tongue, the word came to get him.

The group was tighter now, smaller, but a white face turned towards him again, teeth yellow in the smile, a dark cheek showing through a smudge in the make-up.

The white face spoke. "رجو أن تنضم إلينا"

Jack just looked. Then he heard the voice again, in English, yet heavy with a middle-eastern accent. "Please, join us."

He walked towards the circle; he smelt face paint; he felt an arm slide across his shoulders. *Shakespeare.*

CHAPTER

40

I hadn't intended to go back. The Cenotaph, the place where I'd brooded and tried to find answers was tied to my time with the eavesdroppers. But just one last look. I wanted one final moment at the feet of the empty, white tomb.

Although I had no appetite for lunch, I needed fresh air. The sun was out so I left the office at midday and headed towards Whitehall. Other Londoners had had the same idea and many were perched on the steps of grand buildings with lunch boxes on their shivering laps or take-away sushi held delicately between wooden chopsticks, all of them cold-looking, all uncomfortable.

I had just turned into Whitehall when I heard a sound. A bird said a complete sentence. Not just a chirp, but a fully formed sentence. Twice. *Goeasyonher. Goeasyonher.* When I looked up, the branches were full of pigeons looking back down. I looked from beak to beak, then *Goeasyonher* came again, but not from up in the tree but from somewhere behind me. I turned. Just a plain concrete wall with a fire extinguisher screwed onto it. I waited a few minutes but the words didn't come again.

I wandered up the street and stopped beside the monument on the blind person's piece of pavement and closed my eyes. I thought again of the man inside whom no one knew the identity of. Someone had died, but no one knew who he was. I thought of the soldiers at Lydd. I read the inscription carved into the stone – *The Glorious Dead*.

"Can you move over a bit, mate?"

I turned round. A man stood beside me on the steps. He held a mobile phone, plus a long plastic stick in his hand.

"What for?" I said.

"I want to take a photo."

"Oh, of course."

I moved along the step and watched him clip his mobile phone onto his stick.

"A selfie stick," he said, eyes sheepish.

My stomach did a superior flip as the man leant against the hard wall of the monument, held up the mobile, smiled and clicked.

"Why did you take that?" I asked. "Like that?"

His selfie smile vanished. "I … what's it to you?"

"Oh, nothing. Do what you like."

"I will."

He repositioned himself on the corner of the monument, stretched out his stick and smiled.

"Budge up a bit, can you," he said.

I moved an inch. The man stood right next to me, held up his phone on a stick once more and smiled. I could see myself in the screen – a scowling man next to a smiling one. Behind our heads I could also see the building beyond the Cenotaph at the end of the street. I blinked and rubbed my eyes. They watered and the building seemed strangely distorted; the whole façade looked as if it was on a long, gentle curve.

VIOLET knew the time had come – the time to close her ears and open her eyes, the time for *it* to be over. The old man, who'd been waiting for them in the meeting room, had spoken the truth.

She felt physically sick as she slunk into the cafe. What Bill Harcourt had said was right; they had to close down what they had started.

She sat in her usual chair and waited for the barista to come. But she didn't want her to come. Not now. Not during this private time while she waited, just for him. She had no doubt. She had a lot of doubt.

"What's it to be?"

Violet looked up and smiled. Not herself. No, not herself. "Double espresso.... Please."

"Anything to eat?"

Didn't the girl realise? You can't eat when your heart is ready to be broken. "No, thanks."

Violet fingered her keyboard, and then leant back on her chair, closed her eyes and waited.

Soon.

This was the fifth day in a row she had come to the cafe in the hope, in the fevered delusion that he would return to the spot where they had first met. She needed this. She needed to be able to stop.

"You're late."

Him. Him. Him. The voice was right behind her.

"Sorry, the bus ran out of petrol." A woman's voice. The woman.

"Ha. I don't believe you."

His words curled round her ears, but Violet didn't turn round. Curled right inside her.

"You alright?" said the woman.

"Yeah ... actually no. I think I've got a stalker after me."

The woman laughed.

"It's not funny."

"Oh, come on, John. Who would stalk you?"

John.

"God knows, but I keep getting phone calls. Heavy breathing and all that crap."

The woman stifled a laugh. "Oh, come on, John. Heavy breathing is really dated. Stalking's done online these days."

"How come you're the expert?" What sounded like a menu slapped down on the table.

"Has anything else happened?"

"No, but I do get a creepy feeling sometimes that she's watching me?"

"She?"

"Okay … *it*. Sometimes I feel it's close."

"John, you're freaking me out."

"Sorry. Let's forget it. Perhaps she won't bother me again."

"I'm sure she won't. Sugar?"

Violet's heels sunk into the grass as she crossed the verge. She looked back to see small holes trailing behind her, as if a unicorn had stabbed the ground with its horn. The cafe receded from view and she walked quickly up the road. She came to a small park with a broken fence and grass smelling of dog shit. She went inside and sat on a bench. It had no back so she flexed her abdomen and tried to stay vertical. But her edges were sagging. The great sadness was pulling her down. She'd closed her ears and opened her eyes. He hadn't known her. She hadn't known him.

CHAPTER
41

Time scurried by and I felt a little older every time I thought about its passing. It was two weeks later when James and I went to the pub and wondered what sorrows we had to drown. James ordered two double whiskies and I asked for a bag of pork scratchings, a combination that never failed to soothe stray anxieties. But today I didn't need soothing, I'd already supped on a bellyful of confidence.

"Not so loud, Bill," James said from across the table. "The whole pub doesn't need to hear."

"Sorry."

"Hey, Bill. Do you remember when we were last here?"

My voice dropped. "Yeah."

"We eavesdropped."

"I know."

"We didn't see what was coming, did we?"

"You never know what's coming, James."

"Maybe we weren't listening properly."

"Oh, shut up."

"Bill, what's up?"

"I don't need a lecture. I already feel like shit."

"Sorry, mate. Is that all that's bothering you?"

"It's that bloody ... noise."

"What bloody noise?"

I gripped his arm. "That fucking hum. Can't you hear it? Really?"

James shook me off and folded his arms. "It's probably tinnitus."

"What the hell's that?"

"It's sort of ... kind of when you hear sounds from inside your body."

"Which bit of your body?"

"Noises that your ears make ... inside. You're probably noticing it because you've been a bit, you know, stressed."

I leant back in my chair. "Not any more – it's over. Everything's going to be alright now."

"Is it?"

"James, don't look like that."

"No loose ends?"

"*No* loose ends."

"Did you check?"

"Yes, I checked. I spoke to them. They understood. I went around all their places. All eavesdropper-free." I moved closer. "Really, James. Everything's fine. I've hung on to my job. It's all sorted. Send me some questionnaires, send me thousands of fucking questionnaires."

James sipped his whisky. I sipped mine. We sat in silence as the words in the room, some loud, some soft, floated gently into our ears.

STANLEY noticed one of Beryl's feather's lying on the hall carpet when he went downstairs to get his first cup of tea of the day. Normally he would have picked it up and put it in his feather box, but no, not this time. He had more important things to attend to. He walked past, hardly noticing that a little part of Beryl flew up in the draft from his body and floated back down onto the collar of his winter coat.

She might be on her way.

Stanley put the kettle on, wiped the kitchen top with a spot of neat bleach, then sat down at the table. "I don't feel like talking," he said, in the direction of Beryl's cage. She stared back. He flicked through the newspaper, and then sat silent. He and Beryl and the kitchen. Just they. He picked up a packet of cotton buds and poked around his ear. He admired his haul of wax, and then threw the bud into the bin. Then he sat silent again and tried to listen to the sound of his body. Could he hear the sound of guilt? Would he actually recognise the tones of regret? Later.

Someone knocked on the door. A gentle knock, the knock of a person with small, weak hands. He looked at Beryl. Could she hear his blood pumping?

The knock came again, still soft, the knock of a small person stretching up to reach.

Stanley felt the air pushing out his lungs; he felt his heart go up a gear. He looked again at Beryl. She looked back at him. Such depth to those dark, beady eyes.

Stanley's eyes filled with tears as he lifted his trembling hands slowly off the table and placed them over his ears. No more sound. Nothing. Nothing but the hum deep inside his head.

He looked at Beryl. Beryl looked at him.

CHAPTER
42

I stepped out onto the cold London street at three in the morning. I shivered. I pulled a cigarette out of my pocket and held it in my mouth. A small shape flitted across the sky. The final scaffolding had been removed from the building across from my flat and there it stood, self-conscious in its nakedness. I needed nakedness: I wanted the fresh start of a newborn. Now that the project was over, the files closed and the eavesdroppers had returned to their homes I wanted to find a space where I could forget.

I tipped my head up and took in the whole façade. Rather than being up on a pedestal like other buildings in the area this one touched the ground and curved in a gentle arc. I crossed the road and stood at one corner. Something made me want to measure it, so I paced its length – sixty paces that I almost lost count of – then I pressed my chest against the front wall and looked up. At least forty feet of concrete towered above me. Then I stretched out my arms and spreadeagled myself against it. The wind rushed passed my ears. I could hear my own breath. I could feel my heart thumping in my chest. I could hear the hum of the concrete. What could *it* hear? Was it listening? Was it listening to me …?

ACKNOWLEDGMENTS

I would like to thank Sandy Vincent, Phoebe Chard and LeeAnn Knutson for reading early drafts of the manuscript and offering so many useful thoughts and suggestions.

Thanks also to Quiller Barrett for telling me about the Citizens Advice Bureau.

I am indebted to everyone at NeWest Press for their customary expertise and enthusiasm, especially Doug Barbour, Claire Kelly and Matt Bowes. I am also grateful to Michel Vrana whose design and cover elegantly reflects the spirit of the book.

A special thank you to Nat, Phoebe and Ollie.

Finally, I would like to thank all my friends and family, near and far, who sent me anonymous fragments of conversation from which *The Eavesdroppers* grew.

Rosie Chard grew up on the edge of London, England.
After studying Anthropology and Environmental Biology at university she went on to qualify as a landscape architect and practiced for several years in England, Denmark and Canada. She and her family emigrated to Winnipeg in 2005 where she trained as an English language teacher at the University of Manitoba.

Rosie is now based in Brighton, England where she currently works as a tutor on The Creative Writing Programme Brighton, and also as a freelance editor, writing mentor and English language teacher. Her first novel, *Seal Intestine Raincoat*, published in 2009 by NeWest Press won the 2010 Trade Fiction Book Award at the Alberta Book Publishing Awards and received an honorable mention at the Sunburst Fiction Awards. She was also shortlisted in 2010 for the John Hirsch Award for Most Promising Manitoba Writer. Her second novel, *The Insistent Garden*, published in 2013 by NeWest Press, won the Margaret Laurence Award for Fiction at the Manitoba Book Awards..

She is currently writing her fourth novel.